THE ONE THAT HE WANTS

CHERRY BLOSSOM LANE SERIES. BOOK 2

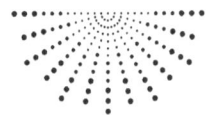

LIZZIE CHANTREE

lemon meringue
PUBLISHING

The One That He Wants is written and edited in British English rather than American English. This includes spelling, grammar and punctuation.

Cover images: ricorico, elenabs
Cover design by Lizzie Chantree

❀ Created with Vellum

This book is dedicated to all of the wonderful readers who keep me writing. Thank you for your endless support and encouragement.

Huge thanks to my editor, Alice. I appreciate your wisdom, friendship, humour and advice.

With big thanks to my amazing aunt, Sandra, who is one of my biggest cheerleaders and who means the world to me.

To my incredible parents and to Enid and Myra. Sending lots of love your way.

Love from Lizzie x

THE ONE THAT HE WANTS

BOOK 2

CHAPTER ONE

*S*asha wrote the final name on the gold and white wedding place card she was holding and then sat back, looking at the neat pile she'd created. A glitzy wedding like this wasn't something she'd dreamed about as a little girl. Most of her teenage fantasies had actually been about the brother of this particular groom. What she had always wanted was stardom and influence. Now she was hobnobbing with the rich and famous in her brand-new job, and it seemed that the lifestyle she'd craved could finally be within her reach – even if Oliver Taylor still wasn't.

Her best friend Poppy's big day was fast approaching and Sasha had pretty much organised the whole shebang. Poppy's business, which involved designing specialist equipment and homes to help with her (often quite famous) clients' mental health, was flourishing. She created breathtakingly beautiful relaxation pods for people to unwind in and sensory panels to bring sunshine into people's homes. She was the interior designer of the moment.

Poppy was marrying her childhood sweetheart, Dylan Taylor, and the essence of their romance *was* something

Sasha had always wanted – finding true love and still having the freedom to be herself. Sasha hadn't had much time to daydream, though, since Poppy had given her the opportunity to work for her. Now her life was full of planning meetings, scheduling public relations, running the social media for the firm and organising their bursting-at-the-seams calendar. Her past jobs were a mishmash of whatever held her attention for more than five minutes. She had often only taken them either to entice or annoy Ollie, who was Dylan's older brother,

Her eyes crinkled at the corners when she thought back to the girl who only took a job if it meant she'd be near enough to bump into sexy, delicious Ollie. Not that he'd ever paid her the slightest bit of attention, other than a quick nod of the head to show he'd seen her... again. She'd been obsessed with making him notice her, and she cringed at how desperate she'd been for his affection.

Poppy had made her see the light, though, and now she was finally free of whatever grip he'd had on her heart. She adored her job, and the little town the office was situated in. Cherry Blossom Lane had a magic of its own and she loved arriving there each day. The tree-lined street was next to a field full of wildflowers in the spring and summer, and you could almost imagine you were in the middle of the countryside, except for the number of new businesses that were gradually creeping into the area. It was a hidden gem that was just starting to poke its head above ground and sparkle in the sunlight. Cherry Blossom Lane was about an hour's drive from where she lived in the town they had all grown up in, in Essex.

Dylan and his brothers, Ollie and Miles, had been the local heartbreakers. Sasha, Poppy and Demi, the third in their group, as well as all the other girls at their school, had admired (and drooled over) the Taylor brothers from afar. In

Sasha's opinion, Poppy's obsession had been even worse than her own, as Poppy had spied on Dylan's house from the balcony of the tower block flat she'd grown up in! Little had she known that he'd always liked her too. Lucky Poppy.

Sasha grinned as Jared Wright strode into the office. She couldn't help but flick her long dark hair from her shoulders and straighten her back. He was so dreamy and made her giggle like a schoolgirl every time they spoke, but he was their main client and completely out of bounds. Plus she was pretty sure that he still had the hots for Poppy – even though she was getting married.

'Hi Jared,' she said breezily, carefully moving the wedding name placeholders to the centre of her desk, so he couldn't miss them. He took a look as he walked past her desk, then threw back his head and laughed, running his hands through his blonde hair and making it mussed up and sexy while his eyes sparkled.

'Subtle as always, Sasha,' he joked. 'I'm on my best behaviour these days, as you well know.'

He then gave her a hard stare, but nothing like that worked with Sasha. She was the one who bossed everyone else around, even if they were their best clients.

He glanced at Poppy's closed office door. 'Is she in? I was passing and need to talk to her about our latest building project. There've been a few minor changes.'

Sasha's face fell, but she motioned for him to sit in the chair opposite her desk. 'She's on a client call at the moment.' Sasha knew not to disturb those, even for Jared.

Jared was always popping in and throwing a spanner in Sasha's carefully planned schedule. Changes to builds meant hours and hours more work for everyone. He held up his hand in surrender at the fire that lit up her eyes and he came round to give her a hug. It seemed everyone who worked with Poppy, or was a client, was a hugger. She surrounded herself with amazing people. Sasha was still getting used to it after so many receptionist jobs where customers shouted at you, and telesales roles where clients lost it too.

She picked up the sparkly old journal that had been constantly at her side when she was at school and shoved it in a drawer. It had a black sequined cover that had lost its shine. She'd found it the previous week and had been looking through it at the dreams she'd once had about running her own business, or of becoming a social media influencer.

She was closer to her dream now than she'd ever been, but the book was packed full of ideas that hadn't quite worked. She'd had strategies to propel herself to fame and she'd followed the hottest trends doggedly. Looking around on a daily basis at the success Poppy had built had jogged her memory about the journal. It was full of childhood dreams, and plots on how to make Ollie take notice of her too. None of them had been successful, either.

She grinned at the gorgeous man in front of her. He looked like he'd just stepped out of a glossy magazine photo shoot, and Ollie was forgotten. She picked up her brand new faux-leather business planner, which was actually quite heavy, and scribbled a few notes about Jared's latest ideas, so that she could transfer them to the main system on the computer later that day.

'Tell me what you need from us, and I'll let you know what we have space for in Poppy's heaving schedule.'

Jared grinned, as he was part of the cause of their success. Poppy and Jared were a dream team who created homes that helped the homeowner relax after a busy day and live in a calm and nurturing environment. Customers often said that walking into one of their builds felt like the house was giving you a hug too. Their technology was life-changing for their clients. Jared ran an architectural firm which built houses and hotels, and Poppy designed the living spaces and layouts to complement his creative vision and improve their buyers' mental health, through light and sound.

Jared spent ten minutes going over the new schedule. Sasha jotted everything down and could feel a headache gathering at the back of her head. Jared's ideas were usually on point and dynamic, and she loved working with him, but he always messed with her plans! She bit her lip and tried not to give in to the urge to kick him under the table. That wouldn't quite fit with Poppy's calm and welcoming ethos for clients. Her green eyes sparkled and Jared grinned at her wickedly, making her pulse jump. He always teased her that he'd love to know what was going on in her head, but he might not like this thought. He got up to leave and came round to kiss her cheek. He smelt divine and it was hard not to lean into him for a longer snuggle, but she didn't want to crease his beautiful deep blue suit and crisp white shirt.

The office door opened and Ollie stepped in, staring at Sasha in Jared's arms and giving them a tight smile. He was carrying what looked like waistcoats over his arm. She sighed and tried to step away from Jared, bidding him goodbye. Jared held onto her for a moment too long, as she knew he loved to wind the Taylor brothers up. She breezily moved out of reach and told him she'd set up a meeting with Poppy in the diary and give his personal assistant a call to arrange it.

Jared politely shook Ollie's hand as he passed and called goodbye to Poppy's account director and other best friend, Billy, who had just appeared and looked sad to have missed Jared. Billy smiled at Ollie and then signalled that he had to get back to his work, by waving around the report he was carrying. Sasha grinned at him, but her smile faded when she was alone with her nemesis – Oliver Taylor.

CHAPTER TWO

Sasha moved back behind her desk and raised her eyebrows at Ollie. Popping in like this was becoming a bit of a habit, but she couldn't have her boss's brother growling at their biggest client.

'He seems to be here a lot,' Ollie said, coming and putting the waistcoats on her desk, his tall frame making the room feel smaller suddenly. She tutted and quickly moved some paperwork out of the way of the clothes.

'Jared is a client and has a right to be here, unlike some…' she said, glancing at the clock on the wall to see how long Poppy would be. Nowadays Sasha stomped around and kept staring impatiently at the door whenever she was alone with Ollie, although it had once been all she'd dreamed about.

Ollie rolled his eyes. 'Dylan asked me to bring these in,' he looked at the waistcoats. 'For you to look at with Poppy. He knows she'll never get to the shop on her own. She's always working.'

Sasha looked up sharply to see if that was a dig at Poppy, but the small worry lines on his usually glowingly handsome face told her it wasn't.

'Dylan's stressing about the wedding, as there's so much to decide on.'

Ollie held up three different waistcoats and she looked at them critically. One was too fussy, the next was ok, but she thought Poppy would hate it. Who knew that being Poppy's assistant would mean practically planning her whole wedding? Luckily being best friends since school meant Sasha could guess at her choices.

'Put that one on for me,' she pointed to the last one. 'I need to see what it looks like on,' she told him, trying not to enjoy his discomfort too much.

Ollie's eyes darted around to make sure that there weren't any other clients about who might see. Then he frowned, hesitated, and complied. She got up to slip the waistcoat over his arms and her mouth watered and her senses went into overdrive. Why did he have to be so damn delicious? He was tall and broad and had a shock of thick black hair. His grey eyes were enticing and running a gym meant that he was muscly, but not in a body-builder kind of way. He was a lean, mean, woman-dazzling machine. It almost made her growl. Other girls' eyes always followed him wherever he went.

Sasha couldn't help but drool a little, even though he was out of bounds and she disliked him immensely for being so nice to everyone else but unavailable to her. It really was his loss, she decided, as she straightened her back and smiled, swishing her hair over one shoulder and noticing with satisfaction that his eyes were following the movement.

He looked divine, but she was glad she didn't *really* fancy him anymore. Years of unrequited love had hardened her heart towards him. He wasn't getting any more of her tears. Sasha missed the way the fourth person in their friendship group, Anne, had always told her to stop thinking about Ollie and get a life. In the end it had helped her move on. Now Anne had done the same herself, by moving to America. The rest of them sometimes felt left behind, but Sasha shook those thoughts off. Anne had also taken enough of their time and energy. She still kept in touch occasionally, but wasn't coming back for the wedding. Sasha tried to hide the fact that she was glad. She just wanted Poppy to relax and enjoy her big day. But Ollie was right, they needed to get organised or there wouldn't be a wedding at all. It was only a matter of months away now.

'That's the one,' she decided, brushing a speck of dust off his shoulder.

'Don't we need to ask Poppy?' asked Ollie.

Sasha shook her head. She knew Poppy's moods changed every five minutes. For a second, she held her breath to make her stomach contract, as he seemed to be looking her up and down. Then she let it go with a huff. She wasn't going to change for any man. She loved her curves.

'Poppy's asked me to sort all this stuff out.' Ollie looked more confused. 'Not every woman dreams of a huge flouncy wedding with a gazillion guests,' she bristled. 'Poppy wants to marry your brother, but she's inundated with job requests and is still building her business. Dylan knows we're pretty much winging it.'

Ollie grinned at last and her heart almost stopped. 'She's lucky to have you. I hear you're super-organised now,' he joked, clearly referring to when she'd worked for him, the git.

'Having a supportive boss helps the staff shine,' she gave him a saccharine smile, making his grin fade and confusion fill his face. Home run!

Ollie took the waistcoat off and draped all three of them over the couch by the wall, which sat beside a beautiful floor-to-ceiling bookcase heaving with books with colourful spines.

'Looks like I need to get back to work myself, to shape up on my leadership skills,' he quipped, turning to the door.

She felt a bit light-headed suddenly and pouted. Why did he always make her say things she didn't mean? He'd been an amazing boss when she'd worked at the leisure centre he owned in their old town. He'd been kind, courteous and treated her the same as every other member of staff. She tutted to herself as he shouted out to Billy, who had gone back to work in his office next door and had his head bent over a pile of papers.

'I'll see you later, Sasha. Say hi to Poppy for me.'

With that, he closed the door and left her standing there, feeling like a mean-spirited hag and an awful friend when he was just being helpful. She vowed to try harder and be nicer to him, for everyone's sake.

CHAPTER THREE

*S*asha forgot to knock and bowled into Poppy's office, stopping short when she saw she was on the phone. It sometimes slipped her mind that Poppy was now her boss and not just her best friend. Poppy was an unassuming person and didn't lord her success over anyone. She might be very career-driven, but she was also happy to take them all along on the incredible ride she'd created for herself. Her business was a hot topic and Sasha fielded calls daily for interviews and new clients craving a conversation with such a specialist designer. They even had one or two social media influencers noticing their work now.

Poppy hated the limelight, but Sasha and Billy loved it, so they made her step out of her comfort zone and attend events, making new contacts and becoming busier than ever. Luckily, Poppy had Dylan to ground her. He adored her and supported her wherever he could, though he ran his own bespoke furniture empire. Sasha wished she could find another Dylan, but then cringed at that gross thought, as he was like a brother to her.

They'd all grown up together and apart from her stupid

and downright embarrassing infatuation with Ollie, and Poppy's practical stalking of Dylan when they'd been at school, they all got on really well. She fleetingly recalled Demi saying she'd snogged the youngest Taylor brother, Miles, once at a party, but that had been swept away in conversation. She'd definitely bring that up another time. Demi's long-term relationship with local lad Allan meant that she'd luckily missed the Taylor brother obsession that others in their group had fallen into. To be fair, half of the town had been, and probably still was, in love with the boys, so maybe Sasha hadn't been that weird.

Sasha stared out of the floor-to-ceiling window that Poppy had designed to maximise the view of the fields beyond. She almost felt like she could be walking through those fields and running her hands along the fronds of grass, as Poppy had so cleverly reflected the outside inside. Wildflowers were growing and swaying gently in the breeze and the lighting inside the room was optimal to keep you energised and relaxed. It never ceased to make Sasha pause for a minute and just stare at the beauty and breathe. That was pretty amazing for someone who rarely shut up or stopped moving.

Poppy hung up the phone and looked Sasha's way, waiting to hear what she wanted.

'Jared popped by to see you.' Sasha said, pulling a pained expression to forewarn her friend. 'He's changed the schedule again.'

Poppy slapped the palm of her hand against her forehead and rolled back in her chair. 'Bloody Jared!' she laughed finally, and Sasha sighed with relief.

Poppy's workload created immense pressure and Sasha hated adding to it, but Poppy seemed to thrive when things were hectic. Sasha's job involved making sure that Poppy had the headspace to create her incredible designs, because if she was stressed, then so was everyone else. Her whole business ethos supported positive mental health and happiness. The first few years of the business had been hectic, but Poppy had learned to manage that better with the help of her friends.

'What does he want done now?'

Sasha glanced at the notes she'd scribbled down in her planner. 'He wants to add another light and sound panel to the annexe on the latest new build, plus the client has requested a relaxation pod in the garden. Is that possible?'

Poppy's pods were small wooden domes fitted with sensory light panels, calming music or water features. They were the perfect place to relax and unwind after a long day.

Poppy chewed her lip and then looked like she was mentally counting stock, although Sasha didn't know how the hell she could do that, with the number of clients they had now. 'We can add another pod to production now the teams know the exact specifications and have got used to demand. They seem to enjoy crafting them and putting them together. Dylan used to hate making them for me as they're domes. He only let that slip recently. He'd drunk a few glasses of red wine,' she said sardonically.

Sasha gasped! She knew how precious those pods were to Poppy. The first one had helped her pay for her mum, June, to stay at the medical sanctuary she'd lived at for years. Poppy's rough start in life had paved the way for her to become the inspirational woman she was now. But now Poppy just laughed and her eyes danced. 'Good job I love him, or I'd have kicked him somewhere painful.'

Sasha laughed too, as Poppy adored that man and every single part of his anatomy was precious to her. She hadn't stopped smiling since they'd got back together, even though she was definitely avoiding talk of her impending wedding.

'So, the changes are good to go?'

Poppy sat back in the beautiful deep blue chair Jared had

given her as a gift to mark their very first big project together, and stretched like a cat. 'Yes. Jared knows we will always prioritise his work. It's to our benefit too. He is a big part of our success.'

'Plus he's so 'interesting' to have around,' giggled Sasha, fanning her face. 'Our female clients start panting when he comes into the office. How the hell he's still single is beyond me.' She winked at Poppy who blushed. 'Ollie wasn't so enamoured by his visit when he popped by just now. He brought in some waistcoats for us to decide on, but you were busy.'

Poppy sat up and tilted her head to hear more, her blonde hair falling in waves over her shoulder, her blue eyes narrowing as she ran her gaze over Sasha's face, making her squirm a bit. Sasha pulled at the collar of her cute short-sleeved dress, which she'd teamed with a pair of Converse trainers for an edgier look. She'd seen the style on a model in a magazine, but was already missing her high heels.

'Ollie seems to be here a lot lately and quite frankly it's getting on my nerves,' said Sasha. She shrugged apologetically at Poppy for moaning about her future brother-in-law, but Poppy didn't flinch. She had a secret smile on her lips that made Sasha want to stamp her feet. 'He keeps sauntering in as if he owns the place and he hates Jared being near you.' Maybe this would make Poppy take notice?

'I'm not sure it's me Ollie's worried about,' said Poppy confusingly, smiling fully now. She laughed at Sasha's blank expression and shook her head, muttering under her breath at her friend's stupidity. Sasha frowned. Did Poppy think she was deaf?

'Ollie's bought the leisure centre complex up the road and he's been revamping it for the past few months,' Poppy continued.

Sasha's mouth dropped open and her skin grew warm.

'Why didn't you tell me?' she asked angrily. Poppy winced and Sasha read her friend's face like a book. 'You thought I'd start obsessing over him again? Poppy! I'm over Ollie. I know I followed him around for years like a lovelorn puppy, but that was the old me.' She could see that her friend wasn't convinced.

'I didn't have focus in my life then,' Sasha said fiercely, pacing around the office and scowling out of the window at a young couple who were strolling through the fields holding hands. 'Now I work for you, I don't have time to lust after Oliver Taylor. I don't need a man. I'm too busy,' Sasha reiterated, in case her friend hadn't got the gist. Poppy pulled a face and Sasha lost patience and threw the pen she had in her hand a little too close to her friend's head. Poppy growled in annoyance, before jumping up and hugging her fiery friend, or perhaps she was restraining her...

'Firstly, please don't throw things at me. I'm your boss and I might fire you,' Poppy said mock-sternly. Sasha just harrumped, but Poppy didn't seem cross. Even though she was so busy, she smiled a lot more these days. Sasha could tell she was nervous but excited about her wedding by the way she sometimes gazed gormlessly into space when she thought no one was looking.

'I know you're over Ollie,' said Poppy carefully, although her tone of voice didn't sound very sure. 'But I didn't want to put temptation in your way when you're being so empowered.'

She sipped the mug of coffee that Billy had brought in earlier and signed in bliss. Sasha wrinkled her nose. It must be tepid by now, but her friend seemed to enjoy cold coffee too. Maybe that should be part of the wedding day, she fleetingly thought.

'I didn't know he'd pop by so regularly. Sorry,' continued Poppy apologetically. 'You're an amazing addition to my team and I value everything you do… except the odd burst of anger,' she looked pointedly at the pen. Sasha had the grace to blush.

'Sorry, boss. It won't happen again. Ollie's a bit of a sore point and I know I behave like a ten-year-old when he's around, but the man winds me up.'

'Don't insult ten-year-olds,' Poppy teased and Sasha poked her in the ribs, making her jump away.

CHAPTER FOUR

*P*oppy went and sat at her desk and peered out at the incredible view, which was full of pink and purple hues as the wildflowers she'd sown liberally outside were standing tall and reaching for the spring sunshine. She breathed in a huge lungful of scented air and re-centred herself. She really loved her job and her friends, but both were exhausting at times. Sasha came and stood next to her and tried to copy Poppy's restful demeanour, with a big sigh. They both grinned at each other for a moment and then turned their minds back to work.

'Talk to me about your new ideas,' said Poppy. Sasha's last initiative with their social media channels had been a huge success, and Poppy loved seeing her best friend shine. The stunning photographs she'd commissioned of their daylight health panels were being shared all over the place and might lead to collaborations in other fields. Sasha had overseen everything, from the hiring of the models to the studio sets. The results were seriously beautiful images of happy people next to her products, in settings you wouldn't usually associate with lighting panels that lifted your mood, like trendy wine bars, dark study spaces, gyms, libraries and doctors' surgeries. Poppy hadn't expected to get any calls straight away and was willing to trust Sasha's vision, but one or two companies and organisations had already begun to reach out to them. It was liberating that the world was open to listening to new ways to support mental health.

Sasha had found a passion of her own and Poppy couldn't wait to help her explore it. She knew Sasha didn't have confidence in her ability yet, but her talent was blatantly obvious to Poppy and Billy. They wanted her to realise it for herself, but they were happy to nudge her in the right direction if she didn't work out how incredible she was at networking soon. They might tease her about her childhood dreams of fame, but if any one of them was going to do it, then it would be Sasha. Poppy was well known now, but she wasn't featured in gossip magazines very often and she'd never been on television. Sasha's personality would shine on a format like that. She won over everyone she met, even when she didn't like them, and her dark Italian looks and beautiful smile had men swooning in her wake, but she barely noticed.

Her last boyfriend had been a complete sweetheart, but as usual Sasha had got bored within weeks. All her ex-boyfriends were now friends, as they could never bear not having her in their lives – which Poppy found weird as she couldn't stand most of hers. Ollie was the only one who had ever got away. Not that Poppy was so sure he hadn't succumbed to Sasha's charms either. He was just as career driven as his younger brother, Miles, and as determined as her own gorgeous Dylan to make his way in the world. Poppy just hoped that he hadn't made Sasha wait a bit too long. She feared that Sasha meant it, this time, and she was ready to fall in love with someone else. If Ollie didn't sort his life out, and soon, he would mess the whole thing up. Demi and Poppy had secretly hoped Sasha and Ollie would get together for years, but it had never happened.

Poppy would hate to lose a key member of staff like Sasha, if she outgrew her admin role in Cherry Blossom Lane, but she wouldn't clip her friend's wings for anyone. Sasha was born to shine. She was even more of a diva than Billy, and his favourite hobby was amateur dramatics. Not that he had much time to spend on that now, which Poppy did feel incredibly guilty about. He seemed to adore his new role in her company, so Poppy hoped she wasn't completely taking over his life. He'd already lost his boyfriend Ed over it, but Ed was coming back from working abroad for the wedding and Poppy wondered if there might be a reconciliation.

Sasha was fidgeting in her seat and Poppy waited patiently for her to spit out whatever was on her mind as she sat back down in her own chair. It was unusual for Sasha not to just blurt out whatever she was thinking. She'd make a useless spy, grinned Poppy. Sasha sat opposite Poppy and put her hands on the desk in front of her, but they were tightly clasped together. The words rushed out at once.

'There's a new social media star who's into mental health… called Devon.'

Sasha waited as if to gauge Poppy's reaction, knowing Poppy was very wary of the effects of social media on people's mental health, even though millions of people found it a positive experience.

'What about him?' asked Poppy.

'He's hugely popular, and would be a great match for either the mood panels you build… or the gyms and sanctuary spaces we want to work with. He's passionate about kindness and his messages are uplifting and inspiring. Look him up,' she nodded her head at Poppy's phone, which was sitting on the desk. Poppy picked up her phone and did as Sasha asked.

'His following's growing every day,' she rushed on. 'People really listen to him. He's got a podcast. Plus he's super sexy and a lot of fun,' said Sasha, as if this would change everything.

Poppy shook her head slowly and grinned. Their life was full of dazzling men now. She'd never thought she'd be in this position, when she'd cried herself to sleep at night as a child, wishing there was someone in the world who could love and take care of her – when her own mother couldn't. Now she did that for herself, but being surrounded by exciting creatives and entrepreneurs was a buzz in itself.

Sasha seemed determined to persuade Poppy to meet with Devon, for some reason. Maybe she just fancied him? Poppy smiled wickedly as she scrolled through her phone and Devon's handsome face smiled back at her. Sasha hadn't really been dating lately and it was about time that changed. Poppy wasn't averse to the idea of working with Devon, but their brand was already popular. This could mean great things for the tech application for phones and computers she'd had built, though, so she was listening with an open mind. She had actually heard of Devon. He'd popped up on her own social media feeds from time to time. She examined his chiselled face, short dirty blonde hair, sparkly blue eyes and lovely smile. She'd been drawn to his posts and had even added him to some lists and saved a few of his quotes for later.

She could see what Sasha meant. His content always resonated with her, and she liked his style. He'd commented on some of their work posts, she'd noticed when she'd checked the timelines. She hadn't thought much of it, as lots of famous people followed her brand now and she refused to get big-headed about it. They were mostly lovely people who had made huge successes of their lives, and she was excited to think that maybe that was happening to her little company too.

'Isn't our schedule already full?' she asked Sasha. 'Especially with Jared and his curveballs? Plus Devon's pretty famous, so why would he want to work with us? What would he want out of it? You'd need more than a common interest to snag his attention,' said Poppy.

Sasha fidgeted, grinned and rested her fingers on the edge of table before tapping her glossy red nails up and down, as if she was going to spontaneously jump up to do a little dance. 'Well, I already follow him on social media and he followed me back!' she said triumphantly.

Poppy was impressed. Sasha's own social media accounts were full of exciting photos. She was creative about her backdrops, even if it was just a flowering hedge from down the road, so Poppy could see why a handsome young man would want to follow a gorgeous girl like her back. Sasha's long dark hair, thick lashes and to-die-for curves had always made men salivate, but they had never really stood a chance. One or two had made it into her affections for a short while, but then Ollie would come back on the scene and she'd be a goner again. Poppy was pretty sure Ollie had kept it that way on purpose in the past, by giving Sasha just enough attention to make her question her relationships when they got even slightly serious. But at the same time, Ollie was one of the nicest men she'd ever met. Perhaps it was something he'd done unconsciously and, if that was it, they needed their heads banging together.

Sasha was still fidgeting. 'Devon made the connection between us somehow and sent me a direct message last week to try and get an appointment with you, to talk about fitting one of your sound and daylight panels to a huge barn conversion he's just moved into,' continued Sasha, clapping her hands in excitement and not letting Poppy speak. 'I think I posted a photo with the inside of the flat upstairs in the background. You installed one of the first panels there. He saw your work in one of the glossies too and he seems keen to meet up. He asked how I got the panel,' she glowed with pride.

'Sasha!' said Poppy in exasperation. 'You shouldn't post photos of your workplace! Not on a personal account.'

'I didn't,' said Sasha quickly. 'The panel was just in the background when I took a photo of some flowers I'd picked from the field. The kitchen's so amazing that I used it as a backdrop. I needed fresh content,' she said sheepishly. 'I know you're already piled high with contracts, but you still want steady growth and if Devon wants a panel fitted, could we nudge him towards trying the panels and pods you've fitted at that gym you worked on last month?' Sasha frowned, and her eyes narrowed as she looked at her friend.

'Um, that was actually Ollie's gym,' Poppy admitted.

Showing considerable restraint, Sasha continued. 'A photo of Devon there would be great for you, as more gyms might call.' She could obviously see that Poppy wasn't convinced, but she ploughed on. 'Plus... it would be perfect for Ollie. He's starting a new business and you'd be helping him without him knowing it, if we used his new venue... you know... the one that just happens to be over the road?' she said, with pure sarcasm in her tone.

Poppy flushed, but Sasha raised her eyebrows and stayed quiet, letting Poppy digest this idea, unable to quite meet Sasha's knowing eyes. 'Why are you suddenly so keen to help Ollie?' Poppy asked, after what felt like ages, but Sasha ignored her question.

For once, Sasha didn't fidget in her seat. She usually joked that she felt like a naughty schoolgirl under Poppy's direct gaze, but today she was defiant.

Ollie had two relaxation pods in the garden behind the gym. Poppy had designed these quiet spaces and four treatment rooms, months ago, as a favour to her brother-in-law to be. She'd done the extensive work for a ridiculously low fee. He'd vehemently protested, but she'd held firm. He'd helped her with emotional and business support when she'd started up her own company, so she wanted to repay his kindness. He'd even let her use an office at his old gym free of charge for a year before she managed to finance her dream project and move to a different space. It had been a tiny, dark room at the back of a solicitor's office, but at least it had been hers and she hadn't felt indebted to anyone. Now she'd repaid Ollie and she felt amazing. Poppy finally met Sasha's gaze. 'So? Why do you want Devon to do a photoshoot there?'

Poppy knew how awful Sasha had just been to Ollie, as she'd opened the door a tiny bit and hidden behind it when she'd seen Ollie. The last thing she needed right now was more wedding shenanigans. She knew her friends could plan her big day with their eyes closed. Sasha was organised and Billy had impeccable taste. If she'd wanted to plan it all herself, they'd only have interfered, so it was actually easier to let them get on with it. She needed to keep her mind clear for work and was careful not to overload herself.

She'd had a moment the previous year when she'd wondered if she'd taken on too much, but Dylan had helped her to see that she could work and play. She was trying to balance everything and she found she actually hated wedding planning. Luckily she wasn't a fussy person. Bossy and detail-driven in her work, maybe – but not fussy! She smiled to herself and wondered if she was weird for letting her friends take charge. Did every woman want to plan their own wedding? She sometimes wondered if it might be a hang-up from her parents' disastrous relationship. Although she couldn't wait to be Dylan's wife, she'd have happily done it in ten minutes with a registrar.

'I… um…' said Sasha, suddenly not so brazen. 'Ollie's almost family… for you anyway… and it would be a double win. Jared's amazing, but he keeps changing the schedule! More diversity would be great for us, so we're not relying on one major client. I know we've had enquiries from the last campaign, but this could be huge.'

Poppy thought for a moment and then patched in a call to Billy, who moments later stuck his head round the office door and tilted his head enquiringly. She beckoned to him and he pulled up a chair. He was looking as smart as ever today in his fitted black jeans and designer shirt, rolled up at the sleeves. His blond hair was shaved into the latest style. He prided himself on being bang on trend and never let them down. Poppy's attire had also smartened up over the past year. She no longer wore big colourful T-shirts and took a bit more care about her style, but she was still a creative and happy for the world to know it. She wore skinny jeans and short-sleeved shirts or tops that fitted her perfectly. They were always from artisans or her friend Verity's shop, which was just down the road in the little town at the end of Cherry Blossom Lane. The detailing of Verity's designs always stood out and the patterns were subtle but eye-catching.

'Sasha…' said Poppy, glancing at Billy, 'in her ever-expanding world of interesting connections with social media superstars…' Sasha smiled, recognising the truth behind her friend's teasing. 'Well, she has had an idea about us working with an influencer. She thinks we should design more gym and relaxation areas – like Ollie's.' Billy shot a panicked glance her way at the fact that Sasha now knew about Ollie's gym build. 'Yes, I told her about Ollie and we're both very sorry for keeping that from her,' she added and she gave Sasha a contrite look which Billy quickly copied.

Sasha rolled her eyes. 'Please don't do that to me again, but I can see you were trying to protect me,' she said, giving them both a stern look.

Poppy let out the breath she'd been holding and then hurried on before Sasha thought twice about being so forgiving. 'Sash also wants to widen our customer base,' she continued. 'So we aren't so reliant on Jared.'

She looked at Sasha for confirmation and got a vigorous nod.

'So let me get this straight,' said Billy. 'Sasha wants to look at bringing in social media influencers alongside your designs to promote healthy living. Will they match up?' He shifted in his seat to stare at Sasha thoughtfully. 'I thought you'd given up on being famous?' he said to Sasha.

Sasha's face flamed and she looked indignant. 'We'll select them carefully,' she said. 'Does everyone know my personal business?'

Poppy remembered well the exact moment when Sasha had been drunk on a night out and pulled her and Billy in for a hug, whilst exclaiming that she was going to be internet famous and they needed to stay close to share in her 'brilliant-ness' as some stardust might rub off on them. At which point she'd started rubbing their arms until they were sore. Poppy touched her arm at the memory and Sasha cringed at their obvious amusement at her antics. She pretended to ignore them and stuck her tongue out at Billy, who laughed.

'I may not feel the need to be famous any more, but I do think an up and coming social media influencer – who is so hot he's almost on fire – could help us all,' Sasha said, sticking her nose in the air. She brushed her hair over her shoulder with one hand, eyes flashing, daring them to laugh at her.

'A hot social media influencer?' Billy perked up. Billy was always online and looking for new trends to watch out for. He was almost as bad as Sasha.

Sasha pushed herself out of her seat and rolled her eyes. 'You have a one-track mind. What about Ed coming back for the wedding?'

Billy's smile faded and Poppy wished Sasha had kept her big mouth shut about Billy's ex-partner. Billy had been an eternal ray of sunshine, until Ed had broken his heart. Billy had been recovering, when Ed had announced he'd be back to see Poppy tie the knot. Ed had been a big part of Poppy and Billy's lives for years, so he was on the limited invite list. Billy had said it was ok, but now he seemed to be having second thoughts, when it was too late! Poppy winced and glanced at Sasha who looked equally worried.

Billy pushed himself out of his seat. 'I don't care if Ed's coming back. We've spoken and he knows that choosing his job over me ended our relationship.' He sighed. 'He might now be regretting his choices, but he lives in a different country. It's all too complicated and I'm over him.' His body language didn't reflect his words and Poppy noted Sasha's anxious expression. It was mirrored on her own face.

'I love the idea of bringing influencers in, Sash,' he said. 'It's exciting! Well done. It really is a great idea and I'm sorry we didn't tell you about the gym. It was a stupid decision, but we were thinking of you, honestly.' He gave her a firm squeeze and she hugged him back. 'If your ideas work, we could contact others in the industry and widen our follower base.' He quickly released himself from her arms, saying he had to get back to work. He was singing the whole way back to his office.

Poppy was relieved that Sasha finally knew about the two

relaxation pods that were already installed at Ollie's gym, but she had another client call to make and a whole list of supplies to order for the changes that Jared had just made. She signalled that she needed to make a phone call and ushered Sasha out, while jotting down a few key points from their chat to check out another time.

CHAPTER FIVE

*S*asha doodled ideas on the notepad in front of her and nibbled on a custard cream biscuit. She put the pen down and thought carefully while she drank some of her hot chocolate. Billy had started off as Poppy's assistant, the job Sasha had now, but he had been promoted to Poppy's associate and worked with her on big projects. Sasha had her own dreams for where this path could lead, but for the moment her brain was whizzing with ideas on how to entice Devon into smiling into the camera beside Poppy's brand and in Ollie's gym. Then she'd feel like she was bringing value to the business and would also be apologising for being bitchy to Ollie recently.

Sasha checked her phone and realised it was lunchtime. She usually arranged for food to be sent in. Although Poppy had turned Billy into a workaholic, they did carve out a lunchbreak, which they spent together in the sunny client area. It was next to the boardroom and had a pretty little secluded patio outside and magnificent views across the meadow. There were four outdoor chairs with sage green cushions around a table out there. Dylan had made a living wall backdrop out of wood filled with green plants and fragrant flowers.

Billy was on a health kick to look his best for the wedding, so sweets in the office had been vetoed. Sasha eyed her own curves and petite frame and shrugged. She loved figure-hugging clothes and was not about to forsake her cheese and chilli-jam sandwich for a lettuce leaf. She added two packets of vegetable crisps to the tray and placed it centrally on the boardroom table, checking that everything else was tidy and in its place. She tutted. Two A4 lined writing pads and some black pens she'd put on the table earlier were messing up her line of vision. She'd been learning about sight lines from Poppy and was becoming increasingly fussy about how things looked, even though this was probably just going to be a casual working lunch where they threw creative ideas around as they scoffed their sandwiches.

They'd all loved visiting the gym Ollie owned in their old town, although Demi always ended up sitting in the coffee shop in her gym gear and chatting to other customers and not doing a workout. That girl found any excuse to avoid exercise, but hated missing out on the gossip. She worked with her dad in the popular garage he ran, half a mile from the gym. It felt weird to think Ollie had a business in Cherry Blossom Lane too, now. Sasha had a feeling that there was discontent at Demi's dad's garage from snippets that her friend had divulged, and made a mental note to check that Demi was ok.

Poppy was looking a bit worn out of late. Sasha eyed the crisps. They would give her friend extra energy, she decided, knowing full well they wouldn't, and Billy probably wouldn't be able to resist eating them all, despite his diet. His healthy eating plan seemed to get conveniently forgotten at meal-times, but at any other time, he'd munch on a Tupperware lunchbox full of raw vegetables he brought from home. The noise was annoying, and he'd end up looking like a carrot at this rate. Poppy needed some pampering and to begin trying on the wedding dresses she hadn't even started looking for yet, even though the actual vows were mere months away. Sasha was already having palpitations about that. Ever the organiser, the wedding was looming and practically nothing was sorted out. The next few weeks would probably whiz past, and Poppy needed a dress!

Poppy might be work crazy, but she was also a mental health advocate and she was always banging on about creative time and winding down at lunch breaks to become more productive afterwards. She said they had to have a balance between work and play. To be fair, it worked. Sasha never felt frazzled with this career. She'd been employed in an array of jobs before, where she'd admittedly tried to be as outrageous as possible, to make Ollie notice her, but it had never worked. He'd not batted an eye, whatever she did, not even when she'd worked at the sports centre he owned as a receptionist. That had been her longest ever job. But he had never done more than politely chat, or frown and move on, even when she'd done a brief stint as a part-time model and had her hair styled into a crazy whirlwind. It was also why she didn't stay long at each place. She'd always been working on how to snare him. Now she was finally free of Ollie, she found she was organised, efficient and she ran Poppy's schedule like a dream. She never overbooked her and in fact she often turned down work. Sasha puffed out her chest in pride, but then popped a button off her blouse and almost took her eye out. She blinked, and then decided that she looked better with the extra button undone anyway, and sauntered out of the meeting room back to her desk.

Being selective about who they worked for meant Poppy was focused on one task at a time while they built up a waiting list of clients. Demand was high, but Poppy wanted to expand in new arenas. Sasha had been learning online about social media branding without telling her friends, and she'd implemented a few changes to Poppy's website and social pages. Now their brand was something people coveted.

You didn't have to be rich to have a Poppy Marlowe mood scheme. You could visit a community pod, even if you couldn't invest in a panel to bring in daylight lighting, mood generating warmth, or music for your own home. On the other hand, you could also fully automate your homes like the big builds they ran with Jared, but that was very upmarket. Poppy's dream was to make that available to everyone.

Now all Sasha needed to do was to create some excitement with the younger generation via social media influencers like Devon, or preferably Devon himself. Sasha got her phone out and looked for his latest post. She followed loads of influencers online and had been learning their craft by observation. Sometimes it was sheer luck that made them famous, but often it seemed more like lots of hard work and a business brain. Devon's gorgeous face came to mind and Sasha thought about how much she'd enjoy working with someone as delicious as that. Her eyes crinkled at the corners as she pictured Ollie walking in to ask her something about the wedding while Devon was sitting in her office, hanging on her every word. She'd read somewhere that Devon was a few years younger than them, but he was certainly a successful entrepreneur already.

Sasha really enjoyed chatting to customers and posting images to capture people's imaginations and make them crave their technology, but she wanted more. The phone application Poppy had developed last year had been genius, and she could retire right now if she wanted to. Sasha had rebranded that too. It now fitted seamlessly into Poppy's work portfolio. Who could have guessed Sasha would have had such a flair for marketing? She'd thought she was rubbish at pretty much everything for such a long time.

Sasha ambled over to one of the big front windows looking out onto Cherry Blossom Lane and gazed out. There was Ollie's building. It was right in front of her. How she'd missed all the work going on there, she didn't know. She always arrived from the other direction, so she hadn't really noticed what was going on just up the hill. She'd seen building contractors turn up regularly, but had assumed that it was some sort of hotel group or industrial firm that were refurbishing the old building. It was a big plot with a huge car park in front, so she'd not walked over to see what was going on. Never in her wildest dreams had she thought that Ollie could be the new owner.

Sasha climbed the stairs to the flat above the office that staff used for occasional all-nighters at work. She felt the tension leave her body there as it was such a pretty space, with a little fitted kitchen and huge picture windows overlooking the fields below with big soft couches next to them. She often took a tea break up there, away from Billy's constant musings and singing. It was a quiet space to scroll through her social media or chat to someone online. She put down the designer sports bag she'd slung over her shoulder, so she could change in privacy before heading over to the gym for a workout. She took off her dainty gold bracelet and put it in the little artisan dish Poppy had bought. It had tiny cherry blossoms dotted all over it and it made Sasha smile each time she saw it.

She occasionally felt a bit self-conscious wearing gym clothes or anything this form-fitting, but her mumma had taught her to love her body, so she flicked her hair over her shoulders and straightened her back. She had curves and she loved them, she reminded herself. She'd certainly never had complaints from boyfriends before about her body, but those heartbreaker Taylor boys were enough to keep most women within a fifty-mile radius primping and wanting to look their best.

Thank goodness Sasha wasn't most women, she breathed out a sigh of relief. She was looking for dependable, solid and uneventful now, not annoying, unexpected and exciting. She quickly scrolled through some of the texts on her phone, but none of the men who were trying to engage her in conversation appealed. Most of them came via her online posts and she was never sure how genuine the responses were, so she ignored them. Poppy thought it was hilarious, but Sasha's heart just wasn't in it.

Perhaps it was time to give one or two a chance, though? They couldn't all want casual dates, or a fast fling. She'd grown out of that stage now and was looking for something or someone more serious. Helping Poppy arrange her wedding had shifted something inside her and she was tired of the flirting game or having sex with a boyfriend she didn't really care about as much as she should.

Although Sasha was a bit still piqued at being the last to know about Ollie being in the area, she could understand why he'd opened the new leisure centre whilst it was still being updated, one area at a time, to keep the cash flow moving. It was something she had learnt about recently with her online course. It said you should grow the business gradually through learning phases, which she didn't fully understand yet, but she guessed meant practice and a bit of trial and error.

So she'd decided to stop being such a cow and go and support Ollie. It wasn't his fault he found her physically repulsive and practically ran away every time he'd spotted her over the years. Her crush on him must've been plain for all to see. She refused to be embarrassed by that. She'd been a young woman with untamed hormones, and it was his own fault for being genetically perfect in her eyes.

Now that Ollie was always popping into the studio in Cherry Blossom Lane because his business was across the road, it seemed churlish to ignore him. Plus she'd have to get used to seeing Ollie as family, what with Poppy being almost a surrogate sister. Her own sisters were incredibly annoying. As Ollie was Dylan's older brother, Sasha had to play nice. She would probably be seeing even more of Ollie after the wedding, especially now that Poppy had admitted that there were already two pods in residence at his gym, and they were building a relaxation garden and four treatment rooms! Poppy and Jared had such a big team of contractors working for them now that they could finish up small jobs in days or weeks and then jump onto their next project very quickly.

Initially, Sasha had felt her blood boil as she was the only one who had been in the dark about the build. It made her look like an idiot, but she'd just have to get over that. What must Ollie think of her, that they had to keep his new business a secret from her? And he must think she was rude for not acknowledging his hard work. She didn't know which was worse. Her skin flushed bright red.

He'd probably assumed Sasha was still in love with him, when Poppy asked him to keep it quiet. That was so embarrassing. It would have been better if they had all been in the loop from the start. Sasha could kind of understand why Poppy hadn't told her, but she was still mortified that Poppy had felt the need to protect her from Oliver being nearby again. Sasha's heart had healed and she didn't have room for him now, so her friends could stop worrying about her. Ollie might even have a few fit friends she could date, since they were going to be seeing more of each other. She'd have to remember to ask him.

Sasha was all about being a powerful single lady, on her

way to becoming a social media influencer. She pictured herself looking sensational, being assisted out of a stylish car by a gorgeous chauffeur, just as Ollie came out of the gym, looking sweaty, his thick black hair dishevelled, his eyes locking with hers. She held her head a bit higher. She could do this. She was determined to start going to the gym again and if Ollie was nearby – which he probably wouldn't be very often, once both gyms were fully operational – she would be polite and walk on by.

Sasha called out to Billy that she was taking her own lunch break, quickly changed and headed towards Ollie's gym. Taking in the front of the building and all the bustle from the workmen and women, she crossed the road. She was impressed that the scaffolding she'd noticed the day before was already down, and the front was freshly painted in white and blue accents. The logo and signage were still waiting to be fitted, which made her tut, but she applauded Ollie for his hard work. She had to admit she was impressed by the number of cars already lined up in the car park, which now had greenery in huge blue urns between the rows to transform the space from drab to inviting.

Sasha had helped design the logo for Ollie's other gym, and she noted that the urns were of the same blue shade. He'd run a competition with staff and customers and her design had been chosen. The end result wasn't exactly as she'd designed it, as her drawing skills had been amateur at best at that point. A professional designer had been brought in to fulfil her vision, but she'd been pleased with the end result. She'd won a huge hamper of goodies which she'd handed to her Nonna, as she called her grandmother, who had given her a big toothy grin and told her she was her favourite grandchild. She said that to everyone, including Poppy, Demi and the dog, but it had made Sasha swell with pride to see her smile anyway. Nonna was the best.

CHAPTER SIX

Sasha walked into reception, where a pretty girl with long red hair tied back in a ponytail smiled a greeting.

The lobby was clean and bright, with modern, comfortable-looking blue plush chairs and natural wood tables, which she bet Dylan had made in his workshop. She could now spot his trademark craftmanship anywhere. The seating was strategically placed along one wall to look comfortable and inviting. There were also a lot of green leafy plants in urns again, which made Sasha feel instantly relaxed and brought the inside and outside together. Very clever, she approved. There was a huge window behind the seating area, and her eye was drawn to a light and airy coffee shop bustling with customers in workout clothes. She could smell the scent of fragrant coffee and hot chocolate mingling together and she had to make herself walk in the opposite direction. She could so easily slump down into a chair and sip a chocolaty glass of heaven, instead of working out.

She approached the redhead and enquired briefly about day passes. She couldn't be bothered to get into the whole membership chat right now. She just wanted to be nosy and see what Ollie was up to. She was mightily impressed by the receptionist's knowledge and threw in a few discreet questions about the build and new ownership. The receptionist was bubbly and enthusiastic, her hair swishing as she talked animatedly about the gym, making Sasha think about the difference between how she dealt with customers now, and what she had been like when she worked for Ollie. She hadn't been perky and friendly like the young woman she was chatting to. Sasha had been frustrated all the time and pretty much barked at everyone.

Now she gazed around in awe. Cherry Blossom Lane was becoming quite the place to work. The pretty little tree-lined road was buzzing with new possibilities and up-and-coming businesses. With just a short walk to the little town at the end of the lane, you had the best of both worlds here. You could have views over untamed fields, or pop into a coffee shop with friends for a chat. Not that any of Sasha's other friends were nearby, as they mostly still lived near to their old town in Essex, as she still did too. The hour-long commute to work wasn't ideal, but she was getting used to it.

She saw movement from the corner of her eye and winced, eyes darting around for somewhere to hide, as Ollie came strolling towards her, looking fresh and business-like. Her pulse leapt and she wondered if she could get behind one of the urns before he saw her. His white short-sleeved shirt showed off impressively tanned skin from the spring sunshine. She could have kicked herself for being nosey and wasting time, but it was too late. He'd clearly spotted her. He broke into a wide grin and briefly touched the arm of the man he was speaking to, who looked at her, smiled and then moved away.

Sasha cringed and her face flamed. The woman on reception frowned as Ollie came through the barrier and hugged

Sasha as if all of his Christmases had come at once. Sasha's face grew hot suddenly. Perhaps he saw her as family, now that Poppy and Dylan were getting married, but he seemed desperate to re-start their dwindling friendship for some reason. She rolled her eyes at the receptionist, to try and laugh off why Ollie was cuddling her when she'd just been asking about him.

'Ollie!' She said shrilly. 'I didn't think you'd be here, your brilliant staff member was telling me how you're getting on because I was being nosey.' She wished the ground would open up and swallow her whole, but the phone rang and the receptionist moved away to answer it, after buzzing both in with another confused glance her way. *Blasted Ollie! Always embarrassing her.*

She looked longingly at the coffee shop, as Ollie's hand touched her bare back, below her cropped gym top. She felt naked suddenly, and a frisson of heat shot up her spine. She laughed and moved away so that he had to drop his hand. He was still beaming, though, and turned to face her.

'Would you like a tour? I'm glad you popped by. I thought you'd gone off workouts, as I haven't seen you at the other centre for ages now.'

She could hear the censure I his voice, but it was under-lined by something else? It was as if he'd missed her or some-thing, which couldn't be right. He barely spoke to her.

Sasha paused and briefly closed her eyes. Even when she'd left her job at the gym, she'd still come in to visit as a customer, as she hadn't been able to bear not seeing him regularly. Now humiliation burned inside her that he'd noticed when she'd finally stopped. She hoped he hadn't known the extent of her obsession and felt a teeny bit glad that Poppy had kept them apart for a while. It had clearly done her good after all. Thank goodness she was over him.

She gave him a weak smile and glanced distractedly at a

workout studio to the right, with huge glass windows on two sides and a wall-to-ceiling mirror at the back. Suddenly Sasha could imagine a giant logo emblazoned across the top of the glass to catch people's eyes. Then, feeling a bit more together, she turned back to Ollie. A small blonde woman was frantically trying to catch his eye as she passed on the way to the studio. Her immaculately highlighted ponytail was bobbing up and down prettily. With bright pink lipstick and a figure-hugging cropped top and leggings combo in vivid orange, she wasn't that hard to miss. Ollie finally smiled and nodded his head at her in greeting.

'Who *is* that?' whispered Sasha, close to Ollie's ear. 'She looks like she wants to say hello.'

They both looked at the woman, but then a tall man with a moustache, who must be joining the exercise class judging from his cycling shorts and vest top, drew her into a conversation.

'So, how come you ended up in Cherry Blossom Lane?' Sasha asked, before he could dodge the question.

Ollie looked into her eyes and for some reason she blushed and pretended to gaze around at the various people who were coming and going.

'Poppy brought my attention to the area when she moved here,' Ollie replied. 'Land is being bought up quickly. At the moment it's affordable, but in a few years it will be way out of my price range,' he added candidly.

'Ever the entrepreneur,' joked Sasha, trying to lighten the suddenly heavy atmosphere. She felt a drip of sweat run down her spine and wondered who'd turned the heating up.

'What about you?' asked Ollie.

'Me?' she asked in surprise.

'Are you going to stay working for Poppy?'

Sasha flushed at Ollie's inference that she didn't stick at much for long. She gritted her teeth and tried not to snarl.

'Actually, I'm very happy there, but I'm thinking of starting my own business too.'

Ollie's eyes went wide and his mouth dropped open, before he saw her warning stare and quickly snapped his mouth shut.

'Aren't you usually too tied up with your latest boyfriend to start a business, or stick with a job for long?' he asked casually, watching her response avidly.

She spluttered and her eyes flashed. 'I didn't realise you'd noticed who I was dating,' she said tightly – although she'd only had boyfriends to make him notice her.

When he didn't comment, she continued. 'I've been taking online courses and I've realised I've got a flair for marketing and social media. I organise Poppy and Billy's timelines, but I'm considering the possibility of having some clients of my own.' She bit her lip and thought for a moment, trying to block out the scent of his musky aftershave as it was making her swoon. 'I was thinking I could run it at weekends for now.'

A couple of beefy guys walked past and looked at her appreciatively, saying a quick hello to Ollie and smiling at her as they went. Ollie responded to them politely before guiding her along the corner and away from temptation, as he seemed to think she was a man-eater who might pounce on his clients. If only!

Perhaps she wouldn't ask him about available friends to date, if he thought she'd eat them alive. A vision of gently biting her way up his neck came into her mind and she shook her head to clear it, cursing under her breath.

CHAPTER SEVEN

'*I* love your business idea,' said Ollie, as they walked along, mentioning that he was keen to show her his office. She nearly fell over in shock that he wanted to spend more than five minutes with her and gave him a hard stare while she tried to work out if he was making fun of her again. She certainly wasn't bothered about spending time with him.

'Can I be your first client?' he asked, glancing at her and then smiling at a customer as they passed. She frowned and stopped walking.

'The social media presence needs updating for both my gyms,' he explained, grinning down at her. He towered over her, at over six feet tall to her five feet five.

Sasha knew she should have been ecstatic at her first possible contract offer, but it would mean that she'd have to see more of Ollie – and she was stronger when he wasn't around. She knew she wasn't in love with him anymore, but she was only human.

Ollie clearly saw her indecision, but wasn't about to let her off that easily. 'How about I give you a tour of the whole building and you can see if there is something that inspires you? There are lots of very fit men here,' he joked and winked at her, making her almost miss her step. Ollie was never playful with her. He was the serious one who had always kept her at arms' length. He mostly growled whenever she as much as opened her mouth to speak.

Sasha checked the time on her phone. 'Such temptation…' she parried back, seeming as he was so sure she was a man-eater. 'But I'd better get back to work,' she added quickly. Ollie eyed her workout gear and raised his eyebrows sarcastically. She was about to blurt out about her idea for Devon and the gym, but she bit back the words, as she suddenly wasn't feeling so generous.

For the first time in her life, she hesitated about what to say. She'd love her first weekend client, but working with Ollie would unsettle her. Maybe Poppy and Billy had been right and knew her better than she knew herself. Poppy had first-hand experience of the Taylor brothers' magnetism, so no wonder she was trying to protect her friend. Sasha felt a bit better about all that suddenly.

Being near Ollie drove her insane with self-doubt. What if she couldn't do the job of running his social media accounts, or wasn't good enough for him again? Not that she ever had been in the first place. Ollie had never chosen her for anything – not as his date for that fateful school party they had all gone to, where Demi had kissed Miles and ended up dating Allan, nor for any work parties or events. She did love the idea of running the gym's social feeds, though, and plans were already flitting through her mind. She instantly conjured up images of where she could improve things.

'I can see that you're already thinking about what to do!' said Ollie, laughing, completely unaware that she'd been thinking of throttling him earlier.

She started heading back to reception, head held high and

annoying men put to the back of her mind, while her eyes darted around making mental notes. Ollie watched her for a few seconds and then caught her up, matching his pace to hers. There was a huge queue for an exercise class as they moved back to reception.

'Wow! You aren't even officially open properly yet and you have classes that are full?' Sasha said.

Ollie smiled but it didn't quite reach his eyes. He was watching the tiny blonde woman they'd seen earlier stride to the front and start chatting animatedly with the line of people, who suddenly started acting as if a rock star had arrived.

'Who is that?' asked Sasha again. 'She's popular.'

Ollie sighed and took Sasha's arm, almost using her body as a barricade. What the hell?

'Yes, she is really popular,' he said. 'A big hit with my customers.'

When Sasha frowned he picked his smile back up. 'Hasn't Poppy told you about Maxine?'

'Maxine? No.' her stomach churned with foreboding.

'She's our most popular aerobics instructor at my other gym.' He thought for a moment. 'She started after you left.'

Sasha gave him a nonchalant glance and pretended that she had no clue when this was. She was surprised he'd even noticed when she'd gone. But then, she'd been almost like his lovelorn shadow. It must have been a huge relief to him when she got another job. She felt her cheeks burn with humiliation at the memory. Thank goodness they could just be friends now.

She straightened her shoulders and looked him directly in the eye. She could finally be on equal terms with a man she'd dreamed about for years. Working on reception to be near him hadn't been her best idea. She'd left after three years, as he'd barely said hello in that whole time. She'd had managers who were annoyingly efficient, who didn't need to call him in much, to her frustration. In the end, she'd made a mistake at work, mis-booking a potential new client, to get Ollie to fire her... because at least then he would have to talk to her. But in fact he'd just looked disappointed and called the client personally to offer them three months' free membership. She remembered thinking *if only she'd been the client!* She'd been that desperate for him to notice her. What a lunatic.

'Anyway...' he continued, watching the class file in and waving tentatively back to Maxine as she smiled widely at him and then indicated she had to start her class with a tilt of her head. 'Poppy started coming to Maxine's classes on the days she used to visit Dylan's place and they became close.'

Sasha's eyebrows shot up. Poppy had mentioned a Max she occasionally went to the gym with, but Sasha had assumed it was one of Dylan's mates. Sasha didn't like the feeling in the pit of her stomach at the thought of her best friend keeping secrets again, although perhaps it was her own fault for not asking more about this Max. Sasha had hated any mention of the gym after she stopped going there, so both she and Poppy usually kept that chat to a minimum.

'She's coming to the wedding,' Ollie said tightly.

Sasha had written the guest list and table plans, so immediately remembered writing the name in gold pen on the pretty placeholders. Poppy had made lots of new contacts over the past year, it was hard to keep up. Sasha sighed and admitted to herself that she hadn't always listened when her friends spoke. The sparkling, new and improved Sasha sat up and took notes.

It wasn't going to be a huge wedding, even though Poppy was almost famous now with her incredible home designs. There was a pretty little church at the end of Cherry Blossom Lane and the door was framed with wisteria during the summer, which smelt amazing and looked gorgeous, apparently.

Poppy had a tiny family and wanted to keep things local to where she lived now, so the venue was close to where she worked and had her new home with Dylan. They lived in a stunning house with grounds that Poppy had designed, while Billy lived in the flat above the garage. Sasha had found out that morning that Ollie was currently living in the house that backed onto Poppy's property, in a development she and Jared had designed.

Sasha had often stayed over at Poppy's house or in Billy's flat, but now Ollie had moved in and ruined it. It would be weird not actively avoiding him, now it looked like they were going to try to be friends, but she definitely wasn't going to seek him out like she used to. But suddenly there he was in every part of her life anyway. Bloody men!

Having Ollie nearby was something she'd have to get used to, as she had her eye on the flat above the office and was hoping Poppy might consider letting it out to her now it had been converted. The commute to work, and then the online training, were taking it out of her. She'd have to make some changes to her life soon. She snapped her attention back to Ollie and quickly checked the time on her phone.

'What's wrong with Max coming to the wedding?' she asked.

Ollie shifted from foot to foot and wouldn't meet her eye for a minute. 'You didn't sleep with her and dump her?' she asked in horror. 'Oh Ollie!'

He looked annoyed at her assumption and shook his head. 'No! I didn't... I haven't,' he sighed and ran his hand through his hair, making it look mussed up and sexy. Then he flexed his shoulders, a movement that she involuntarily followed with her eyes. 'Not for want of trying...' before she could interrupt, he continued. '...On her part. She follows me everywhere. I don't want to offend her, but I'm her boss!'

Sasha didn't like the weird feeling in her stomach, but then anger took over. 'Well, if you will be God's gift to women, Oliver. How can the poor woman cope when faced with such masculine beauty each day?' she scoffed. He gave her a hard stare but she refused to look away.

'You know me better than that,' he said. She had the grace to blush, but still felt like she had an army of tiny ants marching up her back, ready to rile her up further. This man was infuriating. 'I don't date people who work for me as, you well know.'

She frowned. She hadn't known this. She felt her skin grow even warmer when she thought of the number of times she'd practically chucked herself at him when she worked at the other gym. He'd always politely turned her down or hurried away. She'd never considered he was being professional. Loads of people had sex with co-workers. Not that she'd just wanted sex with him. She'd have given anything to have him committed to her, but he was too much of a playboy... she'd thought. She wracked her brain to think of any gossip about him dating a staff member, but there hadn't been any.

'Maybe if you told her that, she'd quit. If she thought you were worth it,' she said tightly.

He seemed shocked, as if he'd never given that a thought, and his eyes met hers. For a second, she couldn't look away – then she coughed slightly and backed up. He took a step towards her and held out his hand, but she jumped as if she'd been scalded and turned towards the door.

'Sasha, wait!'

'I've... um... I've got to get back to work.'

But, before she could leave, Maxine appeared in front of them like an evil genie, swishing her ponytail.

'Hi Maxine,' said Ollie, sounding as if he was pulling teeth. 'How are you?' He inclined his head towards the people waiting patiently for her outside the class.

Maxine turned and called out that she was coming and would just be a moment, if they wanted to go into the studio and wait for her. She waved greetings to a couple of late-comers as they filed in. Ollie nodded his head and said hello to one or two, his smile right back in place. He had taken hold of Sasha's arm again and was standing so close to her she could feel his breath on the back of her neck, which made the hairs stand up. She wondered if he'd fall flat on his face if she abruptly leaned sideways.

'Your class looks busy,' he commented to Maxine, who licked her lips as she regarded Ollie, her eyes sparkling. Her teeth dazzled, they were so white. Sasha almost stepped back, but Ollie was still behind her.

Maxine was like some sort of power source, radiating energy. She bounced from foot to foot as she talked. 'I was hoping that we could have a chat after my class?'

Maxine turned to check that her clients had moved into the gym, then eyed the big clock on the wall by the door. Sasha guessed she was deciding how much time she had with the man of her dreams. Sasha felt weird, seeing another woman clearly feeling the way about Ollie that she had. At the time, she'd assumed she was the only one in the world who could feel such angst and passionate love. What an idiot.

'Um, you'd like a chat, yes, of course!' said Ollie politely. 'But my friend Sasha has just turned up and I'm not sure how long she'll be visiting for.'

'I had been hoping to join that class,' said Sasha moodily, looking through the window, as she saw people warming up. 'But I really should go...'

Ollie laughed a bit manically. 'Oh Sasha! She's such a joker,' he said to Maxine, slipping his hand around Sasha's waist and making her gasp in some air. 'Sasha has asked for a full tour of the premises. She works with Poppy and is interested to see how work's progressing on the relaxation spaces and pods.'

Maxine raised her eyebrows and looked at Sasha in her workout clothes, then remembered her manners and gave them both a bright smile.

'That's wonderful! We'll be seeing a lot more of you, Sasha, and perhaps next time you'll actually get to try out a class. I didn't know you worked with Poppy. We should all get together to talk more about the wedding plans,' Maxine said as if she had the inside track, which made Sasha feel even more grumpy, but she kept her smile in place and agreed. 'Poppy and I are old friends,' Maxine added.

She quickly turned before Sasha could speak, exclaiming that her class was about to start and they were as eager as ever. Her tinkling laugh put Sasha on edge. Maxine walked off to the classroom and was greeted by her clients crowding round her.

'She's popular,' said Sasha tersely. Ollie dropped his hand from her waist and she felt cold suddenly. She really did want to join that class, even if the instructor was weird. Sasha had never had body envy – but she was competitive and wanted to see what was so special about Maxine the pocket rocket.

Ollie steered her away and she had no choice but to follow him back upstairs to a beautiful office suite that was clearly where he worked, with a gorgeous view over Cherry Blossom Lane and the flowering fields behind. It was the same outlook as the one from Poppy's design space. He also had a clear sightline of the front of their office. How the tables had turned! He could now see her coming and going, she realised. Not that he cared or would probably take any notice anyway.

She was about to surrender all will and ask to see the rest of the building, but then noticed the time. She really did need to get back to work. 'It's gorgeous, Ollie,' she said truthfully, leaning in and gently kissing his cheek as she explained she had to go.

As they descended the stairs back to reception, Ollie told her more about how everything worked, but then she heard one of his staff call his name. He had no choice but to turn and hear what they had to say.

Sasha sped up and made her escape, almost keeling into a handsome young man who was walking into the gym. He laughed and held her up, but she blustered that she was sorry and quickly made her way back to the office and slumped at her desk.

She was grateful for once that Poppy and Billy were both occupied, while she tried to make sense of the way her heart was beating so rapidly at being near to Ollie on her own again, and why she'd run away. She was over her stupid crush on him and she'd be damned if she turned into a glob of mush when he fixed those smoky grey eyes on her. She was a strong woman, and it was about time that she gave herself a break from working, had some dates and found a partner to accompany her to her best friend's wedding. If the man she'd just bumped into at the gym was anything to go by, this town was full of hotties, and she wouldn't let herself slide back into her old, pathetic ways. She was strong and feisty and no man – not even Oliver – was going to get in her way.

She quickly strode up to the flat and changed back into her work clothes. After a glass of ice-cold water and a stern talking-to in the mirror by the stairs, her heart had stopped racing. She sat back at her desk and opened the drawer. Her old diary was right there, mocking her, taunting her with her own passionate words about Ollie – and her dreams about being so successful she'd never have to think of him again. She had written all her longing for Oliver Taylor on these pages. She quickly shoved the drawer shut in disgust and got up to make herself a huge hot chocolate with marshmallows, throwing in a shot of coffee for good measure.

CHAPTER EIGHT

'Right, everyone,' said Poppy. 'Let's go to the pub.'

Demi jumped up and clapped her hands in glee. She loved the pretty little pub further up the lane. She had to pick up a car part for her dad, and as the specialist dealer was close to Cherry Blossom Lane she had popped in.

She'd been sitting chatting quietly to Billy while Sasha tapped away on her computer keyboard, pretending she wasn't listening to every word they said. Sasha hated being left out of any gossip. It was hard listening to your friends share their worries with other friends, when you knew exactly what they needed. Sasha wondered about the best way to suggest to Demi that she should think about spreading her wings, and spend a little time away from her dad and Allan at the garage.

Sasha actually felt like stamping on Allan's toes quite regularly, for the way he assumed Demi would always be around, without treating her like a princess. Demi deserved a man who appreciated her, not one who put her down and ignored her ideas for the business he worked at with her dad.

Demi could have run that garage with her eyes closed, but her dad refused to see her potential. He still treated her like a child, when she could strip a car and rebuild it in less time than most of his staff, including him. Sasha sighed and wondered if Demi would listen to her if she told her to jump ship. Probably not. Demi liked routine and however much her dad annoyed her, she loved him to bits.

Billy started packing away some paperwork and shuffling it into piles. Sasha groaned because she knew that pile would be sitting on her desk tomorrow. For a tech-savvy guy, Billy liked writing things by hand and said he felt more creative with a pen. Sasha loved him, but his handwriting was almost illegible and trying to transfer his thoughts into a plan of action took twice as long as it should. For someone who was always telling them how efficient he was, this way of working was infuriating. She'd spent the last half hour Googling pens that wrote straight from a tablet to the computer, and had already sent Poppy an email about buying one. She guessed that was what had made her ask them all to the pub. Sasha winced, as her message had been slightly stroppy.

She gave Poppy a smile of apology as her friend walked past her and put a hand on her shoulder, but it didn't shake the tautness there, or help the headache that had been brewing for days. Perhaps a drink with friends was the solution? Switching off her computer, she picked up her flashy new handbag and slipped her feet back into the towering heels she'd bought to make her legs look longer. Wearing them for thirty minutes felt like ten hours, but she needed the extra confidence right now. Having Ollie nearby again made her want to growl at everyone. She knew she'd been a bit short in her responses when they asked her if she was ok. Could she and Ollie be friends? She hoped so, for all their sakes.

Halfway down the road to the aptly named pub, The Cherry Tree, they stopped to take in the view. The building had cherry trees flanking the walkway to the front door, and deep green ivy trailing over the front porch. It was on the same side of the road as Poppy's office, with the garden set into the fields beyond. It was picture-perfect and they always stood for a moment and enjoyed the scene before moving forward and stepping into the quaint Tudor interior through the charmingly wonky door.

They smiled and said hello to the handsome manager, who winked at them all, which had them giggling like schoolchildren as they found a table. He was swoon-worthy, with just slightly too long dark blond hair curling at the nape of his neck, and tanned arms that were firm and strong. His greetings always made them bump into each other, their eyes glazing over, he was so gorgeous. His gaze always followed Billy around and Sasha decided it was about time Billy started living again. Ed was coming back for the wedding, but perhaps he needed to be shown that he shouldn't have left in the first place. Sasha was fed up with everyone being walked over by their dream men. She noticed Demi looking glum and it fired up her anger again.

Demi, Billy and Poppy exchanged glances as she said she was going to get them drinks. Sasha's healthy new bank balance was a revelation to her. She loved being able to buy a round at the pub and had even begun to treat herself to some new clothes. She'd also bought gifts for her family. Before she'd worked for Poppy, each month had been a strain. Paying the rent on the flat she'd shared with her sisters, when their jobs were also sporadic, had meant juggling what to pay when bills came in. Being the eldest sister had meant the task had fallen to her. She hadn't realised quite how much of a strain it had been, until she'd not had to worry about it. Now she could afford to help her sisters out without worrying.

∼

*D*emi watched Sasha reach the bar to get their second round of drinks and start chatting to Franco, the delicious manager. 'What's going on?'

'I told her about Ollie's gym,' sighed Poppy, watching Sasha too.

Demi winced. 'Was that a good idea?'

'She'd have found out sooner or later. It was stupid not to tell her. He keeps coming into the office.' Poppy tried not to laugh at Ollie's antics.

'Is that a problem?' asked Demi, her eyes wide. 'I thought she was over him now? No wonder her face looks like she's swallowed a goldfish.'

'I thought it might make things difficult, and it seems I was right.' Poppy straightened the beer mats on the tabletop and then put her hands in her lap. 'Now she's not fawning over him, he seems to want her attention. It's so annoying and unfair to Sasha. Perhaps her leaving the area and meeting new people has scared him into his senses at last?'

'I thought you liked Oliver!' said Demi, her mouth dropping open.

'I do. I love him, but he infuriates me,' said Poppy glumly, picking up a petal that had dropped from the posy of wildflowers on the table and popping it back into the vase. 'Sasha would have been receptive to him years ago, but that ship has sailed. She's stronger now and doesn't need anyone looking after her. She wanted Ollie because he's gorgeous, of course, but I think it was also about his passion for life. Her family are rowdy and affectionate, so she has to stand out to find her place. She needs a leader in a partner, or she'll crucify them,' said Poppy. Demi and Billy nodded their agreement.

'She loves how Ollie has fire in his belly for his business, even though I think that's what's kept them apart,' Poppy continued. 'He puts work over relationships every single time. Now she works with us, she's realising that there are plenty of men out there with ambition.' She looked across the bar to her friend.

'None of them are Ollie Taylor, though,' said Billy with a sigh. 'What is it with those brothers? They could bottle and sell it, whatever it is. I'd buy some,' he sniggered into his hand like a child, breaking the tension as they all giggled.

Demi nodded at Franco, who was still looking at Billy wistfully as he chatted to Sasha. 'I'm not sure you need that, Billy,' she said and he flushed and grinned, taking a sneaky peek at the bar manager and sipping his wine thoughtfully.

Poppy waggled her eyebrows suggestively at Billy but he ignored her. 'Sasha only used to flit from job to job because she had no direction,' she said.

'Now she's focused with laser-like precision, I'm not sure she has time for a man. Even if he looks like Ollie,' said Demi, and Poppy was taken aback by her wisdom and insight. They craned their necks to stare at Sasha as she threw her head back and laughed at something Franco said, making them all smile. If one of their friendship group was sad, it affected them all. Sasha was often the one to brighten their days, or physically shake them out of their gloom.

'Ollie still seems to rile her, though,' noted Billy. He waved at Franco, who was weaving between tables and showing customers to a free spot. The smile that lit up Franco's face made Poppy prod Billy in the leg and raise her eyebrows in question. He ignored her again and then made a face at them both. 'Stop trying to fix me up. We're discussing Sasha right now.' But his eyes wandered to Franco, who was pulling back chairs with a flourish. 'Whenever Sasha sees Ollie, she gets grumpy and takes it out on us,' said Billy. 'She needs some passion in her life.'

'We all do,' said Demi, shocking them to silence.

Poppy frowned. 'Everything ok?'

Demi avoided the question and continued discussing their fiery friend. 'She's been fine for ages. It's only since Ollie's decided to come into your office that she's growly again. I think the distance helped. Now he's around all the time, it probably reminds her that she's still attracted to him and it annoys her.'

'You think so? I thought she got over him ages ago,' said Billy.

Poppy looked across to reassess her friend. Sasha was turning to walk their way with a full tray of drinks.

Poppy decided that they definitely needed that second glass, if they were going to get to the bottom of what all three of her friends should do to sort their lives out. She was only glad her own love life wasn't in the mix this time, but she had received a troubling email fairly recently and it had been gradually taking over most of her waking thoughts. She felt the usual heavy weight that had settled in her stomach in the last few weeks and tried to ease it with the back of her palm, by gently rubbing in circles until it eased slightly. Whatever happened, they wouldn't leave the pub until at least one of their problems were solved.

CHAPTER NINE

'What are you all talking about?' asked Sasha as she approached and placed the tray of fresh drinks on the table without spilling a drop, thanks to a previous job as a waitress for a pub near her mum's house. Her green eyes looked around the table suspiciously. Sasha didn't miss much, thought Poppy. Sasha's Italian heritage gave her long dark hair and those striking eyes, plus her skin was currently sun-kissed and always looked healthy and glowing. But when she was annoyed it was as plain as day on her face.

'We were just discussing one of our latest design ideas for a lovers' mood panel, and also saying we all need to inject some passion into our lives… well, not Poppy, but the rest of us are definitely lacking,' Billy joked, making Sasha frown as she glanced at Demi.

Poppy wished she could manage to look fierce and glamorous all at once, like Sasha did. Sasha had a special air about her that commanded attention. Poppy had to work hard to build her confidence to deal with clients face to face. For the first year of her business, she'd hidden behind Billy, pretending to her friends and family that it was his empire she worked for and not her own. Now she looked back and wondered what the hell she'd been thinking, but at the time it had seemed to make sense. How things had changed recently. She'd stepped up and admitted the business was hers, she was proud of all they had achieved, and she wouldn't have been able to do that without the support of her close friends.

They might have had a few hiccups along the way, but with the wedding fast approaching, they really needed to sit down and organise the day. It wasn't something she could do alone and she wasn't about to hand it over to some faceless planner, when her three best friends thrived on challenges like this. She was so busy with her clients that she'd never have found time to do it and that would have upset her gorgeous fiancé. She still woke up some nights in a cold sweat thinking Dylan sweeping her off her feet and asking her to marry him was just a dream. They'd had a great start to their relationship, and then a very stormy middle, but now they were back on track and she couldn't wait to become his wife.

'Right, you lot. No design work tonight, even if it is about luurve,' Poppy winked at them all. 'Talk me through the wedding plans,' she said.

Demi squealed in delight and grabbed a ream of notes from the pretty blue bag that was by her feet. There were pages of dazzling dresses and bridal favours. Sasha rolled her eyes and Billy gave her a warning look. She stuck her tongue out at him, but then took her time to look properly at Demi's ideas, oohing and ahhing in all the appropriate places.

Poppy was glad that Sasha seemed to be a bit happier, and was asking Demi lots of questions about the images. Poppy had delegated separate tasks to everyone. Demi was the best dressed of the bunch, so Poppy had entrusted her and Verity, who owned the boutique down the street, with finding her the perfect dress, so she didn't have to trail round a hundred fittings. She knew loads of brides cherished this, but Poppy realised her mum, June, would want to come with her and it would eventually stress her out. One or two dress shops would be enough for them to enjoy it.

June was doing so well, after years in a mental health sanctuary. She was now working alongside her boyfriend, Chris, at the local café they had all visited most days when they were at school, beside the tower block where Poppy and June had lived in a little flat. It seemed like Chris and her mum were in love, and Poppy wouldn't be surprised if she heard about them moving in together soon.

In any case, Poppy's schedule didn't leave much room for taking time off, if she wanted a honeymoon somewhere hot with Dylan. She'd promised him she'd make time, even though her creative business was filling every hour at the moment. She ran her eyes over the bridal designs and hugged Demi to her side, which made her friend giggle so the freckles on her nose stood out. Her dark bouncy curls jiggled around her shoulders. Men sitting nearby always turned to watch Demi smile. It was a joy and she had no idea of the effect she had on them. Her twinkling soft brown eyes and Jamaican heritage drew them in and knocked them side-ways, but she never looked further than her boyfriend, Allan, who was one lucky man as far as Poppy was concerned. Poppy wasn't quite as sure of that match as she should have been, but in the end it was Demi's choice and the rest of them would shut up and support her. Poppy grinned suddenly as she knew how hard it was for Sasha to hold back and not blurt out how she felt at all times. Sasha wore her heart on her sleeve and was fiercely protective of them all. She'd been the same way at school. It was as if they'd all been adopted into her boisterous brood of siblings.

Sasha was now busily vetoing lots of the dresses. Poppy caught her hand and squeezed it, making her take a breath and carefully place the dress designs back on the table. They had talked about making Demi feel involved. Sasha was a natural at organising and could co-ordinate the whole wedding with her eyes closed – but this was a team event.

Sasha grinned and smoothed the pictures down. 'Sorry, am I taking over again?'

Demi smiled and nodded good-naturedly. 'Yep. Don't worry, we're used to it. It's how you kept us all in order growing up. Without you, we'd have wound each other up and fought more. You're bossy, but most of the time you're kind, so we don't mind, really.' Demi smoothed Sasha's hair over her shoulder and kissed her cheek, making her blush.

'You never have a bad word to say about anyone, Demi!' said Sasha. 'Unlike Poppy and me, we tend to air our thoughts.'

'Don't drag me into it,' joked Poppy. 'Right, you lot. Let's have a look at these dresses – and what on earth are those pages of trolleys all about?' she pointed to images of carts and portable bars, and even some kind of horse box.

'Well, that's depending on whether you decide to stick with the main room at the venue, you know, the Manor House Hotel, or use their outside space. You see, you could have a mobile bar, or sweet carts, cocktails themed for the wedding, pretty signs around the grounds, or a photo booth!'

Poppy frowned. 'Demi. It's a small wedding, not some big extravaganza. Most of the guests are Dylan's family.'

'Sasha even mentioned an iced coffee cart,' said Demi, while Poppy shook her head.

'We don't need any fuss. And I've already decided and confirmed the main room, as a marquee would have been too big.' She wouldn't look at her friend's raised eyebrow, at her having finally made at least one decision on her own.

Demi frowned. 'It's only a few months away now, and so far all you have is a guest list and a venue booked. The invites have gone out, but you haven't decided on anything else – including your own dress!'

Poppy could hear panic rising in Demi's voice. Sasha placed her hand on Demi's in solidarity, and Billy was wriggling around as if he had ants in his pants, and frowning as well.

'You do need to make some decisions Poppy,' he scolded gently. 'You're not having second thoughts, are you?' he asked, his voice tense. This was clearly something they'd all discussed without her.

Poppy felt like she'd has a glass of water thrown in her face. 'Of course not.'

'But you're not making any decisions,' Sasha pointed out. 'Every time we compile anything,' she motioned to Demi's stack of dress photos, 'You put us off. You only finalised the guest list last week and I sent the invites out before you could change your mind.'

Poppy's mouth formed an O and she hung her head.

'You're not thinking about running off with Jared?' Billy asked with a slight edge to his voice.

'What! Oh bloody hell, Billy,' Poppy laughed in astonishment. Was that what they'd all been thinking? 'Jared and I are just friends, as you very well know,' she said, putting an end to this nonsense. 'He's not overstepped the mark since Dylan and I got back together. Do you think Dylan worries about that? Has he said anything?' her stomach began filling with butterflies and she realised how tired she was.

'No. He hasn't,' Billy soothed, clearly noticing the droop of her shoulders. 'But you both need to decide on some things soon, or you'll end up walking down the aisle in one of Verity's designer T-shirts.'

'Has this got something to do with your dad?' asked

Sasha. Poppy's dad had left her mum before Poppy was born and Sasha had once asked her if getting married scared her for this reason. Poppy had wondered about that too.

Now she flushed and hung her head. 'Someone contacted me via email a few weeks ago and said he was my dad. Apparently, he saw me in a magazine and recognised my name.'

They all gasped in horror as Poppy continued. 'He didn't want to know me after I was born... so why now?'

'Is it definitely him?' asked Billy.

'Yes. He's got a copy of my birth certificate. I checked. I daren't tell Mum.'

'And you didn't think to tell us?' said Sasha, hurt in her voice.

'Have you told Dylan?' asked Billy, closing his eyes and sighing deeply, already knowing the answer. Poppy was not known for sharing her troubles.

'He'll want to invite him to the wedding. You know what Dylan's like. He loves family more than anything. Mum will fall apart, and she's just got herself back together.' Poppy felt her eyes well with tears and she brushed them away and took a huge gulp of wine which burnt her throat, making her cough.

'Oh Poppy,' said Sasha, getting up and putting her arms round her. 'What a mess. No wonder you've been putting off making decisions about the wedding.' She took a step back and looked at them all. 'Thank goodness it wasn't Jared,' she said solemnly, making them all splutter out their drinks. 'Right,' she clapped her hands like a schoolteacher and they all sat up straighter. 'We are going to make some decisions about the wedding tonight. Tomorrow we will book them in. You will have two dress fittings this weekend, Poppy.'

Poppy sniffed and wiped a tear from her cheek. Billy reached over and held her hand. 'But for now, go home and tell Dylan,' said Sasha. 'Talk to him about your dad and the wedding, and explain how scared it makes you. Decide between you about allowing your dad back into your life. Let Dylan in,' she said softly.

'You don't have to go through this alone! We're all here for you,' said Billy passionately.

'Then we can come with you while you talk to your mum,' said Demi, taking Poppy's other hand. 'She's got Chris now and this doesn't have to set her back. She's stronger, like you are. She doesn't need your dad in her life. He can walk on by for all she cares,'

Poppy crossed her fingers under the table. She could see Demi wasn't quite committed to what she was saying, but was so sweet and hopeful. Poppy smiled a watery smile and took another swift glug of her red wine, smarting as the alcohol hit her senses.

'I was supposed to be sorting out all of your problems tonight,' said Poppy, her voice wobbling. 'I thought things were finally looking bright, after such an emotional time last year...' she sniffed, brushing her hair out of her eyes with her hands.

'You didn't bank on your dad turning up though, did you?' said Sasha thoughtfully. 'I know we're all a bit of a mess right now, but at least we're in it together,' she joked, making Poppy smile finally.

'Let's get together another night and decide what all of us should do to turn everything around. Billy needs to decide what to do about Ed. You and Demi have both got to make decisions about your dads and I need to move on from annoying old habits that hold me back from an orgasmic sex life with a hot new man.' They all grinned at that. 'For now, go and see Dylan, Poppy,' Sasha said firmly.

CHAPTER TEN

*S*asha pictured the doodles she'd added to her sparkly journal when she should have been listening to her teachers in class at school. Now that she was actually fulfilling some of those daydreams, she could almost pinch herself. She'd spent most of the past week hanging out in spots where famous people and influencers might be, and getting involved and chatting to people. She really enjoyed mingling and networking.

Tonight she was at one of Poppy's events, wearing a sleek new black dress that skimmed her curves, while her hair was a glossy waterfall down her back. Poppy was wearing a fitted silver dress that shimmered as she moved. Sasha had been flirted with, bought drinks and handed business cards, while her brand-new phone was full of exciting numbers, from people who couldn't wait to hang out with her some more, or talk to her about Poppy's latest designs. That was really Billy's job, but Sasha had learned enough about Poppy Marlowe Designs to explain how the panels and pods were benefitting so many people.

Sasha had discovered she was a natural salesperson.

When she loved the product or service she was selling, the words just flew off her tongue and her audience seemed to lap it up. It helped that Poppy's designs were so innovative. Sasha's mind seemed constantly full of ideas to push the business further. Poppy was happy to let her take the reins, as she chatted to customers all day on reception anyway. Poppy's firm was still a small business where everyone mucked in and helped each other, which Sasha loved.

This was her third event in a week, and she utilised the opportunity to make contacts with any young people who were making a name for themselves, just like she was. Social media had a big impact on the success or downfall of businesses and Sasha didn't want Poppy to be left behind. She felt energised and impressed at how hard the influencers worked to achieve their own dreams.

Earlier in the week they had visited a trade show to see what the competition was up to, and Poppy had given a talk on mental health and how buildings could make everyday life happier, and help the mind wind down after work. The seminar was very well received. Sasha had been there to help make sure everything was set up correctly, see the guests had refreshments and ensure everyone left with a goodie bag full of marketing information and a free sample of their app.

While Sasha had been chatting to the guests afterwards, lots of fresh ideas filled her mind about content to post on Poppy's social media feeds. She knew that people could do a whole day of business from their phones, with a multitude of apps to increase workflow. This made Poppy's mood board and meditation app perfect to help people relax and unwind and find a balance.

She smiled and accepted a glass of Champagne from a passing waiter and took a moment to enjoy the dazzling scene before her. The event that evening was for local businesspeople and was being held in the ballroom of the Manor House Hotel, in Cherry Blossom Lane. The high ceilings and crystal chandeliers made it feel extra glamorous. There was a gin bar along one wall, also serving beers and cocktails. Sasha couldn't wait for Poppy and Dylan to get married here. She was mid-conversation about the growth of the town with the twins who ran the local specialist tearoom. They were both wearing elegant wrap dresses with tie sides, in different colours. Sasha had never seen them dress even remotely similarly before, so she'd done a double-take when she'd watched them arrive.

She'd also spied Ollie looking sharp in a dinner suit. He was chatting to various people and spent quite a while discussing something with a beautiful brunette in a striking wine-coloured dress, which had made Sasha even more determined to enjoy herself. When a handsome guy with gorgeous blue eyes, immaculate blond hair and a designer suit approached her and offered to get her a fresh drink, she smiled and accepted just as Ollie looked her way. She put her hand on the man's arm to ask his name and saw Oliver frown from and then break away from the woman and head over to them.

He reached her just as her companion turned away to go to the bar. He put his arm around her waist and kissed her cheek. 'You look stunning, Sasha,' he said, his eyes running over her body, making her skin warm up. She refused to fidget and just gave him a dazzling smile, which made his eyes turn a shade darker and his pupils dilate.

'Thank you,' she said graciously. 'You look pretty dazzling yourself.'

'I didn't know you were going to be here,' said Ollie, his hand still at her waist. 'I'd have looked for you sooner if I had. Is Poppy here?'

'She's talking to the events manager about her wedding.

She hasn't had a chance before now. As they're both here, Poppy grabbed her moment,' explained Sasha.

'Who is the guy at the bar?' asked Ollie, looking over her shoulder and finally dropping his hand to his side.

'I've no idea yet. I just met him,' she replied.

Ollie nodded and their eyes met for a moment, making her shiver. 'Are you cold?' he asked, pulling her into his side just as the guy returned with her drink.

Ollie smiled and introduced himself, taking his time at extracting his arm and shaking the man's hand. Ollie started asking him about his local business and she quietly seethed that he wasn't making himself scarce. She'd been having a great time and it seemed that there were actually lots of interesting and handsome men who worked or owned businesses nearby. She looked up to hear Ollie agree that the other man should pop by and check out the gym, before he said goodbye to Sasha and returned to the small group of people he'd been chatting to before Ollie had arrived.

'What the hell did you do that for?' she asked incredulously.

'Do what?' he asked, with a frown.

'Scare away that guy, he just bought me a drink,' she said fiercely, almost stamping her feet.

Ollie gave her a wide-eyed innocent look. 'I didn't realise you were using a work event to get a date.'

Sasha pushed her body into his and he had no option but to back up against a wall where they were hidden from prying eyes. 'Oliver Taylor. You are not my protective big brother and you don't have to scare other guys away to stop me dating them. I might have wanted to go out with him!'

'Did you?' growled Oliver, his smile dropping and locking eyes with her, which unnerved her slightly. She drew in a sharp breath and stepped back to get in some air.

'I don't know, because you scared him off!'

'How did I do that?' he asked, his eyes on hers as he brushed her hair from her shoulder, his fingers touching her skin. She blinked, and suddenly she couldn't articulate her words. 'How are you getting home?' he asked, serious now.

'I'm staying at the flat above the office.'

He looked at his wristwatch and then at the party, which was still in full swing. 'Do you want me to walk you home?'

'Oliver! I'm going home with Poppy. We're both staying at the flat. Billy is here somewhere too, for goodness sake. I've only been here for just over an hour.'

'Ok, well, let me introduce you to some of my own contacts,' he said smoothly, slipping an arm around her waist again, leading her away from temptation – and not giving her much choice but to comply. 'I haven't seen you much lately and want to find out more about how your business is going,' he added as a softener. It was her favourite subject, and it looked as though Ollie had guessed that, from the wicked grin he gave her. It was full of mischief... and an underlying hint of something more. What the hell was he playing at?

CHAPTER ELEVEN

*P*oppy was smiling more, now that horrible crunched-up feeling in her tummy had eased. She'd decided not to invite Glen, her dad, to the wedding and Dylan had agreed. He'd listened without judgement when she'd told him all about it and held her close when she'd cried. It had been cathartic, and her step was much lighter now. She was even happy to hear Billy singing again. He often used the office as his stage these days, as he didn't have time to go to his local amateur dramatics group any more.

She gave him a round of applause as he hit the high note at the end of his song and he took a bow with a flourish. Sasha rolled her eyes and told Poppy not to encourage him and he stuck his tongue out at her, which she ignored.

Sasha then gave them all a quick rundown of their schedule for the next few days, but seemed distracted and was unusually quiet, which instantly made Poppy worried. They'd just had a very productive meeting with a new client and Poppy was determined to celebrate. They'd had a whole host of work and social events lately. Sasha had stepped up in her role, not only running their diary but taking on a lot more work, including posting to some of their social feeds as part of her regular job and not just as a sideline when she had time. Poppy sighed and, after taking one look at Sasha's face, decided to take action.

'I'm meeting Demi for dinner tonight and I know you said you had loads of work to do, but I want you both to come with me. We've had a hectic few days and we've just signed a new client. You deserve some of the credit for bringing them on board. Your social media posts have persuaded them to ask to look at pods for the grounds, Sash, as well as panels for a hotel they're building.'

Poppy picked up Sasha's lightweight jumper and Billy's jacket and handed them over without another word. Billy opened his mouth to protest but Poppy cut him off.

'I'm your boss and I'm saying no more work today. We all deserve some rest and recuperation, and it will give us a chance to find out how Demi's getting on at her dad's garage.' This made Sasha and Billy stop in their tracks and look at her. 'This is the second time she's been in town in the past two weeks. However much I love her, that can't be good.'

'You're right,' said Sasha as she pulled her soft blue jumper over her fitted dress. 'Demi usually hates being away from Allan for too long. We sorted out your problem with your dad, but we still need to find out the root of the situation with Demi – and you haven't spilled your guts about Ed yet, Billy.' She looked pointedly at him while he put his jacket on and opened the office door for them both to walk through, putting a pause on that discussion for now.

Demi was already seated at the little velvet-lined booth when they arrived at the restaurant in town. There was soft lighting above each booth section, with seventies-inspired glass pendants and brass fittings. The room felt warm and inviting, with plants running along the top of the bar area and then draping downwards, while the patterned floor tiles in soft hues complemented the materials used elsewhere.

Sasha sniffed the air and glanced around, making Poppy smile. Her friend wasn't keen on visiting Italian restaurants unless the food was authentic, so Poppy and Demi always chose carefully. Sasha would happily eat burgers and fries from a fast food place, but her heritage was sacred, as far as she was concerned. Sasha had grown up in a huge family and food was a big part of their time together. Even though Sasha usually left the cooking to her parents or sisters, she was still a food snob. Luckily this little gem was amazing, smirked Poppy. She noticed that Sasha had relaxed and given the place a nod of approval.

Demi started fiddling with her wine glass, so Poppy put a gentle hand on her arm to stop the movement, her face pinching in concern. 'Are you ok, Demi?' she asked.

'Can I stay over at your flat tonight?' sighed Demi, dipping her eyes and staring at the table. 'My dad and Allan are driving me nuts with arguing about Allan taking over the garage. Allan is pretty much running it anyway, but won't take over and Dad wants to step back and retire. Neither of them listen to anything I say on the matter.' Her bottom lip wobbled and Billy slipped his arm around her shoulders and rested his head on hers.

Demi looked around the table with watery eyes. 'I've been running the office for years and can strip a car and replace any of the parts, but they just don't see me as an asset. I could run that place better than either of them, but they only me as the dogsbody.'

'They're so dumb,' said Sasha with such passion that Demi gave her a watery-eyed grimace, but seemed to appreciate the solidarity. 'How anyone can overlook you is a mystery. Are they blind? Half the customers only come in to look at you because you're gorgeous, and the other half want your advice about their cars. They wait until your dad is out of earshot and ask your opinion every time.'

Demi sniffed, but her head was up now and there was a tentative smile on her lips.

'The women are just as bad about going behind your dad's back, because they trust you, Demi.' Sasha went on. 'You are the sweetest person alive and you'd help anyone. Your dad is taking advantage of your kind nature... so is Allan,' she said finally, then winced as they all gasped.

'Sasha!' scolded Poppy. 'Do you really need to be so blunt?'

'What? It's what we've all been thinking for years,' she defended, then saw the tears back in Demi's eyes and huffed out a breath. 'I'm not trying to hurt you, Demi. We all love your dad and Allan, but they don't know a good thing when it's sitting right in front of their face.'

She softened her tone carefully, but Poppy was cringing inside as Sasha was right and it was what they all thought. None of them wanted to hurt a beautiful soul like Demi, though.

Demi smiled, though she was upset. It seemed she was finally getting fed up with being treated like a doormat, when she was a valuable asset. Tears were leaking out of her eyes and she brushed them away and sniffed. Poppy gave Sasha a warning stare, but she ignored her and spoke again.

'Is it time you branched out on your own?' Sasha asked, and Demi jolted in surprise. Poppy and Billy silently communicated with a glance and Billy took Demi's hand.

'I think what Sasha means,' he said slowly, 'Is that perhaps if your family are a tiny bit set in their ways, maybe you could work for another firm that appreciates you, or even start your own business?'

Sasha rolled her eyes. 'That's what I just said!' She took hold of Demi's other hand and held it to her face, as if she was holding something precious. Poppy's heart melted a little for her fearless friend. Billy and Poppy's eyes met again and they both shook their heads and tried not to smile.

'I couldn't leave my dad in the lurch,' said Demi, defensively, shaking off her friends and dropping her hands into her lap. 'But I've been thinking of taking a business course of some kind to give me a better insight into how I can help. I don't think they'll take me seriously until I do. As you know, I've been fixing cars since I was a teenager, and I even did mechanics at college, but though I run the office and bookings, they don't even see me. I'm invisible. It's as if I'm a bit of the furniture.'

'Old and battered,' said Sasha helpfully, as Poppy glared at her and Billy almost choked on his drink.

'I think Demi meant something like useful and familiar,' said Poppy, trying not to laugh at Sasha's antics, though she was clearly trying to lighten the mood. Sasha was sipping the wine they had ordered when they arrived and had almost drained her glass already, Poppy noted, which was unlike her. Sasha enjoyed wine too much to gulp it down and not taste it properly. She would also never hurt anyone intentionally, but she certainly spoke her mind and often blurted out what they were all thinking. She was braver than Poppy and Poppy loved her for that, however forthright she was at times.

'We need more drinks,' said Sasha, getting up and giving Demi a swift hug, laying her head against her friend's for a moment. Demi sighed into the hug and gave a lopsided smile. 'We need to celebrate Poppy reuniting with her dad sometime soon, and Demi standing up to hers. Both of you are strong women and you'll follow the right path, whatever that might be,' Sasha said breezily as she got up to go to the bar, which ran along one wall of the restaurant.

'Did Sasha actually impart some wisdom then?' asked Billy, his eyes wide.

'Without sarcasm?' added Demi.

'I think so,' said Poppy sombrely, and they all burst out laughing as they watched several men turn to watch the sexy Italian sashay to the counter with a flick of her hair and start chatting up the barman.

'I think Sasha's finally getting used to Ollie being around again,' said Poppy, in a hushed voice, even though Sasha was at the other end of the bar. 'He's been helping with the wedding planning and it means they have to spend time together, whether she likes it or not.'

'Thank goodness!' said Demi. 'I hated all that cloak and dagger stuff. He's Dylan's best man and she's your maid of honour…' she left that nugget hanging for a moment, as Poppy did have more than one best friend.

Poppy pulled a face and apologised. 'You're all as important as each other, but there can only be one chief bridesmaid. You know I'd have married in Vegas if I could! I'm sorry, Demi.' Poppy hung her head in contrition and Demi smiled and brushed it away.

'I'm only teasing, and I know you love us all. Sasha was the perfect choice as she'll get things done. Plus, I get to help you choose the right dress. The wedding does push Sash closer to Ollie, though,' she said thoughtfully. Poppy just shrugged.

'Why did he buy that site?' Demi asked, just as Sasha returned with a tray on which was balanced a rich red bottle of wine and four fresh glasses. Sasha handed them out and tilted her head to one side as if she'd known what they would be talking about as soon as she left the table.

Poppy sighed and knew Sasha had a right to know why Ollie was now front and centre in her life again, when she'd avoided him for so long. 'I told Ollie how much property values in this area were staring to rise. Jared and I are buying more land for our local housing projects and we came across the gym site. I hadn't known it was for sale before.' Poppy looked around the table and tried to think of the right thing to say. 'The gym was up and running, but the owners had overextended themselves with the build and wanted to have a quick sale, so they had put feelers out. Jared had his ear to the ground and told me as soon as he heard.'

'So Jared helped Ollie?' gasped Sasha, her eyes lighting up in glee. 'Does Ollie know?'

Poppy rolled her eyes at Sasha's mirth. Ollie wasn't Jared's greatest fan because of the way he'd tried to woo Poppy right under Ollie's brother's nose, but he'd grudgingly admitted that Jared was spot on this time.

Sasha tilted her head to one side and Poppy could visualise the cogs in her brain whirring. 'So Jared told Ollie, which makes Ollie indebted to him, and Jared gets a top notch gym which is up and running for any potential new homeowners to use, without the cost of setting it up himself?' Sasha raised an eyebrow and Billy and Poppy took a huge glug of wine, while Demi's mouth hung open in shock. 'Once again... does Ollie know he's in Jared's debt?'

Poppy's flushed face answered the question.

'Jared made absolutely certain that Ollie understood the status quo, I'm sure.' Poppy grinned suddenly and shuffled up to put her arm around her friend. 'You don't need to worry about the Taylor brothers, Sash,' said Poppy with absolute confidence. 'Ollie's been in business for years and was looking for a second site. He knows full well how it benefits Jared, and he took advantage of the information. It helps Ollie too and he doesn't feel in the slightest bit indebted, unbeknownst to Jared,' grinned Poppy, her eyes shining with love for the family. 'Ollie knows his customers might buy Jared's houses, and that having a complex like his nearby will help them sell. It's win, win. I benefit from both options too. As do we all, with loads of new business.'

Sasha's eyes gleamed at the idea of Ollie having one up on Jared, then she coughed and tried to hide it by taking a huge slug of wine.

'All we need now is for Demi to up sticks and join us,' Poppy continued. 'Do you want to work for me too?' she joked, but she was half-serious, despite knowing Demi would never actually leave her dad.

'I'd love that,' sighed Demi wistfully, 'but my family need me, whether they know it or not.'

Poppy sipped her wine and thanked the waiter as he brought over plates of garlic bread sprinkled with melted cheese. The garlicky scent was heavenly and they all helped themselves to a slice, leaving trails of cheese everywhere.

'Ollie wanted a new challenge and the other centre pretty much runs itself,' Poppy went on. 'He brought over a few key staff to help set up this place, like Maxine and Annabelle, who runs reception, but otherwise he's madly trying to update and employ new staff all at once. It's a lot to take on.'

Sasha halted mid-bite of a piece of garlic bread.

Poppy winced. 'I'm sorry I didn't let you know straight away, Sash.'

'He's going to be Poppy's brother-in-law,' said Billy crisply. 'It was hard for her to let how you feel about Ollie get in the way of a big project.'

'How I feel?' Sasha's blank expression told them that she didn't know what the hell they were going on about. 'I can't stand him!'

'Exactly!' said Billy, looking smug. 'You'd have just ended up as one big ball of stress. We need you at your best – and you're already having to spend time with him while you plan the wedding,' he said kindly.

Sasha curled her lip and looked like she really wanted to

stomp home in a huff. They could see her internal conflict as she took a few deep breaths and tried to calm down.

Demi tactfully changed the subject. 'You're actually letting Billy get on with things now?' she asked Poppy. 'Doesn't it kill you a bit inside?' she joked.

Poppy smiled. She knew she could be a control freak, but that came from growing up with an anxious parent with mental health issues. Still, her mum was doing brilliantly now. She was in love and working alongside Chris in the café. Poppy didn't feel the need to check on her every minute any more, and she was also relaxed about Billy taking on more and more responsibility within the firm.

'I'm enjoying relinquishing a bit of control,' she said honestly. 'Both Sasha and Billy are godsends. Plus you're all helping me plan the wedding so that I can get on with my work.'

Sasha's back was ramrod straight and she ignored the compliment, even though it had been an honest one. She was still glowering at them all. More food arrived and suddenly the table was heaving with plates of fresh pasta in delicious sauces, breaking some of the tension. Billy moved up to make space for her, as she leaned across him to spoon a forkful of the spaghetti Carbonara into her mouth. They all waited while she assessed the taste and then sighed in bliss. Then they sat back in relief, because if Sasha liked the food, it usually meant everyone else would. She had amazing taste buds.

They hadn't tried this particular restaurant before and although it said authentic recipes on the menu, you could never be too sure if it would meet Sasha's high standards. The place was tucked into a side street in the little main town at the end of Cherry Blossom Lane. The area was still quite sleepy, but it was getting busier. Poppy was gratified to see quite a few other diners in the restaurant. It had been a long day and they'd all forgotten to eat lunch. Even Sasha hadn't had time to shove vegetable crisps or coffee their way.

Ever the gentleman, Billy put his arm around Sasha and she sighed and sank into him. 'What's up?' asked Demi, worry in her eyes.

'I still hate Ollie, but I think I'm jealous of you all,' admitted Sasha. 'Even him! He looks too damn good in a waistcoat.'

'What?' they all chorused, looking puzzled.

Sasha scrunched up her nose and then sighed, putting her fork down and looking forlornly at her half-eaten plate of food. 'Poppy and Billy have this amazing business and now Demi is probably going to night school to follow her dreams. Ollie has his own empire in Cherry Blossom Lane too. I've been studying hard too, but only on my own so far – and I don't know how you'll feel about this, Poppy…?'

Poppy waited patiently to hear what she knew Sasha was going to say. Times were changing and however much she'd like to keep everything the same, she knew Sasha would outgrow them at some point. She just hadn't expected it to be this fast. Sasha had never seen her own potential in a work sense, but after being around Billy and Poppy for a while now, it seemed that she'd finally begun to realise her own worth.

CHAPTER TWELVE

*S*asha frowned, because there had been no outburst. If one of her friends had announced they wanted to change the trajectory of their lives, she would have jumped in and asked loads of questions. They'd all been so concerned when Demi had announced her plans, but the response to Sasha's was a bit meh…

'I've been taking online classes in networking and marketing,' she said, her hackles rising. Still no reaction. 'I've been thinking about starting my own little business,' Sasha tried again.

Poppy seemed surprised at this and blanched. Gotcha, thought Sasha with satisfaction. Didn't they think she should run her own business? Then she bit her lip, because her track record at staying at anything for very long wasn't exactly stellar.

Then Poppy recovered and spoke. 'We guessed you must be learning new skills somehow,' she said. She didn't look that upset about losing her most valuable asset. 'I'd happily have paid for your studies,' said Poppy thoughtfully, surprising Sasha again. 'But I wondered if that might upset you, as you're so independent. Your latest ideas about our social media timelines are really impressive, Sash.'

It was Sasha's turn to be shocked. Independent? 'I always rely on you and Demi, or someone else,' she said, frowning, an uneasy feeling swirling around her tummy. 'This is the first job I've held down since that reception position at the gym. That's because of you giving me an opportunity, Poppy. I'm hardly a beacon of inspiration,' she scoffed, self-depreciatingly.

The others exchanged glances and Sasha frowned. 'What's going on?' she demanded to know. 'You all look shifty.'

'We're just confused,' said Demi, quickly spooning in the last of her spicy chicken and tomato pasta before continuing. 'You're the one who taught us how to stand up for ourselves – to move on if we're not happy – although I admit I haven't mastered that one yet. And to love our bodies no matter what shape or size we are.' She thought for a moment before continuing. 'And what about what we chose to wear?'

Sasha checked out Demi's fitted cut-off jeans and raised her eyebrows in jest. They all burst out laughing. But then Sasha spoke more seriously.

'You have a successful business, Poppy. You take immense risks and they pay off – and Demi, you've always known that you wanted to work in the family business. I'm a drifter,' said Sasha sadly.

'You've been subbing your sisters' rent since you started working with me, and helping them out long before that,' said Poppy.

Sasha gasped in shock. 'How do you know that?'

'We care about you, and your sisters love a gossip,' said Demi affectionately. 'It's why you were always broke.'

'Not any more!' cried Poppy, with a grin. 'You're independent, but can still help your family. You just hadn't found your vocation, and wouldn't settle for anything less, that's why you moved around.'

'She only stayed put if Ollie worked there,' joked Demi and Sasha pulled a face and then burst out laughing, before grabbing back her half-finished pasta, as Billy was eyeing it up and gradually moving it closer to his plate. She gave him a victorious stare, then he dipped his fork in and filched some anyway. After taking a few more bites, Sasha pushed her plate back for him to finish off. So much for eating healthily for the wedding! She finally felt some of the angst she'd held, since finding out Ollie was going to be around much more, loosen its hold and disappear. They could work together to plan this wedding and she could be near him without swooning at his feet. Unrequited love was a bitch.

Sasha basked in the glow of her friends' approval and enjoyed the fuzzy feeling in her tummy. They thought she was the independent one? She was floored. Her mum had always told her to be herself and stand her ground, but she knew in reality that she was a bit flaky and bossy. She came from a big family of strong women, but she'd always craved approval from others – well, one man anyway. Ollie had been part of her life since her heart had begun to crave love as a teenager. She had set her sights high, on the town heart-breaker, and never given up… until now. Now her heart had healed and she was ready to meet someone new.

Poppy had shown her that she could be her own woman and that to find love, she didn't need to change herself or compromise. Poppy and Dylan were far from perfect, but were right for each other. Demi and Allan were another matter altogether. Demi was vivacious and the sweetest person Sasha knew, but she had a sneaking suspicion that Allan knocked her confidence to keep her with him. Demi was beautiful inside and out, but she didn't see it, however much her friends told her. She helped elderly people across the street and carried their bags. She took the time to listen to others, plus she was totally beautiful. Her smile lit up a room.

If Sasha ever found the secret to Demi's bouncy glossy hair, glistening eyes and pouty, kissable skin, she'd be a millionaire, but Demi was oblivious and had no self-confidence at all. It was as if it never occurred to her that the glances that came her way might be admiring. She assumed she'd got something on her face or her lipstick had smudged. She'd been with Allan since she was a teenager and he took her for granted and put himself first every time, which grated on Sasha's nerves. He even spoke over her whenever they all met up, as if she wasn't important enough to listen to, Sasha fumed.

Billy grinned and sipped his drink, watching her over the rim of her glass while he patted his full belly, even though it was still perfectly flat. 'So, what are your plans?' he asked the question they all seemed to want an answer to, and her attention turned back to their conversation.

Sasha's shoulders slumped. She could organise Poppy and Billy's life to a T, but when it came to her own, she always hesitated and second-guessed herself. Supposing she messed up? She knew that was why Poppy was the entrepreneur, and not the rest of them. Poppy made hard decisions and went for it. She'd invested time and money, even when she'd had barely enough to get by, and had given her dreams wings. To Sasha, the thought of working for herself terrified her as much as it excited her. What if she failed, when she was finally onto a good thing with her job at Poppy's office?

'I'm not sure,' she hesitated, brushing her hair out of her eyes and hooking it behind her ear so it fell in waves down her back. All eyes were on her and although she loved holding court, she couldn't shift those damn butterflies that seemed to have taken up permanent residence in her stomach since this idea had been brewing. Maybe she should slosh some wine in, and they'd all have a party, she sniggered to herself, imagining drunken butterflies happily bobbing around on a sea of booze.

'I've realised… through the opportunities you've given me,' she looked at Poppy, who smiled. 'That what I'm good at is socialising.' Her eyes gleamed and they all grinned and nodded their heads in agreement, as it was her particular forte.

'You communicate messages about my business really well, and connect with our customers,' clarified Poppy, while she topped up their glasses. 'So if you can do it for me, why not for others?' she asked. 'Is that what you were thinking?'

Sasha was back to biting her lip. She waited for Billy to get mad and tell her she couldn't split her time with other clients, but he was just staring into the void, deep in thought.

'Poppy and I have spoken about you recently,' he said suddenly and held up a hand before Sasha could growl at him for talking about her behind her back.

Poppy joined in. 'We were chatting about how you're wasted on reception.'

Sasha opened her mouth to speak, but she was rooted to the spot. Did they want to get rid of her? She needed time to build her seedling of a business idea into something. It might take her years… decades even!

'You pretty much run all of our social media already,' continued Poppy matter-of-factly. 'Plus our new branding is down to you.' Billy patted her on the shoulder proudly.

It was so tense, waiting to find out what they were going to say, that she started to worry her muscles would spasm and she wouldn't be able to get off her chair. She pictured herself lying prone under the table, undiscovered for months. She grabbed onto the table for support.

Poppy gave her a strange look and then carried on, as she

was used to Sasha's dramatic ways. 'Our social media is an ongoing task, but it's not a full-time job. We could have someone else answer the phones and organise the calendar now.'

When Sasha spluttered the wine she'd just gulped, and almost spat it across the table, Billy patted her back and Demi looked at her with concern.

'Poppy's not saying that she doesn't need you, Sash,' said Demi. 'She's saying you've made the flow of work easier now, so you can train someone else to take over while you begin your exciting new career.'

Sasha's cheeks flamed and she could feel the volcano inside about to erupt. She was getting quite good at controlling her temper. Working in a zen place like Poppy's studio made it hard to get upset about anything... she'd thought. But the simmering inside her proved that wrong.

'You're all in on this?' she demanded to know, feeling like the floor underneath her was tilting sideways. She loved her job! She'd just got used to having a healthy pay packet for once as well. Her throat went dry, and she gulped as her airways were tight suddenly.

'You want me to leave and give someone else my job? Now I've made your life so much easier?' She asked sarcastically, annoyed that they didn't look at all upset and seemed to be laughing at her. 'I just had a spark of a business idea to do in my spare time. I didn't say I wanted to leave,' she huffed. She wanted to accidentally spill a drink into someone's lap, but they were such guzzlers that they'd drunk the lot!

Poppy giggled and Sasha growled at her. 'It's not funny.' This was the first job that she'd actually loved with her whole heart. The office was super-efficient now and that was down to her. She'd be blowed if someone else got to enjoy her hard work. She slumped back against the velvet booth, suddenly unsure that she was even wanted by her friends. She chewed on her lip and started picking at her nail. Her eyes began to mist over. She'd thought that she was irreplaceable part of Poppy's team. How wrong had she been!

Poppy asked Billy to swap seats and scooched over next to Sasha, hugging her fiercely and brushing the tears from her cheeks. 'Sasha! I don't ever want you to leave! I'd happily employ you forever, but you have so many talents that I don't want to hold you back.'

Sasha sniffed and Billy reached out and touched her hand in support. Demi blew her a kiss across the table and said they all needed a fresh drink, before rushing off to get a new round in. They definitely needed another bottle.

'Billy and I were chatting about the flat above the studio in Cherry Blossom Lane,' said Poppy. 'You could move in there. Billy and I are happy where we are, and it would make sense to have you on-site. What we're proposing is that you take a social media course one day a week. Work for us for the first half of the week, still handling our reception and calendar, then train a new staff member to handle that for the rest of the week. You can use your spare days to begin your own business, running social media for other people. As your business grows, you can see what works best for you, but we would always love you to run our network first and foremost. We'll be your first client!'

Sasha wiggled on her chair in stunned silence. It wasn't often that she was lost for words. They had planned it all out without her. She had been thinking about looking for a new flat, and had been imagining her things in the flat above the office, but she hadn't thought it would ever become be a reality. The commute to work every day was tiring, but she hadn't told anyone that yet except for Ollie.

Poppy and Billy were looking at her in expectation as Demi returned with a bottle of Prosecco and four tall glasses.

'Are we celebrating?' she asked candidly, laughing at Sasha being lost for words for once.

Sasha caught her breath for a moment and then felt all the tension leave her body. She couldn't believe how much they were doing for her again, but instead of feeling scared or daunted, she decided to face this challenge head on. She would love to live in Cherry Blossom Lane, as it would mean no travel and much more time to invest in the business. Her, a business owner! When she'd mentioned her ideas to Ollie, she hadn't been sure how serious she really was about it. It had just been pie in the sky. But now she might already have her first two clients!

'I can't believe you're actually stunned Sasha into silence,' joked Demi, pouring the fizzy liquid into the glasses and handing them one each. Sasha tried to look cross, but her face had a mind of its own and she was beaming.

'How did you do it?' Demi asked Billy, making Sasha snap out of her trance.

Billy spoke up, 'It seems that you just have to tell she's amazing and she shuts up!' he joked, jumping as Sasha nudged his leg with her foot. 'Ouch!' he stuck his tongue out at her.

'That's for organising my whole life behind my back,' said Sasha.

'What about Poppy and Demi?' he protested. 'Kick them too!'

Sasha's eyes filled with tears but she blinked them back. Maybe she could follow her own dreams? She held up her glass. 'I love the idea. Living in the flat means I won't be exhausted from the commute each day, and I could also think about approaching local businesses in Cherry Blossom Lane.' They all made approving noises about this idea. 'I might have already mentioned my ideas to Ollie... and he asked to be my first client.'

That stunned *them* to silence for a nanosecond – before they all started talking over each other. Sasha ignored their questions.

'I bumped into him at the gym,' she said mysteriously, shutting down that line of questioning and giving them all a death stare until they shut up and drank their Prosecco. 'Are you sure about this?' she asked, facing Poppy and holding her breath for the answer.

It all seemed too good to be true. She searched Poppy's face, but Poppy's smile was firmly in place and she looked happy, content and slightly flushed from a few glasses of wine.

'Don't get too excited about me not being around so much,' Sasha joked. 'If I'm living in the flat, you'll never get rid of me!'

'Perfect!' said Poppy, chinking glasses.

'To Sasha and her new business,' they all chorused as Sasha blushed and revelled in how amazing her friends were. She peered at Demi.

'Don't think I didn't notice your help in all this plotting. You also mentioned your dreams, and that won't be forgotten when it comes to meddling. We know you haven't been happy for a while and I want to help you too. Are things ok with you and Allan?' Sasha debated carrying on, but decided now was the time.

'Allan and I are fine,' Demi sighed. 'I've got enough on my plate keeping Dad's garage afloat to think about my own dreams.'

Sasha took her hand across the table and gave it a squeeze of support, trying not to mention Allan's lack of it.

'Dad won't listen to any of my ideas to modernise his systems and he's adamant that he can persuade Allan to change his mind and take over. Allan's equally adamant that he won't. It's having a knock-on effect on everything and I want to bang their heads together. I spoke to them about some ideas for re-purposing some of the empty storerooms and finding ways to keep customers onsite, but they vetoed them too. I just needed a night away from it all... if it's okay for me to stay in your new flat for one night before you officially move in?' She didn't wait for an answer, clearly knowing it was fine. 'They simply won't accept change. They say if it's not broken don't fix it, but the business is stagnating and they refuse to see me as an equal,' she sighed. 'I wanted to create a small café or food offering so that customers didn't have to leave the site while their cars are serviced. It would be a double win and bring in more income. Dad won't even look at my plans. He says it will cost too much money, but we already have the facilities and a kitchen area we don't use.'

'That's such a great idea, Demi! Why don't you take over the business, if your dad's so keen to retire?' asked Poppy thoughtfully. And everyone fell silent. Demi didn't have a chance to answer as her phone rang, so she excused herself to answer it, her hair bobbing up and down as she walked away and her backside sashaying so that every man she passed was mesmerised, while she was oblivious to them.

They all watched her exit the bar and then they shared a conspiratorial look about their next big chat. Sasha was thankful that she'd be included in this one and not the hot topic of choice, but also realised that Demi wasn't ready for that conversation, or to step out of her father or partner's shadows just yet.

The adrenaline flowing through Sasha's own veins told her that she was very thankful for her amazing friends. Her head was already buzzing with ideas and potential names for her brand-new business.

CHAPTER THIRTEEN

*S*asha couldn't believe how much her life had changed in the past few weeks. Poppy didn't procrastinate and was like a whirlwind with a new idea. Sasha had sat with Poppy and interviewed a new member of staff and had been included in every aspect of hiring her. Bonnie was stylish, efficient and had lots of qualifications, unlike Sasha, who had spent most of her school life thinking about Ollie, or of ways to make herself famous, to get him to notice her. What a waste of her education! She could now have kicked herself for not concentrating more. She didn't need to be known on social media to have a good life with a great job, but she did love the buzz of someone liking or commenting on her posts, and her new life was weirdly intertwined with her old dreams.

She had reached out to social media star Devon. The house he'd moved into sounded amazing. They'd ended up chatting for hours and, to her surprise, he'd seemed to want to prolong the conversation. They had agreed to meet up at the office. She'd read somewhere that when someone's time-line looked dazzling and like something to aspire to, it didn't always mean that the person behind the page had a full and happy life. She wondered if Devon needed a new and exciting friend and hoped that he could see that she was just as much fun as Poppy was.

Then she frowned. Did she actually feel a bit lonely sometimes, with both of her best friends being so in love and running their own empires? She'd not stopped to think about it before, but perhaps her sudden need to make new friends said more about her than Devon. She shook that depressing thought away before it could take hold and sniffed the prettily floral scent of the fresh flowers on her desk to snap herself back into reality. She sneezed as a bit of pollen made her nose itch, and then cursed herself for wallowing. She wasn't one for self-pity and tried to keep everyone else upbeat, but she'd had a lot of changes to her life recently.

Poppy had already added Devon's panel order for his trendy new barn conversion home to their job list. Sasha could tell that she was excited about the possible collaboration by the way she kept popping her head round Sasha's new office every five minutes, to ask if she'd spoken to him. Maybe Poppy wanted a few new friends too, as the old ones were bossy and annoying, she grinned to herself and got some of her equilibrium back.

Sasha's new little office, next to the reception area, made her smile every single time she sat down at her brand new sleek grey desk. She did miss being in the hub of the office, where everyone came in, but she could go and sit there anytime. Her new workspace was Billy's old office on the ground floor, as he had relocated to a bigger space beside the flat upstairs. But he seemed to forget he'd moved sometimes, and she'd find him pulling up a chair and working alongside her, or leafing through an article from the designer chair that sat by one wall.

Every room had its own bookcase full of interesting

reads. Billy still hadn't moved his collection of books about London theatre shows and voice training that still sat on the third shelf of her bookcase. Sasha was itching to add her own growing collection of books about networking and organisation, but every time Billy picked up a book from that shelf he burst into song, so for now the books were staying. She had to admit that her office was a bit too quiet for her liking sometimes, so the odd song and dance cheered her up. He must get far more done in his new room, she mused, but he was also drawn back into the mêlée from time to time for a gossip and a handful of crisps from the kitchen, which was next to the meeting room. She couldn't wait to move into the flat upstairs and really start to feel at home.

She looked around at the empire Poppy had built from scratch by herself. It was a credit to her entrepreneurial friend. Sasha was determined that she'd have her own successful business one day. At the moment, she spent a lot of her time investigating other online courses and reaching out to make new contacts. Success might have come sooner if she'd applied herself at school, but she had life skills that weren't to be discounted – and it was basically Ollie's fault anyway. It wasn't fair for a man to have looked that good when he was younger. She pictured his thick black hair and handsome face and sighed, before scowling at herself and shaking her head. Not everything got better with age, though the Taylor brothers seemed to. She peeked at her own glossy dark pink nails and imagined trailing them down his back and then closed her eyes and made herself get rid of that image.

She was determined to put Ollie to the back of her mind, where he'd been for months before Poppy's bombshell about his new business across the road. Now he was slipping into her thoughts again, which was driving her insane. She wouldn't be distracted by firm muscles and a handsome face this time. She had learnt how to talk to customers in her varied jobs and she had passion to apply to her new role. That counted for a lot. She mentally patted herself on the back for working out the skills she had that were actually useful, and then applying them to adult education. She didn't want to ride on Poppy's coat tails. She wanted to create her own path. She would accept support and encouragement wherever she could grab it, though. She wasn't stupid enough to be too proud to learn from someone with more experience.

Poppy was lucky Sasha loved her, or she might dislike her for being so successful and having bagged the man of her dreams. But no one could hate Poppy. She was the type of person who would help anyone in a bind, and even if they weren't! Sasha fleetingly thought of their old friend Anne and how much she'd hurt Poppy the previous year, but once again that was down to those dratted brothers. They were certainly not worth losing friends over, but in the end, Poppy's fiancé Dylan had been a better friend than Anne was.

A picture of Devon's handsome face came to mind and she licked her lips. He would be a welcome distraction from the fact that she was starting to feel a bit lonely right now. She picked up the phone and answered a client enquiry, before noticing that Billy was on his way to the kitchen and hunting for food again.

She worried that Billy was becoming obsessed with the fact that Ed was coming home for the wedding, even though he denied it vehemently. He'd cleaned his flat above Poppy's garage to within an inch of its life, even though there was still ages to go until the actual wedding. It was zooming closer, though, and she needed Poppy to make some decisions.

Billy waggled a mug at her and she nodded her head. Her mouth was parched, she was craving a drink. 'Sorry about the pile of paperwork on your shiny new desk,' said Billy as he handed her a hot chocolate. Sunshine shone through the big window to her right, sending spirals of light dancing across the surface of her desk and highlighting the pile of unfinished work. She breathed in the heavenly scent of the drink and smiled at the fact that he'd added a few of her favourite mini marshmallows and a squirt of cream on the top.

Sasha sipped the drink and looked at him with a cream moustache, which made him grin. 'Don't worry. It was worth it for the hot chocolate,' she sighed. 'Have you heard from Ed?'

Billy's eyes shone a bit brighter. 'Yes. He's been texting me most days to tell me his latest news.' Sasha raised her eyebrows at this but said nothing. Billy blew her a kiss and headed back to his own office with a steaming cup of coffee.

Sasha tried to imagine what it would be like to be in an equal and committed relationship. She shook off the image. She didn't need a man to be happy and if she didn't know what she was looking for in a partner, then she could have some fun trying a few dates out. Where she would find time in her new schedule, she didn't know, but if a sexy stranger swept her off her feet – and wanted to fit in with her busy life on Cherry Blossom Lane and not get in the way of her awakening ambitions – all the better. She grinned as she pictured coming in from a hard day's work to a gorgeous man in nothing but an apron, all sweaty from cooking her a delicious meal. If only!

Street smarts had got her where she was today, she decided. Now that she was going to join an online social media course, because her evening classes had finished, she needed to plan how she could find clients and still work for Poppy and Billy in the job she loved.

Devon's lifestyle was so glamorous and exciting that

Sasha wasn't ready to give that dream up quite yet, but she was far more realistic now. Perhaps she'd meet a man who *she* wanted to sweep off his feet, she grinned to herself, although she'd have a job picking up Ollie, who was huge! Sasha wrinkled her nose, as the issue of being overworked and having too many ambitions at once had nearly split up Poppy and Dylan – although look at them now.

That reminded Sasha that she still had to pin down Poppy to try on some dresses that weekend. The two appointments Demi had booked were looming and Poppy would be going, even if they had to stuff her over their shoulders and carry her there, kicking and screaming. What *was* her problem with trying on a few dresses?

She thought of Jared suddenly, and the way he still looked at Poppy when he thought no one was watching, but Sasha shoved that horrible idea firmly aside. Poppy was committed to Dylan. She had almost lost him once, she wouldn't risk it again, would she?

CHAPTER FOURTEEN

*S*asha looked round at the interior of The Cherry Tree pub and realised she felt really at home there now. This was her 'other' local, as she didn't have much time to go out and socialise at home, even though she hadn't moved out yet. Her job and new business idea were all-consuming and her sisters, although mostly supportive, had heard about her dreams many times before and didn't take them so seriously any more. She'd stopped talking about Ollie quite a while ago, so she didn't know how to drop in the fact that he now had a business across the road, without all of her sisters turning up to glare or shake their fists at him every other day, for breaking their sister's heart.

A few people were chatting by the bar and a couple were staring intently into each other's eyes, at a small table in the corner. Sasha had been on a brief date the following weekend with someone who had slid into her direct messages, but he'd spent the whole three hours talking about his car. In the end she'd referred him to Demi and her dad's garage, when the guy had said what was under *his* bonnet needed tinkering with and given her a lewd wink. She couldn't get out of there fast enough and had immediately deleted his number.

Poppy had been talking to her dad recently and she seemed to be open to more conversations. They were tentative, short chats, but a huge step for Poppy. She had told Sasha over a creamy latte and hot chocolate at one of the coffee shops in the town that they only spoke about superficial things, but that seemed to suit Poppy. Sasha had persuaded her to come back to one of Maxine's exercise classes to reduce her stress and they'd actually had a brilliant time. Maxine was an excellent instructor. They'd ended up in the pub afterwards and got on quite well, so Sasha was now a regular there whenever she had a free moment and adored how easy it was to return to her old routines... well, some of them. She still actively avoided Ollie.

Sasha could see why Poppy liked Maxine, although she was always talking about Ollie, which was pretty annoying for someone like Sasha who didn't want to think about him. She knew, though, that a man like him could make a woman lose her mind and was very grateful that it wasn't her this time. So when Maxine invited her to the pub a week or so later, she was hoping there'd be no more Ollie chat. She'd advised Maxine time and again to check out the other gorgeous men that frequented the gym, but she had blinkers on. Sasha knew how that felt and did sympathise. It was like an addiction and Maxine needed help – or an intervention.

Now Maxine touched her arm to get her attention. 'Do you think you could set up an 'accidental' date for me and Ollie? We could bump into him somewhere and then you could disappear.'

Sasha winced. 'I'm not sure that's such a good idea.' She ignored the uneasy feeling that the thought of Ollie and Maxine dating always brought. 'It's too close to home and I learnt that lesson when we meddled in Poppy and Dylan's relationship. It split them up,' she said candidly and Maxine gawped at her.

'Surely not? Poppy confided in me that things were a bit rocky at one point, but that was the fault of that girl Anne,' said Maxine.

Sasha started picking at her fingernails and then drew a sharp breath in when it stung. She put her hands in her lap and twisted a pretty ring round and round on her finger.

'You know Anne's not even coming back for the wedding?' said Maxine, leaning nearer and whispering, as if everyone would be listening to their conversation.

Sasha glanced around, but everyone else was happily chatting amongst themselves and not taking the slightest bit of interest in them. Sasha sipped her red wine and gazed out of the window at the fields of tall grass swaying in the evening breeze. A young couple were walking their dog, hand in hand as they strode forward, trying to catch the excitable pup up. The woman paused for a moment to pick a few stems of the flowers and the man smiled indulgently at her as she showed him her trophies. Sasha sighed and tried to quell her unease that Poppy obviously told Maxine every-thing. How much had she divulged about Sasha's stupid crush on Oliver Taylor, Sasha wondered?

'Poppy's sometimes a bit uptight about how that makes her feel, but she drank quite a few glasses of wine when she found out about Anne's plans to stay in America and had a headache for days,' continued Maxine.

Sasha frowned. Maxine was making Poppy sound like a lush. She stretched her legs out and tried to hold onto calm thoughts. 'I'm glad Anne's moved abroad. Poppy's a nicer friend than me,' Sasha said lightly.

Maxine giggled and topped up their wine from the bottle on the table. 'I can understand how you feel. I'm furious at Anne and I don't even know her!' She swept her hair over her left shoulder and looked around to see if anyone was eyeing her up.

Sasha noticed two guys propping up the bar who were staring their way, and she realised that Maxine was primping for their benefit. Maybe Sasha should sit up a bit straighter and flutter her lashes too, but that wasn't her style.

'I did meet Anne once ages ago at the other leisure centre, but I can't say I took to her,' said Maxine, smiling seductively at the tallest of the guys, who grinned back.

Sasha was furious about the way Anne had tried to muscle in on Dylan, and she knew Demi was too, but what could they do when Anne lived so far away? Poppy had done so much for Anne. The least Anne could do in return was come back for her wedding. Sasha tried to listen to what Maxine was saying, but it was about Ollie again so Sasha was tempted to zone out.

Making new friends was fun, but because of the Ollie connection, this one was a slow burn. Maxine was bright and vivacious but tended to be slightly catty about other women, which Sasha deplored. If she had something to say, she'd tell the person to their face, not behind their back and to someone else.

Poppy thought that Maxine was really fun, but there was a niggling doubt in the back of Sasha's mind that wouldn't go away. She was trying hard not to be biased after her chat with Ollie and make up her own mind. It would be good to have more friends near to work, especially when she moved into the flat. Maxine was only working there as a favour to Ollie. She lived closer to the other gym, but held classes at the new place twice a week and was inundated with requests for further lessons. She was an incredible teacher. Sasha's limbs ached like hell after one of her classes – but in a good way.

'If only there were two of me,' joked Maxine, eyeing the

guys at the bar, before nudging Sasha in the ribs for not paying attention. 'You'll have to take one of them.' Sasha snorted into her drink as both men looked like they expected women to faint at their feet at the sight of them, judging by the amount of posing they were doing. Sasha preferred her men to be a bit more masculine and definitely less narcissistic. She turned back to Maxine, but the girl had already slid out of her seat and was on her way over to chat to the guys. They were now pretending that they hadn't been drooling over her for the past hour, by looking at their phones until she got closer.

Oh, to be that popular, sighed Sasha, actually quite relieved to have been ditched by her new 'friend' and to have a moment's peace. Going to places alone never bothered Sasha and she was actually glad now that her ears could have a rest. She grinned to herself when she thought of the most recent photos of Devon she'd just seen uploaded on social media. He'd been smiling widely at the camera and had a stunning vista of mountains behind him. Wherever he was, she wanted to go too. It looked incredible! She'd chatted to him on the phone for over an hour the previous evening and he'd made her feel interesting and special. She was hoping they would become closer, because she could definitely do with more of that, with friends like Maxine.

She had also been getting on really well with Ollie lately, as they seemed to have come to an unspoken understanding to keep things on a neutral ground and be kinder to each other. They had finally found a level of banter that was good fun for both of them, so she'd started looking forward to his visits to the office. Now there was no edge or frostiness to their conversation when he popped in. She actually liked him as a person and felt quite sisterly and protective towards him. He occasionally slung his arm around her shoulder when he was near and she didn't jump a mile in the air any more or scream at him to back off. The animosity she'd held on to for so long seemed to have dissipated, or perhaps they'd both finally grown up. Sasha had been in shock to find out his strict rule of never dating employees, but in the end it made sense. Him ever noticing her that way had always been a pipe dream. One she'd finally let go.

She eyed Maxine out of the corner of her eye. Her blonde hair was poker straight and so different from the dark waves that cascaded down Sasha's own back. She was also lean, firm and sleek, where Sasha was more like a friendly lion. She grinned to herself as she knew she could be feisty if someone wronged a person she loved. She thought of Poppy's tentative chats with her dad and tried not to snarl, forcing herself to smile at a passing barman, who grinned back. Sasha had cuddly bits in all the right places, but they were mostly hidden under her mane. She seemed tame, but she was watchful and would growl if provoked. She was working on her short fuse and learning it was ok to take a back seat and let others shine.

Maxine was gorgeous, and seemed kind of genuine, so Sasha decided to put her doubts to one side and enjoy the blossoming friendship. She grabbed the wine and topped up their glasses, raising one to salute her new friend as she returned to the table with a wide grin and a glance over her shoulder at the men at the bar. She showed Sasha the two new numbers in her phone.

'You really should have joined us, Sash,' she said, using Poppy and Demi's pet name for her. 'The taller one was a bit boring, but the other one has fire in his eyes,' she joked and gave him a wink from over her shoulder.

'You certainly make them sound appealing,' said Sasha drily, but then looked at the shorter of the two and wondered what 'fire in his eyes' meant. He was certainly good looking and had a nice smile, but he wasn't Sasha's type. She liked broad shoulders and a cheeky grin...

Sasha had a meeting set up with Devon the following morning, as Poppy's social media manager. It would be the first she would be handling alone. She felt proud that Poppy and Billy trusted her, but also knew Billy was dying to meet Devon. To be fair, the man looked like a Greek god. Billy would probably find some excuse to stick his head round the door to ask a question and then barge into her meeting.

Sasha grinned. She felt adrenaline jolt through her veins at the thought of her first famous client. As a representative of Poppy Mason Designs, and possibly Ollie's gym as well, she was going up in the world and was determined enjoy every minute of the ride. She sipped her wine and did her best to listen attentively to Maxine's dismissive comments about the poor guys she'd just spoken to, for not following her to their table. Then Sasha's eyes went wide when Maxine drew a small pad and pen from her handbag and insisted they plan out ways for her to snare Ollie.

Sasha didn't know how to break it to Maxine about Ollie's no-dating-the-staff rule. She sank into the soft fabric of the booth she was sitting in, and decided Maxine could find that out by herself.

CHAPTER FIFTEEN

*O*llie brushed some crumbs off the kitchen counter and felt like kicking the huge potted plant at his feet. He'd already been round and had dinner with Dylan and Poppy and his head hurt from lots of fake smiling and small talk. Billy had been there as usual. Much as Ollie loved Billy, he'd wanted to have a private conversation with his brother and future sister-in-law about Sasha. Billy loved gossip and he would only have teased Ollie about his growing feelings for Sasha.

If Ollie was brutally honest with himself, he'd always had a thing for her, but he'd needed to focus on his business and she had been a constant distraction. He knew he was often grumpy and gave short and sharp responses to her bright questions when she'd worked for him, but being out of bounds by his own code of conduct had kept him in a constant state of angst, when she'd always been what he'd wanted.

When she'd left, he'd been secretly ecstatic. Then he'd worried about dating her in case he wasn't earning enough or wasn't flashy enough for the lavish lifestyle she'd always craved. He'd gone with her once when she'd tried out to join the cast of a local reality TV show, but she'd been so nervous that she'd been extra-loud, and the producers had chosen someone else. He'd thought they loved big characters on shows like that, but this one was about local women who'd done well and they didn't deem Sasha to be successful enough. Ollie had shaken his head at their ignorance. Anyone with eyes could see that Sasha was destined to do well. Her personality shone from every pore of her body, and that body... Ollie dipped his head, closed his eyes and pinched his nose with his fingers to clear his mind as Sasha's body was enough to make grown men cry.

He knew she liked nice things and wanted to be rich and famous, and that drove him to succeed and do better to be good enough for her. But in true Sasha style, she'd landed a glamorous and exciting new job on her own. Occasionally he saw her out with a new man on her arm, which made his blood boil. He felt like he'd lost his chance with her because of his own stupid dating rules. After she'd left, she didn't ever seem to be without a boyfriend, so he'd been at a loss about what to do.

His last-ditch effort was to buy the gym to impress her, but then he'd almost ended up too busy to see her. He'd had to make up stupid excuses to pop into the office. When Poppy had offered to design the relaxation suites for him, he'd hoped Sasha might come round to congratulate him, or even spend some time at the gym, but Poppy had been evasive about telling her, saying she was new to the job and this wasn't her department. He'd thought this weird at the time, but he had complied.

He got himself a cool beer from the fridge and sat on his second-floor deck, which overlooked his small garden that backed onto Poppy and Dylan's house. He propped his legs up on another chair and let out a huge sigh of frustration at how his relationship with Sasha had changed. He hadn't liked her frostiness, but at least that meant she'd noticed him. Now she treated him like her pet dog, and that immediately put his back up when he stopped by to talk about what else needed organising for his brother's wedding.

Ollie had had an on-off girlfriend for a while, but that had ended because he couldn't commit to her. How could he, when he was always dreaming about someone else? He'd been clear that any relationship was casual, but girlfriends always thought they could change him.

Now that both he and Sasha were finally available at the same time, she seemed further away than ever. He just couldn't reach her. He needed to take drastic action before someone else swept into her life and claimed her. Especially now she had exciting plans to be a social media manager and would possibly be mixing with the rich and famous, if Poppy's client list was anything to go by. He'd also seen the way the guy who served their coffee in town looked at her – and he was the reason half the clientele came into the café. Ollie had thought about offering him a job in the café at the gym, then scratched that idea. It was hard enough to get Sasha's attention as it was.

He knew she was working with Poppy and Billy, but he wanted to be one of her first social media clients, so that he didn't have to keep coming up with problems with the wedding that he'd just invented. If Dylan ever found out, he'd string him up! Ollie had no idea about planning a wedding, but knew how important it was to Sasha that every single detail was perfect. He wondered how Sasha felt at having to spend more time with him. She might even realise that he was a nice guy!

When Poppy had suggested the new gym space to him, he'd immediately seen the potential, and he'd hoped that Sasha might soften towards him if she saw him around more often. He wanted to reignite the spark he'd been too young to understand fully. If he was honest with himself, it had always been Sasha in the back of his mind. But what could he do? He could negotiate huge business deals, but when it came to Sasha, he always felt wrong-footed and idiotic.

He got up and placed his beer bottle on the kitchen counter. He stared at the bin next to the pot plant and walked away before he kicked it into the wall. The house he was living in was part of the development that Poppy had built with her business partner, Jared. Ollie was in awe of her creative talents. His brother was a lucky man. He walked into the lounge and sunk down into the deep grey couch and switched the mood lighting on, which immediately dimmed the lights and backlit the bookcase which stood along one whole wall. Soothing jazz music began playing and he smiled suddenly. Poppy was a genius. His mood had already picked up slightly. He gazed out into the moonlight at the glittering stars in the inky black sky. The evenings were getting warmer and he'd left the huge double doors that led onto the upstairs deck open, which let in a light breeze.

He needed to decide if he was going to live here permanently, and whether he should also keep his flat in the town he'd grown up in. The flat was near his first gym and was convenient when he visited, which was frequently. He hadn't realised quite how exhausting setting up a second gym would be. He'd loved Poppy's ideas, but he had also wanted to incorporate her designs to show her other options for expansion that moved her away from Jared. He knew they were just friends now, but Ollie wasn't stupid. He had eyes. The man was still smitten with Poppy, although the way he hugged Sasha made Ollie growl too.

Ollie wasn't meddling by setting up a business opposite his soon-to-be sister-in-law... he reasoned. Poppy was more than capable of looking after herself. He was just watching out for his little brother. Dylan could also sort out his own mess, but Ollie looked out for him anyway. He'd always done it. Dylan was a successful artisan. His work was beautiful and sold all over the world. He built the stunning relaxation spaces that Poppy's panels fitted into at the gym. Between them they'd created a real haven. Ollie was so proud of what they'd achieved.

Even his youngest brother, Miles, was climbing up the career ladder now with his tech background and love of cars. He already owned a small workshop that serviced supercars and the fees he charged made Ollie's eyes water. Lots of these cars were like super-computers these days, so just as well Miles was a tech geek. Many of his car owners were entrepreneurs with their own empires. Miles was fast becoming one of the country's hottest bachelors. He tuned the cars to within an inch of their lives and the owners loved him. Ollie suddenly thought of Sasha and wondered if she could help explode Miles' business, in the same way she'd talked about doing for him and Poppy.

If Sasha slipped through his fingers for a second time, he'd never forgive himself. He kicked himself for not taking decisive action earlier. Now he picked up his phone and tapped in her number, rolling his neck and stretching out his taut muscles.

'Hello?' she answered. He caught his breath at the sound of her voice. She sounded like she'd been running.

'Sasha. It's Ollie. Have I interrupted you at a bad time?' he asked.

'Ollie!' she didn't sound annoyed, so he breathed a sigh of relief. 'I didn't expect a call from you. I was just about to jump in the bath and my phone was in the bedroom.'

His mind went to mush at the thought of her draped in a towel and flushed from the steam of the water. He paused and he could picture her frowning at his silence.

'I wish I was there,' he said cheekily, making her gasp and then go silent. He winced and then gritted his teeth. What an idiot. He tried to slow his voice down. 'I... uh... wanted to speak to you about some ideas I have for the gym's social media. Have you got space in your diary to meet me in my office?'

'Um... sure.' She didn't sound that sure! 'Can we talk about it now over the phone?'

'I don't want to disturb your bath.' That dratted mental image again. He coughed and cleared his throat. 'Can we meet up tomorrow?' he asked, wiping sweat from his top lip.

'I've got a meeting with Devon first thing,' she said, as if mentally checking her diary.

'Devon?' *Who the hell was Devon?* He felt his pulse rate jump up a notch.

She laughed lightly, chastising him. 'You haven't heard of him? He's the hottest thing in social media right now.' Hot? How hot, he fumed to himself. 'I was actually wanting to speak to you about him, too. I think there might be a way we can all work together,' she continued.

He frowned and hated how possessive he felt, when he had no right to. 'Oh? How?'

'You're so impatient,' she teased. 'I thought you didn't want to talk about it on the phone. I'll fill you in tomorrow. He's coming to the office. It will have to be after he's gone, as I've got to run my idea by him first.'

Ollie didn't like being second in line, but what choice did he have? At least they were meeting in a public place. Ollie held his phone away from his face for a moment and tapped Devon's name in the search bar. A thousand images of a handsome blond guy filled his screen and he cursed, exited the screen and slapped the phone back to his ear, wishing he'd brought another beer with him to the couch and jumping up to get one, then deciding on coffee to wake himself up a bit. He pressed a button and a machine rose up from a space in the counter. Poppy and Jared's designs were very minimalist, with appliances hidden away until needed under sleek surfaces.

He heard Sasha step into the bath and closed his eyes for a second to make himself concentrate. 'Ok,' he sighed. 'I know from experience that you're a busy woman, particularly whenever I try to get hold of you.' He left that thought with her and could imagine her frowning and brushing a few stray bubbles from her... chin, while she tried to keep the phone dry. 'I'll text you in the morning and keep my diary free from twelve. How does that sound? You can have me all afternoon,' he said provocatively, picturing her skin flushing. Her flashing green eyes and dark hair made his libido go into overdrive.

His hands always itched to touch her skin, though she seemed oblivious to how her curves attracted men wherever she went. The number of staff he'd wanted to fire, when he'd heard on the grapevine they'd fancied her, was ridiculous. There hadn't been anything he could do about it then, as he couldn't date her himself and keeping everyone else at bay would have made her hate him. But he'd been sorely tempted. He'd even dated other women to get her off his mind, which was unfair as he'd been careful to keep the relationships at surface level which was unsatisfactory for everyone.

Sasha drove him crazy.

He'd had enough of playing games and skirting around each other and he wanted her in his home and his bed. He just hoped that she wanted him too. He tried to hold onto his confidence, but whenever she'd dated someone new, he'd almost felt like she was doing it to punish him and he didn't know why. Then he remembered their conversation about staff and his dating guidelines and could have kicked himself for not telling her sooner. Initially he'd wanted to ignore her, as he refused to be a passing phase when she had so many dates, but in the end he'd shot himself in the foot with his own stupid set of rules.

He should have acted on his feelings sooner. It wasn't a mistake he'd make again. He was going to make it clear how he felt, and then she could decide what she wanted. If it wasn't him, he'd be devastated, but in the meantime he'd do everything in his power to turn fortune, and the beautiful Sasha, his way.

He'd looked at the premises near Cherry Blossom Lane as he'd got so fed up with making up excuses to pop by her office, and he was useless and superfluous at the wedding planning. The day he'd learned from Jared that the site was for sale had been a blessing. The gym was ripe for redevelopment with minimal fuss. It just needed a cash injection and some clever design. He had experience of both from his first gym.

He'd been looking to expand for a while but had become restless. He'd had no idea why. Then he'd begun visiting Poppy's studio more often and he knew he was still lost. Sasha was in his blood, and he'd followed her rather than leave her to find love in her new career.

He'd never had a problem attracting women before, but now that he wanted Sasha to notice him, she treated him like a brother. He was going to change that and either make her his, or lose her forever.

CHAPTER SIXTEEN

*T*here was a soft knock on the door. Ollie got up to answer it, more quickly than he ever had before. Had Sasha decided not to wait until the morning? Maybe she had come round to see him? He flung the door open, only to see Poppy standing there. He let out the breath he'd been holding.

Poppy was looking pretty in a soft cream lounge set with her hair in a ponytail, making her look about fifteen again. They'd grown up together, so she would always be young in his eyes. She reached up on her tiptoes and gave his cheek a kiss. She was a fairly tall woman, but he still towered over her and she always teased him that he was a giant.

'What brings you out so far into the woods?' he joked.

'Hey neighbour,' she replied, looking round at the open plan layout of the house and grinning. 'Sorry. I can't help but smile every time I see a person actually living in one of the houses I helped design.'

Ollie slung his arm around her shoulders and walked back into the huge granite kitchen and rested his hand on the cool antibacterial surface of the breakfast bar, making cleaning so much easier, which sat opposite the sleek black cabinets. 'Rightly so. I was just feeling a bit grumpy and put the light and music on and it's incredible, Poppy.' He waved a wine glass at her and she nodded, so he pulled a bottle of crisp white wine from the glass fridge that was integral to the kitchen units. 'I'm just lucky I can live here for a while.'

'What were you feeling grumpy about?' she enquired. He could have kicked himself, as now she'd keep asking about it.

'I just spoke to Sasha and she mentioned someone called Devon,' he admitted. 'I'm not sure what another good looking guy can do for the gym that a hundred others aren't already doing.'

Poppy's eyes gleamed and he hated her knowing gaze. 'Maybe you should wait and hear what she has to say?' she said carefully, sipping her wine and going to look out at the view of her own beautiful garden, which was now mostly obscured by mature trees she'd had planted to give them both some privacy. 'Sasha has some pretty incredible ideas and if she's got one about your gym, I'd say that's pretty lucky for you.' She winked at him and he rolled his eyes.

'How's things going with your dad?' he asked, changing tack.

Poppy turned back to face him and then went to sit in one of the oversize armchairs next to the huge fireplace that separated the lounge from the study space next door.

'I'm thinking of going to meet him,' she said tentatively, her fingers twirling the stem of her wine glass so that the liquid sloshed dangerously before she stopped and took a sip. 'Sasha said she'll come with me as Dylan's travelling a lot at the moment in the run-up to the wedding.'

'Ok. How are you feeling about the wedding?' he asked, taking one of her hands and giving it a quick squeeze before sitting back in his own chair.

The light came back into Poppy's eyes and she gave him a

dazzling smile, which warmed his heart and eased some of the worry he'd been having about Jared. 'I literally can't wait!' she said with such warmth in her voice.

Ollie sighed. He'd love to have someone that happy about committing to him long term. He'd never really wanted anything serious before, but spending so much time at work, and then at home on his own, was becoming tiresome. His team was great, but it wasn't like having friends around. He had loads of mates, but not many lived in the area.

'How are the therapy rooms going down with the clients?' asked Poppy. 'Are they using the relaxation pods in the grounds behind the centre?'

Ollie smiled as he pictured his waiting list for those spaces. People loved the sensory panels with mood lighting, warmth and music, plus the relaxation spaces gave a bit of distance from other customers. 'They're so popular already that I'm contemplating asking you to build more.' He held up a hand before she could tell him off and laughed. 'I know… that would completely go against the whole idea of putting them in the acres of land behind the gym, so everyone can enjoy a bit of space and tranquillity.'

Poppy sighed and smacked his hand playfully. 'Everyone seems to love the pods being dotted around in that copse of cherry trees. It's so much easier now that the pods are purpose-built by my new teams, they just have to be shipped in and placed down on a base. Before that Dylan had to help me. It was the bane of his life,' she laughed, making him smile.

'He didn't mind,' said Ollie. 'It's helped his business grow too.'

'He's very happy doing things at his own pace, as you very well know,' she reminded him. 'But he has enjoyed the challenge of helping me work out how to facilitate it on a larger scale.'

'Those pods have brought extra income in straight away. They're worth every penny you charge for them, even though I got mates' rates.'

'Family discount,' she corrected, and he clinked his beer bottle with her glass in celebration. He hadn't banked on his latest site being popular so quickly, and it was a headache managing building work and customers. Luckily the front of the gym was already sound and just needed sprucing up. But the project was getting bigger by the minute. If this Devon got involved in some way and loads of glamorous people suddenly descended on the premises, how would he cope?

'I just happened to spot an article about the district's dashing new business owner and how he's making waves in the fitness world,' Poppy said, opening her bag and pulling out a copy that looked well read.

Ollie rolled his eyes again and tried to ignore her teasing, but he wasn't used to having his photo taken or being splashed across glossy magazines. This was new territory for him and he wasn't sure how to handle it.

'Maybe I should give this copy to Sasha,' said Poppy as she got up to leave, quickly rinsing her glass in the butler's sink and putting it on the stone draining rack set into the granite.

'Why? She wouldn't be interested in that,' he said, suddenly grumpy again.

'It says you're a hot property,' teased Poppy as he threw a tea towel from a kitchen drawer at her head and she jumped out of the way with a squeal. 'Sasha's always dreamed of hanging out with the rich and famous, perhaps she could start looking a bit closer to home!'

Ollie made a grab for the magazine but Poppy held it just out of reach. 'Anyway, why are you ringing my best friend this late at night, Oliver Taylor?' she asked, suddenly serious, her eyebrows raised and a don't-mess-with-me look on her face.

His eyes met hers and he tried not to wince at her penetrating gaze. 'Oh, bloody hell, Ollie!' She said suddenly. 'Seriously. You'd better do something about it this time, or I'll castrate you myself.' He did wince at that, and she didn't break eye contact.

'I won't hurt her,' he promised, solemnly.

'If you do, she'll probably kill you before I get a chance,' she warned, without laughing.

'I won't hurt her,' he said again, more clearly. She simply nodded her head, then pulled him into a hug and kissed him goodbye, leaving him standing on his doorstep as if a hurricane had just been through his home, upturning everything and leaving devastation behind.

CHAPTER SEVENTEEN

*S*asha sat back in the chair Jared had commissioned for her, after she'd complained that he'd sent Poppy a designer chair. He'd laughed uproariously at her cheek, as she knew full well it had been a gift to say well done on the completion of a big housing project. The next day, a sleek and beautifully padded office chair had arrived for her with his compliments. Poppy had just raised an eyebrow and left Sasha to it, as she was swinging around and around on the swivel chair and singing at the top of her voice. Billy had sulked like a sullen teenager all week, as he'd wanted a gift from Jared too.

Now Sasha got to her feet as Bonnie showed Devon into her office. A wide grin spread across her face. His build was slim and athletic, his blond hair was artistically tousled and his eyes crinkled as though he was genuinely happy to be there. Their personalities had immediately clicked, online and on the phone – and it looked like he wasn't going to be a let-down in the flesh.

Devon's blue eyes scanned the room and took in the relaxing atmosphere and discreet splashes of bright colour that she'd added to the otherwise muted décor. Sasha's desk was in the middle of the room, so she could still keep an eye on reception, while the floor-to-ceiling bookcases in every room lent an air of calm and interest. Sasha had enjoyed slowly filling the bookshelves with her taste in books to put a stamp on her own office and had found as many colourful spines as she could, arranging them by size and tone, so that you had to stop and stare. She'd spent weekends scouring local bookstores and vintage markets with the budget Poppy had allocated her for her office redesign. Devon strolled over and ran his fingers across one or two.

'Great collection!' he said, laughing at the sizzling romances that nestled next to serious design books, networking and marketing reads and celebrity biographies. 'I do love a good romance read.'

She raised one eyebrow to see if he was mocking her, but he was avidly scanning the blurb of one vibrant book, before pushing it gently back into place. He looked like he'd just stepped out of a photo shoot and her eyes couldn't help but track his movements around the room. She knew some people just oozed the X factor, and with Devon it shone from every pore. She caught her breath and motioned for him to take a seat opposite her, stopping herself from fanning her face to cool her blush down.

After a few minutes of small talk, she was surprised at how well informed he was about their brand. He really seemed excited to work with them. Sasha kind of felt as if she knew him already, from their chats and following his timelines on social media, so she had to remind herself that he wasn't her friend and that this was a business meeting. Delicious Devon wanted a panel in his new home and she needed to be professional. She was the one who had persuaded Poppy to fit in an extra design, so it would be her fault if it all went wrong. She quelled her butterflies at meeting someone famous. Wasn't this what she'd always dreamed of, and written about in her sparkly planner?

Devon liked to respond to his followers and they'd struck up an easy friendship, which she had been surprised about initially. On meeting him, she realised she wasn't that special – he was just as friendly and personable to everyone he met. She felt a quick stab of disappointment, and then grinned at her own silliness. Being equally nice to everyone was Devon's way of being professional.

Bonnie had practically swooned when he'd walked in and said hello, and Billy had drooled unattractively. Devon had then propped his delectable derriere on Bonnie's desk and had her in fits of laughter about something or other. She was already smitten by the time Sasha had called him into her office.

Billy was always commenting about how on-trend Devon's online presence was and was just as excited as Bonnie about meeting the man in person. If he hadn't had another meeting, Billy would be sitting on her lap right now and gazing into Devon's eyes like she was. The man was dreamy. He wasn't her type, but she could appreciate beauty when faced with it. It shone from him and he also had an innate kindness, which drew her to him even more. He'd kissed her cheek when he'd arrived and said she smelt divine, but it hadn't been cheesy, she could see he actually meant it and she had to admit she'd preened a little.

Now they were finally sitting opposite each other, she smiled to put him at ease, but he was already sitting back in his ergonomic chair and enjoying the view of the fields from the huge side window, whilst sipping the coffee she'd got him from their fancy machine.

'I've spoken to Poppy about your order for a mood panel and she's agreed we can squeeze you in as a favour. I told her there might be potential to work together in the future,' she said, carefully choosing her words.

His eyebrows shot up in surprise, but he didn't shout at her or run for the hills. 'I certainly wasn't expecting you to say that!' he laughed, his eyes sparkling. 'As you know my expertise in is mental health. That's what I trained in, even though most people seem to think I just make up the stuff I post online!' he laughed self-depreciatingly.

Sasha knew he'd studied psychology for years, which was why, she assumed, he was so interested in what they were doing at Poppy Mason Designs. 'I can see how our brands complement each other,' he mused. 'We're pretty much an ideal fit.'

His face was animated and he seemed keen to know more, which made Sasha sigh with relief. She laid out images and figures that she'd meticulously worked on to show him how she saw them working together.

'Wow!' he said, leaning forward to take a closer look at her mood boards. 'You've really put a lot of thought into this. What does Poppy think?'

'She loves the idea!' she grinned a bit manically, as that was a slight exaggeration – but Poppy was interested at least.

Sasha already liked Devon from his social feeds, but in person he was even more magnetic. 'I have lots of ideas for the barn I've just moved into. Will Poppy be able to consult on that, if we're working together on other projects?' he asked. 'The recent homes she built with Jared are gorgeous and I'd love to come home from work and for it to feel like paradise,' he smiled.

Sasha winced and explained that Poppy had huge waiting lists for panels, but did want to expand in the phone application arena, as it wouldn't mean more building work, which they were already snowed under with.

Devon thought for a moment, but didn't appear too fazed.

She assumed he had a team he'd have to consult over any branding decisions, so this was just an opening conversation as far as she was concerned.

Devon sipped his coffee and then placed it back on her desk. 'Ok. So you squeezed me into your schedule because you think we can do this mutual branding thing where I go to your venues and you promote me too. Is that what you were thinking? Or a paid partnership deal?'

Kudos to him for asking! Sasha was impressed by how quickly he got to the point. She'd assumed they'd skirt around it for months. 'So, we would fit the panel for free, and then you'd be obliged to appear at three of our events. How does that sound?'

Devon grinned and he didn't take long to make his decision. 'That sounds like a good deal to me, as long as the events are local and I don't have to travel. That bumps costs up,' he mused. 'So, I don't have to wait for the panel, but I get to chat to the public and help your business too. My only stipulation would be that the venues are on brand and about wellbeing, but I'm assuming you've got that covered?'

Sasha's pulse started to race. 'Of course! Do you need to pass this by your management or branding experts?'

He shook his head. 'They might not like it, but I do. It's my decision in the end and I really want that panel!' he grinned, making her smile too, her heart finally settling back into a normal beat.

'Um… I was thinking that we could take some photos at the gym across the road. It's run by Oliver Taylor.'

Devon frowned and looked over his shoulder as if he might be able to see the gym, but was just met by a blank white wall. 'Why would you want to involve the gym? I'm assuming you'd want me to promote your mood panels, or the app you just spoke about?'

'That's right,' said Sasha, and then rushed on before he

could follow that train of thinking and veer left. 'Ollie's going to be Poppy's brother-in-law in a few months. He owns a few gyms across the country,' she said, crossing her fingers behind her back because this was mostly true, his gyms were both in different counties. 'Poppy's designs are incorporated in his latest venture, which is over the road from this office. There are incredible relaxation spaces for people's mental health and mood pods in the grounds at the back amongst the cherry trees. It's a stunning location.' Or it would be once the building work was out of the way, she thought, before continuing.

'We're considering diversifying from doing so many house builds. This would fit with your follower base, and it might help other gyms see the potential of Poppy's work. Win, win!' she said finally and sat back in her chair in exhaustion.

No wonder Billy needed a rest after each meeting. Poppy just ploughed through hers as if they energised her, which they probably did as it was her own business. Sasha had never quite understood that before. If this became her business, and she had clients like Devon, would it fill her with excitement too? She spent another thirty minutes going over the finer details with Devon, but she could see he was won over and liked her ideas.

As expected, Billy joined them and was explaining how they could fit further possible health elements into Devon's home at a later date. This was the first time for a while she'd seen Billy smile genuinely, and Devon was avidly listening to everything he said. Billy adored an audience. He knew the products inside out, and she was grateful to be able to sit back and let him do his sales pitch.

They were showing Devon how Poppy's app worked, and going through some photos of Ollie's wellbeing suites on her computer, when she noticed the time. She'd been having so much fun with Devon that she'd almost forgotten Ollie!

'I love these ideas,' said Devon, as he added a few of his own about how the collaboration could work. It had been an informative morning. Before Devon left, he booked an appointment to come back in and see the gym. Hopefully he'd become one of their long-term clients, and maybe a friend. It seemed weird that for so long she'd craved being well-known, and now she was mixing with the rich and famous. She hadn't lost the need to be heard, though, and was determined that her own business would grow the way Poppy's had, even if it was on a smaller scale.

Once Devon had gone, Sasha grabbed her bag and headed to the door, reminding Billy she had a meeting with Ollie and waving to Bonnie as she went.

Bonnie was a great addition to the office, and having her help would free up lots of lovely hours for Sasha to build her own brand and work for clients like Ollie. She stopped short when she thought of him as a client for a moment, then picked up her pace or she'd be late for their first official meeting. She wondered if Maxine would be working there today, and if she'd managed to wear Ollie down. Sasha didn't know what his problem was when it came to feisty women. Maybe he couldn't handle them?

CHAPTER EIGHTEEN

*S*asha waved hello to the girls on reception, used to being let in without a pass now. Ollie had instructed all staff that she was working with him and had access during opening hours. It made her feel special and she pushed her shoulders back and smiled a little more widely. This was how it felt to be in charge of your own destiny... well, with a little bit of help from her friends.

She grinned and headed for Ollie's office, catching sight of Maxine's packed exercise class and fleetingly looking at herself critically in one of the mirrors. Her new fitted trousers and cute short-sleeved shirt looked good, but she stopped and ran her fingers through her hair to tame it a little. She'd visited a few gym classes lately, as there was no excuse now she literally worked next door to this beautiful space. Working two jobs made her feel exhilarated, but bone tired. She needed to work on organising her own schedule the same way she sorted out Poppy and Billy's.

She peeked her head round Ollie's door. His personal assistant was on his lunch break, so there was an eerie quiet around. Ollie lifted his eyes from his computer and his face lit up when he saw her. He smiled and got up to give her a hug, pulling her in towards his chest so that she had to breathe in, and then got a noseful of his spicy aftershave. Not very professional, she grinned to herself, but she wasn't complaining, he smelt divine. Ollie was a great hugger, plus his body was moulded like a god!

She felt adrenaline flow through her veins and knew she was excited about what she was going to say to him. She shoved away the thought that it might be his proximity that excited her, and sat down at his desk, waiting for him to return to his seat. He settled down, his elbows resting on the arms of his chair, looking like the king of his domain. She kind of liked his authoritative air... which was now sizzling with a few extra hormones. His shirt was rolled up to show off his impressive forearms and she had to drag her gaze away.

'So, what's the plan?' he asked.

'Plan?' her mind wouldn't focus for a second and that annoyed the hell out of her. She was a serious businesswoman.

'I can tell from the way you are sitting that you are planning something. Spill,' he grinned.

She began to smile as her focus sharpened and then she sat forward, eager to share her exciting news. She just hoped he could see the value in her ideas. 'I told you last night about Devon?'

Ollie stilled, then sat back and watched her for a moment, like a sleek panther about to pounce. She frowned as an unsettling feeling filled her stomach. Perhaps he would hate her plan. 'I looked him up last night,' he said, giving nothing away. 'He seems popular...'

Her heart started beating a bit faster and she flushed. 'Um... he is! That's the point.' What was his problem with Devon?

'How did you manage to set up a meeting this morning? Isn't he famous?' he frowned, although half Poppy's clients were famous, so it shouldn't surprise him that much. 'Isn't he some kind of internet star? What does he want from you?'

Sasha wanted to pout. She had skills! Ok, Devon was a big fish, but Sasha knew how to handle talent. She'd done it for Poppy – and she could help Ollie, too, if he wasn't so grumpy and sullen. 'He doesn't want anything from me...' she frowned. 'We started chatting online.'

'Sasha!' He got up and went to look out of the window. 'Didn't your parents teach you not to talk to strangers online?'

She rolled her eyes and wanted to stick her tongue out, suddenly. Maybe she didn't need to help him out? Then his face wouldn't be quite so smug when everyone else did well. She bit her lip and stood up too. If she didn't know any different, she'd think Ollie was the teeniest bit jealous of her meeting with Devon. She would have kind of enjoyed that – but she knew it couldn't be true.

Ollie turned back to face her with a sigh. She could see tiny worry lines under his eyes and wondered if taking on this gym had been a step too far. She pictured Maxine standing behind his desk and massaging his tense muscles, and shivered. It made her even more determined to make him listen.

She sat back down, pushing the chair away from the desk and crossing her legs, not seeing his eyes follow the movement. 'Look, Devon's into mental health and wellbeing, just like you are,' she scolded gently. 'He follows the pages I run for Poppy and I noticed he'd liked a lot of my posts for her business. It was natural for me to thank him and then think of him for a collaboration.'

'Collaboration?'

She shook her head, as he was dumb. 'Yes. His involvement could help us all. He's so popular right now. Everyone wants him to advertise their products or work with him.'

'How can you afford him, then? I know Poppy's doing well, but this sounds like another ballgame?'

Sasha tried to curb her anger at his negativity. He hadn't even heard the plan yet. She was so tempted to leave and let him carry on being as exhausted as he clearly was, trying to do everything on his own. But she was his friend and now they had gotten rid of any sexual confusion, she wanted him to succeed.

'We don't need to 'afford' him,' she said in exasperation. 'He's just bought a barn conversion. He wants Poppy to help him with a redesign and a lighting panel. She's booked out for the next year and beyond, but does want to explore options of working with influencers for her app. So we've offered him a panel in exchange for his endorsement.'

His eyes widened as she could see that he finally understood what this could mean for Poppy without overworking her and keeping her in the office even more. His brother would be ecstatic! Sasha knew Dylan worried about how hard Poppy worked, and fleetingly wished she could find a man like that of her own.

'Ahh. Ok. I can see the benefit of that,' Ollie paused while he thought it through. 'Great idea,' he said suddenly. She could see the tension leave his shoulders and as he smiled, his eyes began to twinkle at her. She caught her breath.

'Plus, it could mean that we entice other big clients, beside Jared…' she added cheekily.

His mouth dropped open at this and then he threw his head back and laughed out loud. This man really was too handsome for his own good. 'Oh Sasha. Only you would think of how to do that. I've been worrying about Poppy lately,' he said. 'She's had so much going on with her dad and the wedding. You really are amazing! So what do you need me for?'

He left the question hanging and she felt her mouth go dry. She gulped in some air and looked out of the window, trying to refocus her brain. 'It's not really what I need you for, it's what you might need me for...' she parried, suddenly remembering this was just Ollie and he was her friend. They'd had loads of banter recently, but somehow the room suddenly felt tropical. She pulled out her collar and tried to let some air in.

His eyes narrowed and she felt her skin grow hot under his gaze. What was it with this man and her bodily reactions? He was looking at her like he'd like to eat her alive and she shifted uncomfortably in her seat, but kept her eyes on him, refusing to back down.

He smiled and leaned in. 'There are many things I want you for, Sasha,' he said huskily, 'but for now I'm willing to listen to your plan, as it seems to involve us all.'

Sasha let her breath out and felt like she'd earnt a reprieve from something she didn't understand. It was so stuffy in his office, she looked around and then turned his desk fan on without asking if that was ok, which seemed to amuse him further.

'I think it would be great for us all if we did a photoshoot with Devon in one of the relaxation pods in the gym grounds,' she said all at once. 'Although it is ironic that you all hid the gym's existence from me, and now I'm the one who is trying to promote it,' she huffed.

Ollie frowned for a moment and she knew she'd hit a home run. He'd hate the idea at first, of course. 'I didn't know you weren't aware I'd bought the gym, and was building the pods,' he said, frowning. 'Poppy said because you'd immaculately arranged their schedules, and the installations here were not on the lists, it wasn't fair to mess up all your hard work. I was so confused as to why it mattered that much, but you weren't really talking to me anyway, so the topic didn't come up,' he joked, and she ignored him.

'Why take photos here?' he continued. 'Poppy has relaxation pods everywhere now.' She could picture the images in his brain of hordes of screaming fans wanting to know where Devon was, but she also saw the moment when he calculated how much exposure that would mean for his new gym. 'Ok, don't answer that,' he said after a minute or two. 'Why would you do that for me?' His piercing gaze was back to hers.

Duh… she thought. 'That's what friends do for each other,' she said, licking her lips and then stopping as he was still watching her. 'It means Poppy doesn't have to do anything, as the pods are already popular and fit with Devon's brand,' she added haughtily. 'He might even become a regular, as his new home is not far from Cherry Blossom Lane. Plus it helps my new business, as I can share it on social media. And you're now my second client, if that's what you still want? If you're happy, then I'm doing a good job.'

'I didn't expect you to bag a celebrity client when we spoke about you updating my brand and social sites!' he laughed. 'You really are incredible.'

Sasha enjoyed the warm feeling of praise. Then he came round and pulled her into another hug. She snuggled into his chest. He smelt warm and inviting and it had been a while since she'd had a hug from a gorgeous man. None of the few dates that she'd been on recently had lit a fire under her, or made her want to see them again. One of the guys had offered to show her a home-grown toadstool collection he kept under his bed and had seemed devastated when she'd been less than keen.

'It would work well for all of us,' she mumbled into his chest, when he didn't seem to be letting her go. Her hands itched to slide into the waistband of his trousers under his shirt. She pushed against the solid wall of his chest and he leaned down and kissed her softly on the lips, making her gasp and stand back, her heart racing and her eyes wide.

'I shouldn't have expected anything less,' he said as he walked back behind his desk as if nothing had happened.

Did he kiss all his clients? Sasha tried to brush it off, but she could feel the indignation bubbling inside – even if she'd happily go back for more of those hot kisses. Then she pictured him kissing Maxine and had to bite back a sharp retort.

She quickly said she needed to get back to work, breezily waving goodbye to his surprised face as she rushed out and then nearly bumped right into a vending machine. She only just about preventing herself from opening a window and yelling at the world for carrying on regardless of the monumental thing that had just happened in her life.

What the hell was he playing at, kissing her like that and then acting as if it was nothing?

She should have slapped his silly face and left him wondering what the hell had just happened. She stomped back to her office and then held a hand up to Billy as he knocked on her door. He raised an eyebrow and then backed out, leaving her to fume quietly while she messaged Devon telling him that her plan had been given the green light from their end.

CHAPTER NINETEEN

*S*asha peered around her brand-new home and spun round in circles with her arms out wide. How was this her life now? She'd never loved a job as much as she did this one, and this flat was designed like everything Poppy did, with style and thoughtfulness. The windows were huge, with double doors leading out to a small balcony with a pretty metal balustrade, giving a view onto the fields of wild-flowers below. She could literally see for miles without stepping out of her lounge. The little kitchen was lit up like the morning sun with low lights, up-lighting and music that could be set to play as you walked in.

The lounge had an L-shaped couch in deep moss green velvet, which also faced out over the fields through a giant window. There was a TV, but the view was the focal point. Who needed television with something like that in front of you?

Sasha sighed and ran her hand along the back of the couch. *Her* couch, for now. She grabbed her bag of toiletries and carefully emptied them out in the bathroom. The flat was a good size, as it ran across the top of their offices and meeting rooms. There were also two offices upstairs. The shower room had a full bath that sat by another floor-to-ceiling window.

As there was no one overlooking her, she could dance around naked to her heart's content. People did occasionally stroll in the fields, but the section behind the offices was all pretty untamed. Ramblers tended to stick to the paths further along.

Now she climbed into the empty bath fully clothed and leant back, letting the tension of the last few days float away. She was in. This was her new life and she didn't have to fight one of her sisters for a soak in the tub. She'd lived with two of her sisters for the last few years, but the third was also always popping in, and the place had felt like a railway station half the time. The flat had been tiny and if any of them had a boyfriend over, it was mightily embarrassing bumping into them in the kitchen in the morning. Sasha needed her own space. She adored her sisters, but they were noisy and demanding. She was lucky she didn't have the diva gene, she mused, grinning to herself.

Hoisting herself out of the bath, she wondered why she wasn't sipping Champagne to celebrate her momentous move, but her sisters were a bit peeved she'd moved so far away and wasn't just round the corner. Her mum and dad had said they might pop in the next day, as they'd assumed she'd be celebrating with friends. She had a huge family, but not one of them had taken the time to stop by the first flat she'd had on her own. She supposed that it wasn't exactly a ten-minute journey to visit her now, and it was her own fault for moving away. She sniffed a little and went into the kitchen to see if Poppy had left any food there. Sasha had forgotten her bag of provisions, which she'd left on the table of the flat she'd shared with her sisters. Sasha couldn't imagine it lasting for long with them around. They'd assume that she'd left it for them and scoff the lot.

Poppy and Billy were at a glittery work function that night. That sort of thing was usually like nectar for Sasha, who loved a good party, but she had been determined to move in as soon as possible, even though it was exhausting and a teeny bit lonely on her own. Poppy had asked her to join them so that she could meet potential clients for her new business, but Sasha hadn't wanted to impose on her friend's generosity again. This was something she knew she could build up on her own. She already had Ollie's brief from their initial phone call, and very confusing meeting, and she was happy to get working on things. Now he knew of her plans with Devon, he would already be thinking of what it could mean for his business.

She was determined to show Devon her potential and make him want to engage her as his social media consultant, too, although he probably had a team of staff already, judging by how popular he was. She knew from recent experience how time-consuming presenting a perfect image to the world could be. As both Poppy and Devon advocated mental health, their social media posts were less 'look at me' and more 'this is what I can do for you'. She could probably learn a thing or two if she studied Devon's timelines in more detail, although her work for Poppy was what had drawn him to them in the first place. She checked Poppy's follower and engagement statistics regularly throughout the day and the account analytics told her what was working and what wasn't. She knew she could do a good job.

She thought for a minute about how that felt. She'd never really cared too much about any of her other jobs before. This one felt right. It felt empowering and full of possibilities, even if her family had the hump with her for moving out, and was ignoring her for now.

If she had more clients like Ollie, she'd be quite well off for the first time in her working life. She'd tried to give Ollie a concession on the rates that she'd worked out with Poppy for her blossoming business. He was almost family, after all. But he'd refused and offered to pay her new set fees. It still blew her mind. She'd have had to work for a month in her old jobs to earn what she could in a few hours now. Getting qualified with her online studies would also make her feel more comfortable in her new role, as at present she had crippling imposter syndrome and spent hours scrolling through uplifting quotes on her social media feeds to counteract it.

She knew she had talent, but could she really do this as a part time job, and mesh it with her work for Poppy? Friends like Ollie were one thing, but would strangers pay her fees? The only proper work history she had was so recent, from her time with Poppy. Ollie was probably paying her because he felt sorry for her, with high-flying friends like Poppy. Sasha had done loads of research about what customers at this level and in this industry were used to, and kept reminding herself that she had won two clients in as many weeks, and even bagged Devon for a client's campaign. That certainly wasn't shoddy for a newbie like her.

She was waiting for someone to jump out of a cupboard and yell 'surprise!', then tell her that this had all been a wind-up, that she was useless at her job and she would have to move home with her mum and dad. She loved them dearly, but they would kick her out again for being too messy within ten minutes.

She flinched as the doorbell pealed. It wasn't a sharp sound as, of course, Poppy had even thought of that. It was melodious and welcoming. Pulling the door open, she was shocked to see a tall, sexy man standing there. She sucked in her breath and wondered if she'd remembered to brush her hair since she'd slouched in the empty bath. He grinned and held up a bottle of sparkling wine in a cut glass bottle. She looked at it in confusion.

'To help celebrate your new home!' Ollie said, handing it to her and bending down to kiss her cheek. He smelt of patchouli and musk again and she reeled back and held onto the doorframe. Her face flamed. Did he expect a flat full of revellers? How embarrassing!

He glanced over her shoulder. 'Are you going to let me in?' She had the grace to blush and scooted back to let him inside. His shoulders were so wide and firm that she had to reach up to help him out of the lightweight jacket he was wearing over a pale blue shirt and smart jeans. He grinned and pulled her into a hug. 'Congratulations on your new home.'

'Thanks,' she said, backing away before moving over to the kitchen and pulling out two Champagne flutes, silently thanking Poppy for kitting out the kitchen with what she classed as essentials, before Sasha moved in.

Ollie walked over to the window and exclaimed how beautiful the view was. She knew he'd been to the flat before, so it must seem weird with her few items now placed around. She hadn't exactly had time to sort it all out, so suitcases and boxes were randomly dotted here and there. She might be a tad messy at home, but she wasn't a hoarder, and didn't own many possessions. Her family end of terrace home was still full of boxes of her childhood things waiting to be collected from the loft, though. She hadn't moved any of them to the flat she'd shared with her sisters.

The thought that her parents might want her childhood possessions out of their house depressed her for a moment, then she brightened up. They had never actually encouraged her to come and get them, and loved it when she went back home. Her dad was a neat freak, which wasn't ideal in a house full of messy women, but he just laughed and shook his head at their shenanigans and let them get on with it. It was a house full of love.

She grinned suddenly. A very handsome man was standing in her living room and he'd brought her Champagne. He might not fancy her, but she'd happily have one of those kisses on the lips to keep her going. It seemed Ollie kissed all his friends, so she had to understand he was just being friendly and not make it a big deal. She handed him a glass of the sparkling wine and then kissed him fully on the lips, making him gasp in surprise and his eyes dilate, as she walked away and began talking as if nothing had happened. Touché!

'Is Dylan on his own tonight?' she asked lightly, suddenly enjoying herself. 'Poppy and Billy are at a work event and I didn't want to join them. Too much to do here,' she gestured to the boxes. When he didn't answer straight away, as he was just staring at her, she hid a smile.

'Do you want anything to eat?' she asked, walking into the kitchen and knocking into three boxes, almost toppling them over. She cursed under her breath and wished she'd got back earlier so everything was tidy and in its place. Then she pictured her old flat and winced. It had never been tidy. She vowed to change that from now on. This flat was too pretty to be covered in plates and dirty coffee mugs. She looked at Ollie expectantly.

'No thanks,' he replied, but he was still watching her as if he didn't know what she would do next. She wasn't about to pounce on him, for goodness sake! It was only a kiss.

'Dylan's gone to the pub with a few friends,' he said as he inclined his head for her to join him by the window. They could see for miles across the fields behind the offices. 'How are you feeling about your new home?'

Her face lit up as she stood next to him, enjoying his obvious pleasure at the view. Surely he had other plans for tonight, or could have joined his brother in the pub, though? 'Are you on your way somewhere?' She touched his arm to regain his attention and felt the soft fabric of his shirt. 'You look smart,' she smiled up at him, trying to quell her nerves at him turning up at the flat.

His big frame seemed to fill the space. She was about medium height and curvaceous, but she felt tiny next to him. He seemed to enjoy riling her up lately, but now she'd wrong-footed him. She had wondered if he'd been flirting with her at his office, but had quashed that idea as stupid.

'She gives me a compliment!' he joked, staggering slightly. She laughed and grabbed onto his arm. Then he pulled her to him and their chests touched. He brushed her hair out of her eyes gently and she drew in a sharp breath, but couldn't look away from his eyes.

'I knew everyone else was out and wanted to make sure you celebrated this momentous occasion,' he said simply, as if that explained everything.

Her skin felt hot suddenly, though she hadn't touched a drop of the wine. 'What momentous occasion?' her mind seemed to have gone to mush and she couldn't work out what he was talking about.

'Your first home of your own!' He drew her with him as he went to sit on the couch and instead of letting her sit next to him, he pulled her onto his lap. She squeaked and didn't know what to do. He picked up his wine from the pretty artisan side table that he'd put it onto earlier and she quickly sipped her own, thinking she must be like a dead weight on his legs! He clinked their glasses gently. 'Cheers to your new place,' he said before taking the glass and putting both on the table.

He turned towards her and slid his hands into her hair and gently inched her face towards his own. He was staring deeply into her eyes and for the first time in a long while she felt scared for her heart. What the hell was he playing at?

She tried to push herself up and way, but her hands seemed to have a life of their own. They were winding into the hair at the nape of his neck and pulling his face to hers. She just had time to see the passion burning in his eyes before her mind was filled with ecstasy as his lips met hers and her body moulded into his. She turned so her knees were either side of him on the couch and she could hear his laboured breathing and feel his response to her touch.

Her senses were on fire as his hands slid around her back and cupped her backside, pulling her closer to him with a low moan. She'd never been kissed with such longing by a man before and although she wanted to give into it and never let him go, she unwound her arms from his neck and gently pushed on the wall of his chest. His eyes were glazed and he dipped his head for one last kiss before he dropped his hands and let her go. She slid onto the couch next to him in stunned silence, her breathing laboured. His hand caressed her face and she couldn't help but sigh and lean into the contact, then anger began to fizz inside. What the hell did he think he was doing?

She stood up shakily, but couldn't face him. She'd dreamed about this for half her life, but she wasn't about to be used. 'What just happened?' she asked quietly, looking out as the sun dipped below the horizon and the sky turned a darker shade of blue.

'You kissed me,' he joked lightly. She gasped indignantly as he came and stood behind her, but she could hear his laugh and suddenly his arms were around her. He turned her to face him and lifted her chin with his finger. 'Then I kissed you,' he said.

'But why?' her brain was heavy with confusion, but she

felt weirdly at home in his arms. He laughed gently again and kissed the side of her neck, making her shiver with longing

'I've always wanted to kiss you,' he said simply. She sucked in some air and felt the room spin. He guided her back to the couch and handed her a flute of wine, sitting close enough so that their legs were touching.

She frowned. 'I don't understand.'

He shook his head and then picked up her other hand and kissed it tenderly, making her pulse jump.

'We were friends, then you worked for me. We were never single at the same time,' he said as if that explained everything.

'So you never bothered trying?' she asked pointedly, finally looking at him. He blushed this time. 'I didn't want to lose your friendship. You've always been important to me, no matter what you might think.'

'You didn't think I was worth fighting for?' Her cheeks were hot from anger now and she stood up and walked to the kitchen, eyes filled with fury, as he got up and followed her.

'I think about you all the time, Sasha,' he said gently, reaching for her, but the fire in her eyes warned him away and he dropped his hand. 'I always have,' he said, moving closer to her, so their bodies were almost touching.

She reeled back slightly in shock at his words and then pushed him away, her breath coming fast and her eyes dilating. 'So what changed?' she really wanted to know. 'Is it that now I won't be a drain on you, as I can support myself, or that I've shown I actually do have a brain? Or is it that since I'm not following you around like a lovesick puppy, you suddenly think I'm a challenge?'

Ollie stepped back in shock, his arms dropping to his sides as if he'd been stung. She could see the hurt on his face but she was confused by the emotions flowing around her mind and it was too late to take the words back.

'I've always admired your drive and determination, Sasha,' he said, watching her coolly now. The passion from seconds earlier had left the room and she felt the chill. 'You're right, perhaps I should have told you how I felt sooner, but I was working every hour of the day and night to build my business and didn't think it would be fair on you. My friendship with you was too important to mess up. All of us were friends, You, me, Dylan, Poppy, Demi, Anne, Allan and Miles. Plus you always seemed angry at me as we got older and I could never figure out what I'd done wrong.'

'So you stayed away, even if it meant I ended up with someone else?' She thought back to the loser boyfriends who had made her feel like a second-class citizen.

Ollie winced and took the hit. 'I hated you being with anyone else.'

She could see from his expression that he meant it and this was hurting him. But her eyes glittered and she felt her fists bunching up. 'Not enough to give me a smidgeon of hope, or stop me dating them? You knew full well how I felt. I'm not stupid enough to hide my feelings, but I *am* stupid enough to hang around for years for a man who thinks he can pick me up and put me down when he feels like it.'

'Sasha...' pleaded Ollie. 'You know that's not true,' he said, moving to take her in his arms, but stopping again when she took a step back.

'I think you should leave,' she said with finality.

Ollie didn't argue, and grabbed his coat from the rack by the door, attempting to slam the door behind him. Poppy's soft close door design was having none of that, though, and it swished silently shut as he left the flat.

Sasha grinned in triumph for a moment, then tears spilled over her lashes and onto her cheeks. She sobbed noisily and threw herself down on the couch, her body wracked as sobs escaped her. Bloody men! Who was he to decide when the time was right for them?

While she cried, she thought of the words he'd said, and she remembered that he'd said he'd always liked her. The fact that he'd left her in pain for so long was just too much to bear. Her heart had finally healed and she'd been over him – but now she was back to square one. She'd never get past the feel of his lips on hers and his arms around her. She buried her face in the prettily patterned fabric of the cushions on the couch and hoped she wasn't leaving mascara trails everywhere.

She sniffed and sat up, wiping her face with the back of her hand. She grabbed the bottle of fizz and her glass and walked over to run a bath. She wasn't about to let the moment of moving into her first home of her own be ruined by Oliver Taylor. She'd spend the evening pampering herself and sipping the delicious wine he'd paid for – and think about ways to make him sorry he'd ever let her go.

CHAPTER TWENTY

llie pulled into the parking area behind Dylan's house and stared at the empty space next to him. Getting out and opening the door to his plush home above Dylan's new workshop, he cursed his own stupidity at not being clearer with Sasha sooner.

All those hot glances, and that stolen kiss, hadn't brought her to him, so he'd decided tonight was the night to tell her straight about how he felt. He was fed up with living in an empty flat and with putting work first. He knew he had succeeded at the gym but it was stretching him emotionally. He was tired of being alone. Casual hook-ups just weren't for him, whatever the reputation he and his brothers had for being players. Sasha had held his heart in her hands for years. She just didn't know it.

He pictured Sasha's angry eyes and winced, then a fire lit in his stomach. He would make her see the light. He'd known that she'd had a crush on him but, without being big-headed, so did a lot of local women. He and his brothers were known as heartbreakers, but mostly that was just down to the townsfolk gossiping. In fact, it had made them all wary of jumping into bed with strangers. He certainly didn't want that sort of reputation, but it seemed it had happened anyway. He'd had to concentrate on his business, but now he was on track to fulfil his dreams commercially, he found his mind was full of Sasha. He'd treated her lustful stares as a bit of a joke in the past, to protect his own heart, sure that she'd tire of the crush and move on. It seemed now, though, that her feelings for him had always been genuine, and he was a bloody fool waiting this long to tell her how he really felt too.

He cursed and walked into the sleek shower room, stripping off in seconds and pressing his face into the blast of water as he turned it on. He gritted his teeth as the cold jets hit his skin and washed the frustration from his heart. He leant his head against the cool tiles and the water flowed over his body as he formulated a plan to win Sasha's heart. If she wanted him to fight for her, then that's exactly what he'd do.

Once his anger and libido had cooled down, he slung a towel around his waist and walked into the lounge. He switched the daylight panel onto evening mode, which immediately dimmed the lights and made him feel less snarky. He put some jazz music on in the background, grabbed some food from his fridge and picked some fresh herbs from the living wall by the door. He thought of Sasha's offer of food, but all he craved was her.

Poppy and Dylan's wedding was coming up soon, so he ran through several different ways that he could try and persuade Sasha that he wasn't an ogre so she would be happy with him. He was sure Sasha would want everything to flow as smoothly as he did. His eyes narrowed for a moment and he smiled suddenly. Maybe a family wedding was exactly what they needed to bring the maid of honour and the best man together.

CHAPTER TWENTY-ONE

*M*axine waved at a member of her exercise class and ushered them inside for the next session as she stood on the threshold. Everyone wanted to stop for a chat, but she was determined to catch sight of Ollie.

She was wearing her best gym outfit, bright pink form-fitting leggings with detailing to show her firm muscles and a tiny, cropped top in a slightly lighter tone. The man must be blind if he couldn't see her in this. He'd been courteous and had work meetings with her, but she hadn't been able to get him on his own, much to her growing frustration.

Maxine glanced at Sasha, who had joined her class as soon as there was a vacancy. She was limbering up. Maxine eyed her curves under her lashes. Sasha didn't seem fazed by her shapely behind, and men seemed to like it, judging from the stares she got from those in the class.

Maxine enjoyed her own taut lines and, although there was growing demand for classes that built up certain areas of the body, her workouts had always been aimed at overall tone and fitness. Plus she'd often seen Sasha relaxing in the coffee shop after a class, with a hot chocolate and a slice of gooey coffee and walnut cake next to her on the table! Maxine rolled her eyes. What was the point in doing the exercise class if you were just going to stuff your face afterwards? She huffed and then took in a deep calming breath. She didn't like to appear rattled. Her clients expected perfection from her. It gave them something to aspire to. She shook out her glossy blonde hair and then pulled it into a sleek ponytail. Glancing in the mirror, satisfied that she looked just right, Maxine nodded her head to a gym member who strolled past and waved.

Maxine had asked Ollie to help her plan a new class as demand was so high, but he was focussed on the build and revamp of the gym, and she'd heard Sasha was now their social media manager or something. It was why they always seemed to be in an office together with heads bent over a file of some sort. Until recently, that was. This was the first time she'd seen Sasha in a week.

Sasha worked hard in the class as it progressed, her long black hair swept off her face. She was now a bit pink-cheeked and sweaty. Maxine was desperate to ask her about Ollie again, but needed to pick her moment, as Sasha seemed to avoid the topic when they met up. Every conversation was about Poppy and Dylan's wedding, and it was boring Maxine to tears.

As the previous class filed out, Ollie passed and Maxine pulled her flat stomach in and thrust her chest forward, swishing her hair and laughing gaily at something a client said as they left. Ollie was about to stroll past when Sasha walked out. Maxine grabbed her arm and pulled her to one side, making Sasha frown, but she was evidently too tired to pull away and quite used to Maxine grabbing her for a hushed chat about men by now.

Ollie stopped and was looking straight at them, indecision on his face, which was weird. Maybe they'd had a falling out about the wedding plans. Sasha's face fell, and seeing this Maxine's lit up with glee. She could be the one to fix whatever was wrong with their friendship, and then Ollie would be forever in Maxine's debt. Perhaps Sasha was rubbish at her new job, she speculated spitefully.

Maxine beckoned Oliver over and he hesitated, then smiled and headed their way. His smile didn't quite meet his eyes and suddenly Sasha was fidgety and saying she needed to get back to work. Maxine was happy that he could see the contrast in their appearance and didn't let go of Sasha's arm until he was right in front of them.

'Sasha and I were just talking about our flats,' said Maxine gaily. Sasha's mouth dropped open but Maxine carried on regardless, knowing her friend would back her up. 'Unfortunately my car's broken down outside my place, so I had to catch the train to work. I wondered if you might know anything about cars and could help me? I'd throw in dinner.'

Sasha's eyebrows flew into her hairline and she moved away slightly to stand back, while both girls waited to see what his response would be to such a blatant invitation. Sasha went very quiet, but Maxine was confident and didn't doubt she could persuade Ollie of her charms one way or another. She just needed an excuse to get him alone.

Perhaps she should take notes from Sasha, Maxine thought, as men always approached her, but she never returned their interest. Maybe that was the key, and Maxine should ignore Ollie for a while?

All Sasha ever blathered on about these days was Devon and the social media campaign she was working on with him and Ollie. Sasha needed to up her game to bag an attractive man like Devon, he was famous, for goodness sake. Ollie had been featured in a few magazines lately, too, and his profile was rising. She wondered if Sasha had had anything to do with that and fleetingly wondered if she could magic up some public relations for her as well. Maxine was getting tired of posting the same old content to her timelines, and if Ollie became famous, she'd need to have a higher profile as his girlfriend.

Maxine was sure Ollie would take her up on her offer of a date. She hadn't planned on blurting it out in front of Sasha, but as Sasha already knew how Maxine felt, she didn't really care. These were times of female empowerment and she wasn't scared to ask a man out. Plus she wanted the whole world to know they were interested in each other, so other predatory women would back the hell off.

Ollie looked directly at Sasha and then back at Maxine. 'I… uh… I'm useless with cars. Um… maybe Sasha can recommend someone?' He stepped closer to her and pulled her out of the shadows to stand beside him, their sides almost touching.

Maxine had no choice but to turn to Sasha. She gave her a tight smile before another customer said hello and went into the next class. Sasha looked like she wanted to run away and Maxine frowned. Whatever Ollie had done to upset her, it couldn't have been that bad. She'd just have to get over it as Maxine intended for Ollie to attend the wedding with her, and Sasha was Poppy's oldest friend, so falling out was not an option.

'Demi can pretty much fix anything,' said Sasha, helpfully. 'Her dad owns a garage. I can drop her a text to see if she'll help?' I know there aren't any garages close to here, but that one is nearer to your flat and the other gym.'

Maxine smiled tightly and said thanks, glancing at the clock on the wall. She only had moments before she'd have to go in to run the next class. She didn't have much time. She gave Ollie her most seductive smile, as Sasha seemed to be daydreaming and was looking at the floor. 'The wedding is coming up soon,' she rushed on. 'Poppy has mentioned that I can take a partner with me,' she said, staring straight at Ollie so he got the message loud and clear. Sasha made a gurgling sound in her throat and Ollie patted her on the back before slipping his arm around her shoulders, making her almost choke. He handed her the bottle of water he'd been carrying and she sipped it gratefully.

'The wedding?' he asked, looking relieved, which made Maxine frown. 'I look forward to meeting your date,' he said. 'Sasha's promised to accompany me, as she's chief bridesmaid and I'm the best man.'

Maxine's face fell and they both turned to Sasha for confirmation. Humiliation burned in Maxine's chest, but she tried to push it aside. Had Sasha liked Ollie as well this whole time? Surely not? Maxine could understand the obligation of formalities at a wedding, but she was still not happy and her cheeks flushed.

'Oh, right?' she said to Sasha with a frown.

Ollie didn't give Sasha a chance to respond. 'Since you're here, Sasha,' he said, 'I need to speak to you about our latest social media campaign… in my office.'

Then a customer called Maxine's name, so she had to leave them to it. But she'd seen that Sasha did not look happy, so perhaps she hadn't been given a choice in the arrangement.

Maxine's eyes narrowed as she looked back at them, but she plastered on a smile as she moved forward to begin the class. Inside she was fuming, and decided to call Poppy that evening to see if she knew what was really going on with her friend and her future brother-in-law.

CHAPTER TWENTY-TWO

*O*llie followed Sasha into his office and shut the door behind them. He could see she was angry. She'd barely spoken to him since she'd moved into her flat and they'd argued, and that had been a week ago. He was fed up with her ignoring his texts and calls. He'd been tempted to stroll into her office, but the latest renovations at the gym hadn't left much time to take a break. He ran his hands through his hair and sighed with relief that she was finally in front of him.

Women were an enigma to him. He'd grown up in a house full of rambunctious boys. Their mum and dad were equal heads of the household and although their mum was very proprietorial over the kitchen, she hated the mess they all made and they had to muck in and help clean up. They were all very self-sufficient boys, but as their mum wasn't overly emotional around them, Ollie didn't really know how to handle Sasha's feelings.

Had he let Sasha down? Maybe he should have made time for her, but his business had been his priority and she had been pretty flaky back then. She was always announcing that she was into some new trend or other, or had a shiny new boyfriend that she paraded around like a prize poodle. Now he found her newfound confidence attractive – but she'd always seemed pretty sure of herself to him. She just had never been interested in furthering her career. That hadn't mattered to him, as it was her life and he liked her as she was, fiery outbursts and all.

This new Sasha had even more spark, though, and he was like a moth to a flame. He couldn't get enough of her. He'd always been attracted to her before, but now she was like blood in his veins. He needed her. He craved being near her and was distracted when he wasn't, which was a brand-new feeling. He couldn't believe his luck when she'd agreed to work with him, but now he was jealous of other clients, and basically anyone who spent more time with her than he did. He hated Devon and he'd never met him. He was probably a very nice guy!

Ollie needed to get a grip and get a life, or get Sasha out of his system, but that hadn't happened in the past ten years. As he'd reminded her, they'd never been single at the same time. He had a horrible feeling that now he'd kissed her, there was no going back. He'd sensed that danger when they were younger, so perhaps that was why he'd steered a different path. He'd been determined to build a strong foundation for his future. He'd known there'd be passion, but he hadn't banked on even stronger feelings. He'd also been wary of messing her about when neither of them was ready for anything serious, especially as their friendship group was so tight and Poppy was marrying his brother.

Now Sasha spun round and looked at him, face flushed and fists curled, which amused him until he saw the glint in her eye and realised that she meant business. This was not good. He winced and tried to look cute and apologetic. It didn't work.

'What the hell are you playing at?' she stormed as she began pacing the room. 'If you don't want to go to the wedding with Maxine, man up and tell her! You know she's obsessed with you. Anyone can see it! Stop using me in your games.'

She was gesturing angrily with her hands and he caught one and backed her up against the door. She gasped and her eyes went wide like saucers. Before she could say anything else, he swooped his head down and kissed her. He couldn't help it. He was a man in love with this fiery, independent woman. As soon as their lips met, fireworks exploded in his brain and he groaned deeply.

Her hand was still in his, but suddenly she moaned too and her spare hand slid into the top of his trousers and touched naked skin at his waist. He drew in a sharp breath and took a moment to lean back and look at her face. Her eyes were open but glazed. His had a question in them and she leaned forward and captured his mouth again, pressing her hand into his back to push his body into hers. He felt like a horny teenager and after a few more moments of bliss, they heard someone in the corridor and sprang apart. Both of their faces were flushed, their breathing laboured and he quickly pulled her to stand next to him as someone knocked on the door. Ollie tucked her long hair behind her shoulder and could see the questions in her eyes.

'I'm sorry if I embarrassed you with Maxine,' he said in a rush. 'It was the first thing that came into my mind, but I do want you to be my partner at the wedding if you'll have me? Just as friends… if that's what you want… for now. I know I've behaved like a Neanderthal idiot, but I can't seem to stop kissing you now I know what you taste like.' Sasha drew in a sharp breath and heat blazed in her eyes.

The person knocked on the door again and Ollie stepped back and opened it, so Sasha could exit the room. He said hello to the guy who she'd bumped into on her very first day there and Ollie told him to go into the office and sit down. Closing the door behind him for a moment, he took in a few breaths of air to calm his body and mind from the fire that was raging inside.

'I need to think about it,' was all she said, still looking glazed and not as enthusiastic as he'd have hoped. His ego took a hit.

'Poppy's going to need us there to support her and if we're together, it'll make things easier for her. Fewer guests, less worry?'

Sasha spluttered a laugh at this finally and he grinned bashfully, but wasn't about to give up.

'She's only got about thirty guests anyway!' she said. But she was smiling now at least. 'Most of the guests are your family.' She paused in thought. 'Together?' she frowned, watching him closely.

'Yes. Together…'

CHAPTER TWENTY-THREE

*P*oppy was wringing her hands in her lap. She'd finally agreed to meet her dad and she was feeling shaky. Sasha had shyly dropped the bombshell that she was going to partner Ollie to the wedding (for convenience's sake, whatever the hell that meant), but she'd also tentatively mentioned Maxine's feelings for Ollie! What a mess.

Poppy knew Ollie must have had an ulterior motive to keep popping into the office, although that hadn't happened much lately, but she'd hoped it would blow over as he'd danced around Sasha for years and never done anything about it. But by his latest antics, it seemed as if he was serious this time. Why now, for goodness sake? When Sasha seemed to have finally got him out of her system and moved on. Poppy loved Ollie, but if he broke Sasha's heart, she would hurt him.

She sighed. She knew Sasha was more than capable of looking after herself – over everything except Ollie. He was her Achilles heel and Poppy wasn't sure if her heart could withstand the full force of being loved by a Taylor brother if it didn't work out. Poppy knew very well the devastation that could cause, from personal experience. She'd barely survived it herself and she didn't want that suffering for her best friend.

Poppy tried to still her hands and pictured herself in her zen-like office and not in a bustling café in the centre of a small town thirty minutes from her home. She controlled her breathing and attempted to quell the urge to pick herself up and rush back to the car. She wished Demi was with her, as well as Sasha who was ordering their drinks, but she'd had to work at the garage, as her dad had double-booked something. Demi had been furious with him, but he didn't seem to like her mixing with her old friendship group so much these days.

Poppy made a mental note to make time to pop in and see her friend, to make sure she was ok. She hated the thought of Demi silently suffering at the hands of her family and vowed to be more supportive. They were kind people, but their recent business troubles appeared to have put Demi and her mum on one side of the battle lines and her dad and Allan on the other. For such a close family, this was a disaster.

Poppy hoped that Sasha and Maxine wouldn't fall out over Ollie, either. Maxine was a sweetheart, but was a bit like how Sasha used to be with men. She went doggedly after her latest beau with laser-like precision, overlooking scores of suitable partners who were usually milling around her every day. It seemed that Ollie brought out determined devotion from women who would do anything to capture his attention.

Poppy smiled finally, as she pictured Dylan, with his broad shoulders and secret smile. She could definitely understand the attraction of the Taylor brothers.

Her stomach squirmed, though, at the thought of Dylan actually meeting her dad. She'd begun to search for him online quite a few times over the years, but had always stopped herself. Why bother when he wasn't interested in her? When he'd contacted her recently, she'd finally succumbed, but his social media pages were private. She had found a few articles about his art and seen a couple of images of him, but she'd found out very little about the man himself through the printed paragraphs and the few sparse telephone conversations they'd had, where they'd been incredibly polite and mostly talked about their respective work.

Thoughts were tumbling through her brain as Sasha came back with their drinks; a cappuccino for Poppy and a hot chocolate piled high with cream and marshmallows for herself. She placed them on the geometric patterned, wipe clean tablecloth. Poppy grinned at last and Sasha's eyes were crinkled at the corners with mischief. 'If your dad disapproves of my marshmallow tower, he can piss off,' she stated and Poppy snorted a giggle behind her hand, feeling some of the tension dissipate.

Sasha was wearing a pretty pale blue short-sleeved shirt, buttoned up to the top, which strained across her ample chest. She had on a fitted cream skirt, which accentuated her curves and made her look like a very sexy schoolteacher! Poppy had never seen her wear an outfit like it and she giggled at her friend clearly trying to look professional and imposing in front of Poppy's dad. How she loved this woman! Sasha usually wore tops that swept across her shoulders, sat wide across her chest and cinched in at the waist, cute little dresses with towering heels, or perfectly tailored trousers that looked like they'd come straight off a catwalk. To be honest, with her growing list of contacts, they probably could have!

Both Sasha and Demi had jaw-dropping curves and they were both quite body confident, which helped Poppy to feel better in her own skin. She was skinny and lithe and the polar opposite of her vivacious friends, but she was growing in self-confidence herself since starting up her business, especially as its success was developing at such an exciting rate. Dylan was also a big part of the way she felt about herself. He loved her, quirks and all.

Poppy was wearing skinny jeans and a long white cotton shirt. Her blonde hair was swept up into a high ponytail and she had added colourful earrings that tickled her neck as she moved her head. She let out the breath she'd been holding as another person came into the café. But it was just a harassed-looking woman who was trying to manoeuvre a pram between the tables.

Sasha darted a look of sympathy Poppy's way and took her hand, squeezing it in solidarity. Then the door opened again. A tall man with a shock of thick grey hair walked in and looked around. Poppy and Sasha waited in trepidation as he turned and noticed them. He sighed with relief, hurrying their way. He hovered by the table as if unsure what to do. Sasha let go of Poppy's hand and asked him to join them.

'I assume you're Glen?' asked Sasha. He nodded his head absently, with his eyes fixed firmly on Poppy. Poppy couldn't take her eyes off him either, and for some inexplicable reason she felt like crying. Not in anger, as she'd thought, but in sadness for all the lost years, which muddled her mind even further.

Sasha took charge, as Poppy had known she would. She wished Dylan was there. He'd offered to move his morning meeting, but it had been booked for months and it was important to finalise the contracts for that particular project before the wedding and honeymoon. The thought of her impending nuptials threw her into a spin as always. But finally seeing her dad was nothing like how she'd pictured it, practically every day of her life.

'I'm Sasha,' said Sasha brightly. 'Poppy's asked me to sit in for this first meeting,' she said, making Poppy smile finally at the formality. It was as if they would be interviewing him, which in a way Poppy supposed they would. What did he want from her after all these years?

His shoulders were hunched and he put his hands on the table. They were clasped together, as Poppy's had been, and she realised this meeting might be difficult for him too. Then she hardened herself against any sympathy for him. It had been his choice to leave her and her mum.

'I'm glad to meet you, Sasha,' he said, smiling finally. He shook her hand and then looked longingly at their coffee. 'I'm sorry I'm a bit late. Traffic was horrendous. I hope you weren't worried?' he looked pensively at Poppy.

Sasha pushed her chair back and Poppy panicked that she was leaving them alone. Sasha put a reassuring hand on her shoulder. 'I'm just getting Glen a coffee,' she paused. 'Unless you're partial to a hot chocolate and marshmallows like me?' she smiled his way kindly.

He took in the tall drink and his eyes sparkled. 'I'd love a coffee any way it comes, but maybe I'll try that next time,' he joked, nodding his head towards the mountain of confectionery on Sasha's drink. The tension eased from Poppy's shoulders a little more and she sagged into her chair a bit and relaxed her spine. She decided to treat this like any meeting with a new client and smiled reassuringly at him. He meant nothing to her, she steeled her brain. They both watched Sasha expertly weave between the tables.

'She seems like a lovely friend,' he commented. His voice was soft and had a slight Essex accent. The thought that he might have been just around the corner her whole life made her suck in some air to her parched throat. She sipped her coffee, eyeing him over the rim of the wide cup.

'She is,' she replied. 'She's the best. So. Tell me why we're here? I'm not into apportioning blame and, as you can see, I'm all grown up and ok – so what can I do for you?'

His eyes glistened and he cocked his head to one side and watched her for a moment. 'It won't have ever felt like it, but I'm immensely proud of you. You've clearly become a strong and successful woman and I'll always be sorry that I wasn't around to see you when you were little.'

Poppy sat back in shock. That wasn't what she'd expected him to say. But then she had been so muddled about why he wanted to meet her that her whole life was pretty much upside down right now. Her work was suffering and the wedding had stalled. She was trying to ignore how much she'd missed her dad growing up, even though she'd never met him. Her mum had said he was a waster who ran off the moment he'd found out she was pregnant. People could change, though, and through her work, Poppy had come to understand that the obvious reason for something wasn't always the truth.

'Why weren't you around?' she asked simply. 'Mum said she told you she was pregnant and then she never saw you again.' She couldn't help the bitterness that had crept into her tone, however understanding she'd hoped to be. He flinched as if he'd been slapped.

Sasha came back with a coffee for him and sat back at the table. He drew some money out of his pocket, but she told him to put it away. He protested but then gave in and said thanks. He took a quick fortifying sip, seeming unsure where to start and then sat up straighter.

'It's time you knew the truth. I've stayed away for so long, but I heard through an old friend who moved back to town that your mum is happy now and I can't keep my life on hold for her again.'

Poppy felt like she'd been slapped and held onto the table for support. What the hell did he know about her mum?

Sasha frowned and looked at Poppy to check she was ok. She took her hand across the table and told Glen to go on. His eyes were glazed and he frustratingly took his time to decide what to say.

'Your grandma didn't approve of my relationship with your mother and caused all kinds of issues,' he winced and watched her from under his eyelids before continuing. 'Your mum's mental health was delicate and your grandmother was worried that I was negatively influencing her. She kept stopping her medication. I was a penniless artist and couldn't exactly offer the kind of stability your gran wanted for June.' He blew on his coffee and took another tentative sip. 'I can understand why now, but at the time I was young and reckless and we wanted to travel together and see the world.' He chewed his lip, a trait Poppy had inherited, so she quickly stopped gnawing at hers.

Poppy looked down at the table and frowned, trying to clear her muddled thoughts. She knew her gran and mother had fallen out long ago, but understanding was dawning. 'Gran was worried about her child's mental state?'

Poppy suddenly realised that her mum must have grown up with the same issues, and that they hadn't been caused by Poppy's own birth. If she'd been on medication way back then, it must have been an existing condition. It was freeing to finally realise she wasn't the cause of her mum's problems. Or she wasn't the only cause, anyway. Maybe she should reach out to her grandma before it was too late? So many conflicting feelings flew round her body. Tears seeped out of her eyes and she brushed them away with the back of her hand. Glen's eyes were full of unshed tears too and he sat back in his chair, watching his daughter. Sasha squeezed her hand and said the words Poppy hadn't dared to.

'Did you know June was pregnant?'

Glen didn't shy away from the question as Poppy had feared. He faced it head on. 'I did,'

Poppy felt like she'd been punched in the stomach and sat back in her chair, winded. She'd always dreaded those words. She'd held onto the hope that whatever her mum had said, he'd not known about her, or surely he would have stayed. Sasha flinched and she stuffed some of the marshmallows into her mouth, chomping angrily.

'Your gran told me to stay away, otherwise she wouldn't help with the baby and June. I had no money, and nowhere to live. We were both living at home with our parents, and I'd already booked to host an exhibition of my art abroad. I begged June to come with me, but in the end, her mum persuaded her to stay. Your gran didn't think she'd cope with the constant travelling and a newborn, and in hindsight, she was probably right.'

Poppy hung her head at the pain her mum must have gone through. It had clearly caused another huge fight with her gran after Glen had left, as they hadn't spoken since. Why had she lied and said Glen hadn't wanted his baby, though? Poppy felt tears fall from her eyes and Sasha held out a napkin for her, which she took gratefully. Glen reached for her hand, but then stopped himself.

'I hated myself for not trying harder, but June was diffi-cult to be in a relationship with and I was worried about how defying her mum would affect her. I knew your gran would look after you both, when I couldn't.'

'She didn't, though, did she?' said Sasha sarcastically, spooning in more cream and the last marshmallow.

Glen's brow creased and he turned to face her, his complexion paling. 'What do you mean?'

'June and her mum had a massive argument about some-thing after Poppy was born – which it would now seem was probably about you – and they've not spoken since. June brought Poppy up on her own and then tried to kill herself, which Poppy also had to deal with alone.'

Glen looked horrified and Poppy wanted to kick Sasha to shut her up. This was sharing too much, but Sasha was on a roll and was like a lion protecting her cub. Glen's face told her it was a lot to take in at once!

'Poppy kept all this to herself and then worked every hour to find a safe place for her mum to stay while she lived alone a lot of the time,' said Sasha, sombre now, her own lip wobbling with emotion. 'She hid how bad it was from her best friends and social services because she was so scared she'd be taken away from her mum. June often only stayed away a night or two, but as she got older, Poppy bartered with a sanctuary and got her a room. She lived there for years, until recently.'

'Sasha! That's too much information,' said Poppy, pushing her chair back and bracing her legs to jump up and leave.

Sasha caught her arm and made her stay put. 'He needs to hear this, Poppy,' she said seriously. 'And you'd never say a bad word about your mum to anyone.' Sasha turned towards Glen. 'I'm sorry if it seems disloyal, but Poppy needs someone in her corner. Life hasn't been a bed of roses for her, and half of that is your fault!' she said, staring directly at Glen and refusing to back down, while his face flamed. 'She's too nice to tell you the truth and I'm not about to let her brush over how hard it's been for her. She's the woman she is, despite her parents,' she growled.

Sasha ran out of steam then and sipped her drink, but she never took her eyes off Glen, staring at him over the rim of her glass.

Glen bowed his head for a moment, but then brushed his hands across his eyes and faced them. 'I did try to reconnect with you both, over the years. I sent June money as often as I could,' he sighed, worry lines etched across his brow. 'My first exhibitions didn't come to much, but I did offer to help, and have always paid what I could afford, which admittedly wasn't much.'

Glen put his hands on the table in front of him. Poppy couldn't help but stare at his interlaced fingers, noting a wedding band there.

'I tried to see you a few times when you were little.' Poppy's mouth hung open in shock. 'Your mum was so angry with me. She told me to stay away and threatened to kill herself if I tried to make contact with you. I found out later that she had tried,' he nodded sheepishly at Sasha, who scowled at him and brushed her dark hair over her shoulder so he could see clearly how annoyed she was with him. 'I never dared do it again. I didn't know she'd been in an institution, I'm so sorry, Poppy.'

'Maybe you should have asked?' said Sasha, gravely. Poppy gave her a look and she finally shut up. Poppy's heart was racing as if she'd run a marathon. She didn't now how to feel. He'd known about her, he'd left her, and then he'd tried to come back – but not hard enough, it seemed. Her mum had also fed her a mountain of lies. Her dad had wanted her and he'd come back for them both. She knew first-hand how scary it was when her mum threatened to harm herself, so she did have some empathy, but she'd been his child and she'd suffered her mum's ill-health alone. She wondered how different her life would have been with her dad in it, but then perhaps she'd have followed a different path and not had her incredible career and fiancé, so she did have something to be grateful for in this mess.

'And now?' she asked. 'Why are you here now?'

Glen ruffled his hair with his hand and placed his empty coffee cup back onto the saucer. 'Your grandmother finally caved and told me you're getting married.'

Poppy didn't think her poor heart could take much more

of this. Her gran knew about her marriage? How? The town grapevine, she guessed. Even though Poppy didn't live in their old town anymore, Dylan's family did and so did her mum and her partner Chris.

'I didn't want you to think I'd never thought about you,' continued Glen, looking at her and giving her a half-smile. 'I think about you every day,' he sighed. 'I also decided that I couldn't let your mother, or grandmother, dictate our relationship any longer. I'm so sorry to hear about what you've been through. If I'd known, I'd have come and brought you home with me.'

'Where to?' asked Poppy seriously, biting back the bile in her throat at the image of a perfect family life that she could have lived.

'I… uh… I don't know. I spent most of my time travelling and trying to find customers for my work. That finally happened, but not until recently. I've now got a home on the outskirts of London, and a regular client base. I've been following your career and knew I had to be financially sound so you wouldn't think I wanted anything other than friendship. If you would even offer that?' He glanced at her hopefully and Poppy hung her head. This was all too much.

Sasha smiled and it was more genuine now, but Poppy pushed her chair back and stood up, so Sasha and Glen followed suit.

'Uh… I think maybe Poppy needs a few days to consider all that you've said,' Sasha said, picking up both of their handbags and looping them over her arm. There was a couple craning their heads to find a free table and she indicated that they were just leaving. 'Poppy has your number so perhaps you might arrange to meet up again or chat on the phone?'

'Good idea,' said Glen, sounding weary. He caught Poppy's eye. To her, his face seemed so strange, yet familiar.

She could see similarities with the shape and structure of her own, and she'd noticed his blue eyes with the tiny gold flecks in them like hers. She smiled gently at him and his eyes lit up a little and filled with hope.

'I'll call you,' she said gruffly. 'I promise.'

A grin stretched itself across his face and he got up to kiss them both on the cheek, leaving a scent of coffee behind. Sasha took Poppy's hand and guided her out into the bright sunshine and then pulled her into a fast hug as they watched her father walk away further down the road.

'We need to call Dylan to tell him what happened,' said Sasha, holding Poppy at arm's length suddenly and peering into her eyes as if she meant business. 'No more dodging your feelings, ok? We are going to see your mother and she is going to tell us both why she lied to her only daughter, and I am not going to leave your side until this whole damn mess is rectified.'

She looked so fierce and demanding that Poppy couldn't help but laugh. It felt so good to let the tension of the last hour float away, but Sasha was actually right. Poppy's mum had a lot of explaining to do and for once, Poppy wasn't worried about how June would be affected. This was about Poppy and her feelings, and she'd be damned if she left their next get-together without some honest answers.

CHAPTER TWENTY-FOUR

*S*asha woke up in her new flat and forgot where she was. She listened to the quiet and for a moment missed the raucous behaviour of her sisters in the mornings, where one of them was always cooking a big Italian breakfast and another would be washing her hair or shouting across the hall for someone else to get out of the bathroom, or accusing them of stealing the last of the shampoo.

She felt awful for the predicament Poppy had found herself in. True to her word, Poppy had spoken to Glen a few times since their meeting and she was trying to understand his reasoning. Sasha could feel a gap widening between Poppy and her mum and when June phoned, which she did frequently, Sasha now found herself having to field her calls. She hated lying to anyone, especially Poppy's mum, even if Sasha was annoyed at her too.

In the end Poppy had caved and agreed to meet her mum that weekend. She'd refused to go unless Sasha joined her. For once, Sasha didn't relish being in the middle of every-thing, even though she was the one who'd suggested the summit meeting in the first place, partly as the wedding was only a couple of months away and she was starting to panic. Sasha did kind of like being the chosen one, though, as Dylan was too furious with June to go and Demi hadn't been mentioned at all. Everyone was so busy these days that they hardly ever got to meet up regularly for a coffee like they used to. She missed the chats in Chris's café. The modern places nearby weren't quite the same. They didn't have Chris and his hugs in them for a start… or his giant marshmallows. The new café in town did have an exceptionally good-looking barista, though, and she'd caught his eye a few times.

Sasha thought Demi might be a bit hurt at not being included, but her work at the garage was furious right now and she was battling her dad and Allan every day over seemingly inconsequential decisions. Why the hell they didn't listen to Demi's incredible ideas for the place, Sasha didn't know. It seemed Demi's dad was old-fashioned and felt that the business should be run by a man. The fact that he deferred to Allan all the time was driving Demi nuts. If they didn't take note of her soon, they'd lose her. Sasha and Poppy had listened to her incredible ideas about revamping the business in awe, but her family's response had been far more muted. Adding a small café to the garage was genius, as there was nowhere nearby for people to go to while waiting for their cars, but her dad wouldn't listen or invest. Poor Demi!

Sasha shook her head and sat up. She didn't have the energy to sort out the lives of two of her friends at the same time. Demi would have to wait.

She walked quickly into the bathroom and threw some scented petals into the bath, turning on the taps and hoping the soothing fragrance would calm her down, then turning them off again and deciding she ought to tidy her bedroom a bit first. She folded a few tops and grabbed a pair of jeans slung over the chair by her huge king-size bed, and put them in her fitted mirrored wardrobe that ran along one whole wall. The room was decorated in sage green with lots of brushed copper and leafy plants. There were three throws on the bed in different shades and textures, and she straightened them out. Next she picked up the soft suede cushions in tones of gold from the floor and piled them up by the head-rest. Satisfied everything was in order, she looked out of the window over the tree-lined road, deep in thought. Ollie had asked for another meeting, but she was annoyed with him and already working diligently on his social media, so Poppy was her priority right now.

Sasha didn't know how she felt about Ollie anyway. One minute he was on fire for her, the next he was popping into the office and talking about the wedding plans and Poppy's dad as if they were just friends. He kept apologising for annoying her and then kissing her when no one was looking, so now she felt like she was walking around in a frenzied ball of lust. She tried to resist but she adored his lips on hers and couldn't seem to stop dragging him into the stationery cupboard to ask him about something to do with the impending nuptials and then sliding her hand up his leg and planting a kiss on him too.

People would start to talk if they didn't stop this now. It was embarrassing not knowing where she stood. Now they were partners at the wedding too. What would everyone think? Ollie hadn't asked her on a date so, as far as she was concerned, she was still footloose and fancy free, and fed up with waiting for him to make up his mind about what he wanted. Was he embarrassed to be seen with her in public? Then why had he asked her to partner him to the wedding? Although she knew that was mainly to avoid Maxine. So many thoughts flitted in and out of her mind and it was exhausting.

She was beginning to feel mentally drained with the extra paperwork for her own new start-up and the marketing ideas she was developing with Devon. He made her belly-laugh and he always picked unusual places for them to meet, so she was burning the candle at both ends and running out of energy. Devon had invited her, Poppy and Billy to a few events recently. Poppy and Billy had occasionally ducked out, but he hadn't seemed to mind. They were all getting closer by the day. He was a beautiful soul and he treated her like a princess. He also seemed to enjoy helping her fledgling business by introducing her to loads of famous faces. He was beyond excited for her and encouraged her to step out of her comfort zone every day, which she relished.

She had been propelled into the world of social media much faster than she'd planned and her own following and that of her business was suddenly bursting at the seams. She had rows of glitzy dresses in her wardrobe and boxes of sparkly heels. It was something she'd dreamed about for most of her life, but it felt a bit hollow compared to what her friends were going through right now. She needed to get Poppy and her mum together for a chat and then do the same for Demi and her dad.

She adored Devon, but he wasn't Ollie. The photos of Sasha and Devon when they were out and about with their new friends were attracting a lot of attention for them both and people were starting to ask who she was. It was a real buzz and she had to ensure that the wedding, her work and Poppy and Demi came first. It was becoming more of a daily battle than she'd realised. How the hell Devon did it, at his level of popularity, she'd never understand. He had a team working for him, but still handled his social media alone. They organised his public relations opportunities and events, but it seemed to Sasha as if he steered the business on his own.

Perhaps she'd need her own personal assistant soon? Then she almost tripped over a box of wedding favours and some rose petal confetti that she'd ordered the week before. She swore under her breath and danced out of the way, before tripping and face-planting onto the wooden floor.

She sighed but then froze as she heard a crash somewhere else in the flat, which made her nearly jump out of her skin. It sounded like it was coming from the living room. There was swearing and someone was hopping around bashing into things. She looked around for a weapon, and grabbed an empty wine bottle from the corner of the room, before rolling her eyes and remembering. She'd told Devon he could crash on the couch. She hadn't meant literally crash! He'd been rolled up like a caterpillar in her woollen blanket last night and she'd completely forgotten he was there.

She rushed into the lounge and laughed at the sight of him rubbing his foot, bare-chested, and then falling over again and toppling onto the couch. He eyed the bottle she was brandishing, and she relaxed her arm and put it down.

'You scared the hell out of me! How much did we drink last night?' She noted another empty bottle on its side near the couch and winced.

'What about 'poor Devon' and 'have you still got a foot?'' He held up his sore toes and she laughed and came over to examine them, before giving him a hug.

'Poor Devon,' she soothed, kissing his cheek. He appeared slightly mollified and sniffed theatrically, pulling his grey marl T-shirt over his taut abs and tucking it into his jeans. 'What did you step on?'

Since having her own domain, she'd found herself tutting at any detritus left around and spent ages scooping every-thing back into its usual place. The flat was designed for calm and Sasha made use of every element, especially now she was becoming busier with her new start-up. The flat helped her to relax after a hard day and the view outside never failed to make her smile. Right now, the sexy man on her couch needed her attention, though. How could she have forgotten about him? Maybe it was because Ollie was commandeering her every waking thought.

'I trod on my car keys,' said Devon, his eyes alight with mischief. 'Must have slipped out of my pocket. How come you didn't let me share the bed?'

He gave her a lewd wink and she sank back into the sofa with a giggle. She knew they were nothing more than friends, but she had grown to love him dearly. She felt a bond with him that was weird for such a new friend. He seemed to understand her and never judged her sometimes left-field creative ideas and assertive ways. She'd had to stand up for herself with three noisy sisters.

'Your big bum wouldn't have fitted into my bed,' she poked him in the rump and he pretended to look affronted as they both eyed his perfect posterior. 'You told me you're a fidget and I needed some sleep. You're lucky you got the couch,' she said, as she examined his foot again, decided he would live and got up. 'Coffee?'

'I thought you'd never ask,' he said, gazing out at the view of the fields and looking at a white board covered in photos. This was Sasha putting her own stamp on Poppy's very cool interior design. Sasha loved the photographic reminders of her friends and feisty family. 'The design of this flat is incredible,' said Devon. 'No wonder Poppy's so in demand. Your ideas for promotion are amazing too,' he added and she frowned for a moment. A couple of things he'd said about Poppy recently had begun to niggle and she wasn't quite sure why.

He picked up a small photo of herself, Poppy and Demi in a gilt frame from the side table and stared at their interlinked arms and smiling faces.

He got out his phone and took a snap of them both and smiled. 'I'll send this to you and you can add it to your photo wall,' he inclined his head towards her collage. Sasha grinned and snuggled into his chest to take a look at the photo.

'I know you love Poppy's work,' said Sasha over her shoulder as she moved away to grab two mugs and turn on the coffee machine. 'I do too. Coming home to a place like this every night is like a dream come true. You can't help but smile when you walk in. It's beautiful. Poppy's so clever to have seen the potential when this corner of the universe was pretty quiet and run down. I'm trying not to wreck the vibe with my mess,' she laughed self-deprecatingly.

'Whereas you,' he waggled his eyebrows at her as she watched him place the other photo back in its rightful place. 'You spent your wayward youth ogling men and daydreaming.'

Sasha threw the pen from the kitchen notepad at his head. He ducked and laughed. She sometimes wished that he didn't have such an easy manner. She'd pretty much told him her whole life story on the second day she'd met him. Now he teased her mercilessly about her choice in dodgy men and jobs. He also stayed by her side on nights out and told anyone who would listen about where she worked and her new business idea, so she felt a swell of pride in her chest. He paraded her around like a proud parent, even though he was younger than her, but kept admiring glances from other men at bay with a warning stare or an arm loosely slung around her shoulder.

Other than Billy, she'd not had a close male friend before. The Taylor brothers were an exception, but the feeling within that group was always mixed with hormones and history. Devon was a revelation. His life was full of new experiences, opportunities and excitement and, like Poppy, he seemed happy to share this with the people he cared about. She did wonder occasionally how she'd become so lucky.

Sasha was determined to do something for him too, and introducing him to a few of her friends was the place to start. She mentally went through a list of the people she thought he'd like, but no one immediately came to mind. She smirked at his off-key singing and wondered how many people in the world would give their last dollar to be sitting drinking coffee with him right now in their flats, after a night on the tiles together. She giggled that most of them wouldn't ask him to sleep on the couch, though.

Ollie's grey eyes and brooding face came to mind and she brushed away the thought that he might not like the idea of another man in her flat. But they weren't dating and he had no say over who she invited to stay.

She added some sugar to Devon's coffee and topped up her own drink with frothy milk. She was actively getting used to drinking coffee after so many business meetings with Billy and Poppy and their clients, plus she'd run out of hot chocolate and didn't want to appear gauche in front of Devon. Grabbing both mugs and her notepad, she told Devon she needed his help with the last few details of the wedding planning and let any thoughts of the red-hot male who worked across the street drift from her mind, and be overtaken by the delicious man in her lounge.

CHAPTER TWENTY-FIVE

$\mathcal{T}$he meeting with Glen seemed to have opened the floodgates for Poppy. Suddenly she was excited about her wedding and wanted to finalise every single detail. They had spent a week making sure all their design clients were happy so that Poppy and Dylan could enjoy their honeymoon in peace.

Everything had now been ordered, from the table linen to the flowers. Sasha sighed with the contentment of a job done well and was glad it had been Glen, and not Jared, that had held up the wedding plans. Jared still loved winding up the Taylor brothers, but he was casually dating a stunning brunette supermodel and had swung by the office on his way to a party, with her on his arm. Poppy hadn't batted an eyelid and had drawn his date into a conversation about how they both knew Devon, and Jared had rolled his eyes and made their excuses to leave, much to Sasha's amusement.

Now Sasha pushed open the door to Chris's café, which Poppy's mum helped to run. It had just started to drizzle and she almost had to shove Poppy inside with the hand that wasn't full of last-minute bridal shopping bags. She knew

Poppy wasn't looking forward to this, but her friends and her fiancé had persuaded her that it had to be done.

The moment had come for Poppy to confront her mother about Glen, and Sasha's insides were going round like a washing machine on spin dry. Billy had left them to do more shopping as he knew this chat was coming and didn't want to overwhelm or outnumber June too much. Sasha worried about that too and dreaded to think what Poppy must be feeling like. Sasha rubbed her tummy and hoped that Chris had made them all some sandwiches as it was nearing lunchtime. Poppy quickly took her to one side. 'It's got to be today,' said Poppy, under her breath. 'I can't take the stress of not telling her any longer.'

'Thank goodness for that!' said Sasha. 'I feel like a naughty schoolgirl as June keeps giving me funny looks. She knows something's going on.' Sasha looked over her shoulder to where Demi was helping June with a customer's order and couldn't help but smile. Demi was one of nature's nurturers. June was milking it by having her carry a heaving tray for her, though! 'Demi is with your mum. Are you ok with all of us being there, or would you like to be alone?' Sasha had no intention of leaving Poppy alone, but offered anyway.

'No!' said Poppy a little too vehemently. 'You can't leave me. I think its best if we are all together. Then we don't have to go through it all again later.'

'Does Demi know about you seeing your dad?'

'I met Demi for a drink the other day and told her everything. You were out with Devon.' Poppy said, looking round and signalling to Chris that they were going into the little staff room at the back of the café. He called out that he'd bring them all some coffees and hot chocolate.

Poppy sighed and dumped her bags on the floor. Sasha tutted and straightened them out, which made Poppy smile a little at this new side to her friend.

'I know you're tired and worried about this chat with your mum, but don't squash the wedding accessories! It's taken ages to finally decide on them,' scolded Sasha gently, making Poppy's eyes glisten with what Sasha hoped weren't unshed tears.

'I can't believe it's all finally happening. I'm going to be Dylan's wife soon,' said Poppy dreamily and Sasha grinned at last. Then Poppy sat still for a moment, as if considering something. 'You and Devon seem to get on well?'

Sasha smiled. 'We do. He's amazing. We all get on, don't we?'

'Absolutely,' said Poppy, sitting in one of the padded armchairs and looking up at her friend. 'I'm actually surprised how easily he's slotted into our group. It's as if he's always been there. He seems to spend a lot of time at our office. I'm thinking of offering him a room,' she joked.

Sasha grinned. 'He loves coming to Cherry Blossom Lane. He's so fascinated by your designs. I think he has a little work crush on you,' she teased Poppy, who smiled shyly.

'He does adore the technology. He'd have me fitting out his whole barn conversion if I had time. He's become my number one fan,' she joked.

Sasha paused for a moment. Something had been troubling her recently. 'He really has. I absolutely love him…'

'But?' Poppy frowned and looked up from rifling through one of the bags at her side.

'I'm not sure. You don't think he's trying to steal your technology or something?' Sasha hated saying the words out loud. She'd had them going around in her head for a while. She'd grown closer to Devon, and he spent loads of time at her flat and often stayed over. He was helping her with her own business – but first and foremost came her friendship with Poppy.

Something felt off about how keen Devon was to hang

out with them. Even though Sasha would love to take the credit, and really wished that it was her magnetic personality that was the draw, she didn't think so. A niggling worry had been growing. Although she'd happily ignore it and enjoy her new lifestyle – the one she'd always dreamed of – it had fallen into her lap a little too easily, considering how many years she'd been trying to break through into the industry.

Sasha knew that sometimes it took just one tweet or TikTok post to go viral, but the reality was that social media was usually a hard slog. Not many people were handed fame. Poppy had helped set her dreams on the right road, but Devon was setting them on fire. Why?

The old Sasha would have accepted the help and run with it, but Poppy's reputation was at stake and that came before any aspirations of her own, however hard she'd worked for them lately. She'd been around for long enough to be able to take a step back from the excitement and glamorous events and ask a few questions of herself. She loved Devon, but she also felt wary of how much he loved them all back, and so quickly.

Poppy was like another sister to her, but Devon was the teeniest bit too keen on the minor details of Poppy's life. Sasha hadn't been able to confide in Ollie, as every time she saw him lately it had been fleeting glances while she built her business and he dealt with the final construction and design at his new gym. He'd called her many times, but she was still confused about how they both felt. They hadn't even slept together yet, but she was worried she might be just a quick fling to him. Now Devon was round so often, they hadn't had any time alone at all. Ollie was polite to Devon, but a bit growly, so she tried to keep them apart.

Poppy sat back in shock. 'What? What's made you think Devon can't be trusted?'

'I just think it's weird that he knows so much about us

and wants to spend all his time with us. We aren't that cool,' Sasha joked feebly, wringing her hands in her lap.

She'd kept these doubts to herself, but she had to be honest now with her best friend. However much she enjoyed the limelight, she would protect Poppy with her last breath, not that she was dramatic at all....

Devon was always trying to ask subtle questions about Poppy. Sasha had a feeling that Devon might have his sights set on her friend. Jared had tried and failed to win Poppy over. And, no matter how gorgeous Devon was, he wasn't for Poppy either, she hoped... Plus Poppy had been in love with Dylan since they were teenagers! She was getting married imminently and Sasha wasn't about to let another dreamboat try and cause trouble, however much she liked him as a person. She prayed she was wrong, but she didn't think so.

Poppy sank back into her chair as Demi rushed through the door and slumped down in a seat.

'For someone who hates going out of her comfort zone, your mum has rediscovered socialising!' sighed Demi as she let go of the bags in her hand and they fell at her feet in a pile of plastic and tissue. She looked from Sasha to Poppy and frowned.

'Your mum's getting the drinks with Chris. What's up... are you sure you want us to be here for this chat with your mum?' Demi's curls bounced around her ears and her face showed her concern, however exhausted she was.

'I was just telling Poppy that I think Devon might be a bit obsessed with her,' said Sasha, darting a glance at the door. 'I know now's probably not the best time to bring this up, but it's been worrying me.'

Demi looked between them again and then threw her head back and burst out laughing almost hysterically, much to Poppy's confusion and Sasha's chagrin. 'Devon and Poppy? I don't think so. Devon and Billy... definitely.'

'What?' said Poppy and Sasha in unison as they both sat forward in their seats. Sasha's brain was whirring and then Poppy was laughing out loud. 'Of course! I knew it wasn't me he was interested in, but you're right, he's obsessed with Billy!' Then she slapped her hand over her mouth, her eyes wide. 'They'd be perfect for each other, but Ed's coming home for my wedding! Argh.'

Sasha let out a huge sigh of relief. How come Demi had seen it and she hadn't? It made perfect sense. He often flirted with her but they both knew it was harmless, they were just friends. He never spoke about anyone he liked and he encouraged her to follow her heart and date more. Maybe he was talking about himself! No wonder he was always sighing dreamily and staring out of the flat window. He was probably hoping to catch sight of Billy on the office patio. Billy often worked late and occasionally joined them for drinks – when he always talked about Ed's impending arrival. Poor Devon! Sasha knew all about unrequited love, with her years of pining after Ollie.

They all jumped as June came in, followed by Chris, who towered over June's small frame. She leant up to give him a quick kiss and he blushed and backed out of the room, after placing the drinks and a round of sandwiches on the little brown table next to them.

'Is Chris not staying?' asked Poppy.

June looked around and her hands were shaking slightly, so Poppy drew her into the seat next to her. The staff room wasn't that big and was more functional than fancy, and with four of them in it, it was starting to feel a teeny bit claustrophobic to Sasha. She knew June well enough now to realise she had something to tell them and it would be a bombshell.

'Poppy's got some news,' she blurted out before they all backed out from mentioning it. They always put June first, but this was about Poppy.

June turned to her daughter and handed her a sandwich, which Poppy took and bit into, putting off the inevitable chat. Sasha grabbed one and stuffed it in her mouth too. She was suddenly ravenous. June smiled and passed the plate to Demi, who thanked her and nibbled at the edges of hers, her nerves showing too.

'I've met my dad,' said Poppy and June's eyes bugged out. Her hands started to shake even more, so she had to put the plate down.

'I know about your dad. My mother called me,' said June croakily. Then she spoke again. 'Chris and I are getting married this weekend,' she said, before all hell broke loose and they started speaking over one another all at once.

CHAPTER TWENTY-SIX

'You're getting married?' said Poppy, as she drew in a sharp breath and sat back in shock.

'This weekend,' clarified June under her breath.

'You spoke to Poppy's grandmother?' asked Sasha, her jaw dropping. June turned to Poppy and winced at the sight of her pale face.

'Not only that, but you know about her dad?' asked Demi in exasperation, throwing her hands into the air.

Poppy counted under her breath for patience, like she used to do at school when they all messed up. 'Why didn't you say something?' Poppy closed her eyes for a moment and tried to re-centre her emotions, because if Demi was annoyed then her mum had just done a very bad thing and it wasn't just her own imagination that the world was conspiring against her.

'Why do you think I've been calling you endlessly lately, Poppy? asked June, a bit waspishly. 'You haven't been answering my calls.'

'Why do you think that might be?' parried Sasha, clearly

trying to keep her voice neutral and not shout at June, which was almost impossible for any of them right now. It was finally clear to Poppy that her mother was a tad self-centred.

'I don't mean to usurp Poppy's wedding, but Chris and I want to be married.' June stressed. 'Because of my past, I didn't want any fuss.'

'So let me get this right,' said Poppy. 'You spoke to Grandma for the first time in almost thirty years when you found out your ex is back in town – and now you have a burning desire to be married?'

Demi's eyebrows shot up and Sasha's eyes were as wide as saucers, but they stayed silent.

'Did you, or did you not, tell my dad to stay away from me or you'd kill yourself?' Poppy went on.

Sasha gasped and Demi looked like she wanted to faint. June's eyes welled up with tears but she sniffed them away.

'I'm sorry, darling,' said June, taking her daughter's hand. 'If I could take it back, I would…' she stuttered. 'I've already spoken to Glen and apologised.'

It was Poppy's turn to freeze for a second in surprise. Her mum hardly ever admitted to being in the wrong.

'I was on all kinds of medication for my mental health at that point,' June explained. 'I was terrified he'd take you away from me. In my muddled mind it was the only way I could guarantee he wouldn't file for custody. There was no way I'd win if he did,' she sighed heavily, as if the burdens of the world were on her shoulders.

The anger in Poppy's chest dissipated slightly and she blinked back tears.

'Now my medication's correct, I can see things more clearly,' said June. 'I know what I did was terribly wrong. I'm so, so sorry.'

She hung her head and Poppy got onto her knees in front of

her mum and pulled her into her arms as her body was wracked with sobs. Poppy tried to quell the terrifying panic that rose up inside of her every time her mum was upset and pulled her mother in closer, stroking her mother's hair as she had as a child when she cried. Tears filled Sasha's eyes and Demi quietly rooted round in her bag and produced some tissues for them all. Poppy and June stayed hugging for a while, then tearfully eased apart and smiled a watery smile at each other.

'I'm glad you're getting to know your dad,' June said carefully after a few sniffs and a blow of her nose. 'He was always a good man and it's broken the stalemate with your grandmother,' she added, her eyes still full of emotion. She took a big gulp of courage and continued, her eyes telling Poppy that this would hurt too. 'Mum and I finally met up. Chris was with me. Your grandmother's been to the café. She cried for hours and we had to move in here because she was scaring the customers,' she tried to joke but it fell flat. 'I didn't know how to tell you without ruining your big day.' Poppy sat back on her haunches and didn't move for a moment, her face frozen in shock.

'Your grandmother would love to meet you,' said her mum, as if this was the most natural thing in the world.

'I'd love that, I think… I just need a minute to get used to the idea,' said Poppy quietly, exhaustion making her bones feel like lead.

'I'm getting married next weekend and Glen and your grandmother are both invited to the café,' said June quickly, as if she was rushing it out so they might miss it.

'Why?' asked Poppy, incredulously. 'What on earth were you thinking?'

'I wanted us all to move on… I couldn't think of another way to get you all together before your wedding,' admitted June as they all sat back mutely and shook their heads. 'I don't want you to be stressed about all this on your own wedding day.' Poppy saw Sasha roll her eyes.

'Is getting married so quickly a good idea?' Poppy got to her feet, her back aching and her mouth set in a grimace.

'Probably not, but I love Chris and he adores the idea.'

'Of course he does,' smiled Sasha, finally. 'He's loved you forever!'

June blushed and started fussing with her hair and mumbling about looking in her bag for a comb before giving up and sitting back in her chair.

'We're going to get married at the registry office down the road and then come back here for a cream tea. No fuss. Just how we like it,' June said carefully, as if she had got every detail planned out in her mind. 'I really didn't want to rush into it like this before your wedding, darling, but Chris has been asking me for ages and I know I'll back out with fright if it's any other way.'

'It's your birthday at the weekend,' said Poppy, who looked slightly dazed. This was not the outcome they'd all been expecting.

'It will be a double celebration,' said June hopefully. 'Triple if you are all there too.'

Poppy looked at Sasha and she grinned. 'I'm on it,' she laughed suddenly. 'Why plan one wedding when you can have two in the same family within a couple of months? What have you organised so far?' she asked June, whose skin was flushed. She was smiling slightly now, although she hadn't let go of Poppy's hand.

'Nothing much,' said June. 'We don't want a fuss. I just want to invite Dylan's parents, Fiona and Don, his brothers and a few café regulars, plus Gladys of course.'

Poppy smiled as she pictured her old neighbour from the flats she grew up in just behind the café, then her mind went to Dylan's parents' house across the road, and the three boisterous boys who had lived there. But she grew serious again when she pictured Sasha being in such a small space with Ollie again. Poppy's blood started to boil, as he still hadn't let Sasha know where she stood from what Poppy could gather. She grabbed another sandwich and wondered if it was already too late to get Sasha out of organising and attending June's wedding. Surely she had other plans with Devon next weekend and, if she did, that was a good enough excuse for Poppy.

CHAPTER TWENTY-SEVEN

The following weekend was full of bright sunshine. Sasha rushed around trying to fill Chris's café with bridal flowers and checking the cream tea was ready and waiting. All previous activities for the day had been set aside and rescheduled, even though Poppy had weirdly said Sasha didn't have to change her plans for the sake of her mum's wedding. As if she would miss June's big day! Chris had been baking especially for the event all week and had insisted on doing everything himself. Luckily he had years of experience, so she let that one slide.

Everyone else was still at the registry office, but Sasha had dashed away after a few photos to check the café looked perfect. She knew June didn't want a fuss, but with Poppy's grandmother and Glen both being at the wedding breakfast, Poppy had asked Sasha to make the café shine. It had been deep-cleaned by professionals the day before and Poppy and Dylan had bought them new furniture as a wedding gift. Everything had been moved in the previous night, and the place looked cosy and functional.

The old wooden chairs had been replaced with cushioned

velvet ones and the tables that Dylan had ordered from a supplier were easy to clean but beautiful in natural beech wood. Each table had a delicate linen cloth that Chris could use if he ever decided to open on Sundays for themed cream teas, which he'd been talking about for ages. Demi and her family had bought the pretty sculpted vintage floral plates and cake stands that were on each table, filled to bursting with petit fours and tiny delicious sandwiches. The happy couple hadn't wanted a big wedding cake, so each table had a selection of cupcakes with 'C&J' scrolled in icing on the top.

Sasha sighed and took a step back to admire everyone's hard work, hoping June and Chris would love it as much as she did. She jotted down a couple of notes in the leather planner she always kept in her bag these days. She was becoming a dab hand at organising events. Perhaps that could be another string to add to her new business later. She grinned to herself and wiped her brow, wondering if she had time to freshen up her make-up, when the bell above the door dinged. She looked up to see Oliver coming in, dressed in a smart suit in midnight blue with a crisp white shirt. He was wearing a bridal buttonhole, a single pink rose with sprigs of gypsophila and eucalyptus.

She smiled up at him as he drew closer and he took her hand as if it was the most natural thing in the world. 'Is everyone else here too?' she asked, her pulse jumping.

He smiled into her eyes and then glanced at the door, nodding to a member of staff who was putting the last cake stands on the tables. 'They're on their way. I wanted to check you were ok, or if you needed help.'

She loved the feeling of warmth she got from the simple pressure of his hand in hers, but as more people came into the shop, they let each other go and she turned in welcome.

'I've missed you,' he whispered into her ear as she moved, his voice making the hairs on her neck stand up. She took a deep breath, but leaned back into him for a moment before going to greet the bride and groom. She looked over her shoulder briefly to find him still watching her and her stomach did a somersault.

Chris and June were glowing as they walked around with Poppy and Sasha. June was wearing a soft blue, knee-length dress, with little flowers sewn around the collar and Chris had on a deep blue suit and a crisply ironed shirt. They were ecstatic about the changes to their precious café, as everything had been done with love and care. Dylan, Miles and their parents were there. Ollie pulled out a chair for his mum and sat down next to her, which made Sasha look away. She'd known Fiona and Don since she was a child, but suddenly those butterflies were back whenever she thought about talking to them. Supposing they found out that she'd kissed Ollie? They might not approve of her for a start. She knew they loved her like a daughter, but it might be different if they thought she had her sights set on Ollie again – even though this was the first time she'd even admitted that to herself. Weddings did weird things to her brain.

Poppy's dad Glen was sitting with Demi and her family, and they seemed to be chatting about cars. Miles had joined them and was in a deep discussion with Demi's dad about something or other. Sasha hoped Miles didn't rile him, he'd always looked out for them all and he'd probably heard that Demi wasn't happy.

Sasha watched Demi and Allan for a moment, but she could see that Demi's smile didn't quite reach her eyes. She walked up behind her friend and put a hand on her shoulder for a moment. Demi's own hand slid onto hers in silent thanks for the support.

Sasha plastered on a bright smile and went to see if Chris and June needed anything, rather than do what she wanted, which was to tip Allan off his chair, so that Demi could breathe. He had draped himself all over her as soon as Miles had joined them.

When Sasha had signed up to be Poppy's maid of honour, she'd had no idea it would mean putting out emotional fires, and helping Poppy's mum as well! Poppy was currently in deep conversation with her grandmother with their hands entwined, their heads close together. Seeing this made Sasha let go of some of the tension in her stomach and she finally smiled.

Ollie caught her eye a few times as the meal progressed. 'Do you need my help with topping up the cakes?' he asked as she passed his table. Demi was already helping, but she handed her plateful to Ollie with a wink, and said she needed to go and ask her mum something.

'Can you also grab some napkins and a spare chair from the storeroom?' Demi added, clearly trying not to laugh.

Sasha frowned and handed a few more cakes out before following Ollie to the storeroom, which was just a cupboard in the staffroom. As soon as the door was shut behind them and Sasha was about to ask why they needed a spare chair, Ollie's arms slipped around her waist and he rested his head on hers and sighed.

'Why are you so hard to get alone?' he grumbled, kissing her eyes, then her nose and then her mouth. Her own lips rose up to meet his and her hands looped around his back and pulled him in closer while he groaned and deepened the kiss. Her mind went blank for a minute and she sank into his embrace before reluctantly pulling away. Both of their eyes were glazed, but Sasha knew they couldn't stay there, even though she definitely wanted to.

'We have to get back,' she said huskily.

'We need to talk about this, whatever it is,' he said, but she wanted more from him than stolen kisses.

She picked up some napkins and put them in his hands

and then decided that they didn't really need a chair. She turned him towards the door, but couldn't help a quick cheeky feel of his backside, which made him growl and look like he wanted to back her up against the door again.

'Come round to the flat,' she said before she changed her mind. His eyes darkened but he nodded, a slight smile on his face. 'We can talk then,' she said.

CHAPTER TWENTY-EIGHT

here had been a bit of a crisis at the café after the wedding. A pipe had burst in the kitchen. It had meant all hands on deck, and that chat with Ollie at the flat hadn't happened. He'd popped by a couple of times since then, but Devon had always been around and Ollie had reluctantly left after a quick drink both times. Maybe she should tell Devon of her fledgling feelings for Oliver, but she'd told him about their history, so there was no way he'd take the hint and leave them alone. He acted like a protective big brother and although she appreciated it, she really wanted to get Ollie alone. The frustration was making her grumpy. When would she finally find time to sort out her own messed-up love life?

With only weeks to go until Poppy's wedding, they had shot Devon's campaign at the gym. Sasha had timed everything meticulously and as soon as the posts went live on all their social media feeds, it had been a smash hit. They were a bit stunned about how well it had worked. It was great news for everyone, but now they had ten times as much work and loads of customer enquiries, at a time when they should be relaxing in the run-up to the wedding. The phone was ringing off the hook and the number of emails they had to deal with each day was eye-watering.

Poppy stuck her head around Sasha's office door to see if she was busy. Sasha beckoned her over to come and sit down. Poppy was holding a mug of coffee in each hand, so she was even more welcome. 'You look exhausted,' said Poppy sympathetically.

'Thanks,' said Sasha sarcastically, but then she grinned proudly at what they'd achieved.

'We need more staff,' said Poppy, mirroring Sasha's thoughts exactly.

Sasha inhaled the fresh aroma of the coffee. It instantly revived her, then she took a sip of the heavenly liquid. It was a caramel latte from their fancy coffee machine and Sasha smiled at Poppy gratefully.

'I agree, we need more people,' said Sasha. 'We have the room, as there's two offices empty upstairs since Billy seems to prefer the other one down here, or sitting on the edge of my desk.' She rolled her eyes. 'I guess I could move somewhere else for the days I'm concentrating on my own business, and you could have a new person here.' She frowned slightly as she didn't like this idea even as she said it.

'No,' said Poppy immediately, which was gratifying. 'It's so useful you being here. Running your own jobs from this office doesn't make a difference and we like having you around,' she came and nudged her on the shoulder before standing and looking at the view through the doorway into Billy's office, which used to be a meeting room. 'I want to keep us as a core team, if you're willing to stay and work both jobs? I know you're inundated with social media requests, but you keep us all on schedule, even with Bonnie here.'

Sasha felt relief flow through her veins. She was far from

ready to jump fully into her new role yet and she adored working with Poppy and Billy.

Ollie's gym was now fully staffed and they'd had a grand opening party, which Sasha had also organised since they'd started working together. She'd gone from tentatively thinking about setting up her own business, to finding it now took up two full days a week. She worked part time at Poppy's studio, but now ran her own enterprise from her desk there too.

Her new business was now registered and called STELLA Social Media. It meant 'star' in Italian and began and finished with the same letters as her first name. Sasha adored her new life and did wonder if she'd need to perhaps rent a room from Poppy if she did go full time at STELLA. She might even need an assistant of her own.

At the party she'd barely spoken to Ollie. Although he had given her a hug and thanked her profusely for all her hard work in his speech, there had been hundreds of people there, including Devon. It had been bedlam! Luckily everyone had enjoyed themselves and the tours of the gym that Ollie had lined up worked beautifully. It got people moving around the centre. The star of the show had been the relaxation garden and pods, which everyone was raving about. They were booked out for months in advance now.

Ollie had already spoken to Poppy about building more pods, and had also mentioned adding them to his other gym. This meant that Poppy was diversifying and widening her customer base from just the contracts she had with Jared. Jared had actually taken it in good part, saying he'd known he couldn't keep Poppy to himself for long. This had aggravated both Ollie and Dylan, but in the end the party had been a resounding success. They were now all looking forward to the stag and hen nights as a way to let loose and relax after months of gruelling hard work.

CHAPTER TWENTY-NINE

*S*asha made a very reluctant Poppy pose for a staged photo, and then posted it to social media. Poppy hated being in front of the camera, but it was her hen night and her customers would be keen to know that, as they'd all heard about her impending nuptials. They often asked about the progress of her wedding plans when they phoned or popped in.

Sasha made sure Poppy was standing in front of the light panel she had designed in the flat above her office, and managed not to include the kitchen counter heaving with booze that was just beside it. Dylan and Ollie were having some drinks at a wine bar in a town near Cherry Blossom Lane, with their younger brother Miles and a few mates. Poppy had mentioned that they might all meet up later in the evening, which had scandalised Sasha, as usually hen nights were strictly best friends and close family of the bride, but Poppy had only laughed. She'd been so happy lately that Sasha really didn't care who came to the hen night, as long as her friend was pleased. The boys had even invited Jared, and he had said he'd join them for a drink later.

Poppy treated her clients like part of the family. Sasha sometimes wondered if this was because her actual family was so small. Luckily she had loads of close friends, and they had made sure she would have a night to remember

Poppy reached up to her hair and straightened her plastic and diamanté crown. 'Do I really have to wear this all night?' She pulled the veil around her shoulders and her eyes twinkled with laughter. Since Poppy had had that chat with her mum, and met her dad, she'd been lighter somehow. She smiled more and now she couldn't wait to get married to her gorgeous fiancé, Dylan. Glen had even been round to her house and she'd met his wife. He had a son who she'd not met yet, but that was set up for the following week, so it was all systems go!

Billy popped open the Champagne and handed them all a crystal flute. Sasha took her glass and smiled at how far they'd come. Billy was wearing beautifully cut trousers with a waistcoat in a deep blue fabric, with a pale grey shirt. The shirt had subtly embellished cuffs you couldn't help but admire. His blond hair was cut into his trademark quiff and his beard was trimmed to perfection. On his lapel was a silver and crystal brooch that completely contrasted with his jacket and gave a hint at his creativity – well that, and the Converse trainers he was wearing, even with his suit. He pulled Sasha in for a hug and she received it gratefully. Organising a hen party took a lot of work and although Demi had helped, Sasha was having none of the quiet and sophisticated theme that Demi had wanted. She grinned wickedly at Demi, who was stunning in a fitted silver dress that moulded to her body and was quite daring for her friend's usual subtle tastes.

Demi grinned back and moved away from Billy's ex-boyfriend Ed. He had arrived back from his home in Portugal the night before and that morning he had announced he was joining them for the hen night. Sasha caught Billy watching Ed from under his lashes, so she nudged him to regain his attention and he almost spilt his wine on her shimmering dress. It was bronze silk and edged at the neckline with crystals. Her stipulation for the dress code had been silver, bronze, gold or sparkles and everyone had gone all out. She was happy to see Ed's white shirt had a pressed collar and he looked handsome in jeans with swept back hair. It had grown quite a bit since he'd been away and with his dark glasses, he looked a bit pensive, but he had a sparkly silver wand in his hand and he was swigging back the Champagne as he spoke to Poppy. Sasha winced. She wondered how his chat had gone with Billy the night before and nudged her friend again.

'How was last night?' she said quietly, observing Ed smile at something Poppy said and then lean in to hug her, which she sank into, before leading him off for a tour of the flat with Demi in tow, a bottle of Champagne in her free hand. Billy watched them go.

'He wants to reconcile,' he shrugged, as if that wasn't something he'd dreamed of for months. 'But he still expects me to move my world to fit his. He told me he'd come home for me, but he's settled in Portugal now and once again he's asked me to uproot my whole life for him.'

Sasha frowned as Demi returned on her own and caught the tail end of the conversation. She quickly topped up all their glasses, lines forming on her forehead too. She was wearing a crown with a bridesmaid sign but it had slipped into her bouncy curls so you could barely see the letters. Sasha couldn't help but grin. Demi was so beautiful, but she'd never been demure or girly, she was a tomboy through and through. She loved pampering and getting her nails done here and there, but her beautiful shimmering dress was complimented by a pair of trainers. Comfort over fashion was her mantra. Why get blisters when you could just wear your Nikes? Somehow her look always worked.

'Would you move for him?' asked Sasha, feeling like her heart was in her mouth. They'd all be devastated if Billy wasn't around to offer advice or cheer them up, but they did want him to be happy.

'Not with Devon on the scene,' laughed Demi tipsily, then stuck her hand over her mouth as Ed and Poppy wandered back in, arm-in-arm. Billy flushed and tried to glare at them, and Sasha raised an eyebrow.

'He's certainly a spanner in the works,' was all that Billy would say as he left them hanging and went to answer the door to let Maxine and a couple of other girls in.

Suddenly the flat felt tiny and Sasha decided that they should all move to the pub, where a room had been set up for them in the back, with a DJ arranged for later in the evening. Sasha and Demi had been there earlier in the day and spent ages filling the room with gold, silver and bronze balloons. They had also blown up photos of them all as kids and growing up. The Taylor brothers featured heavily and she hoped Dylan, Ollie and Miles didn't show up there later, as they'd all get even bigger heads about how good they looked.

She had to admit that Poppy and Dylan really fitted together, though. Demi had escaped the Taylor brother magnetism… she hoped. Meanwhile, Ollie confused her so much by stealing kisses whenever no one was looking and then being totally unavailable due to his workload. So she'd decided to step away from him and start dating again… If she could ever get her head straight.

When they entered the pub a round of applause went up from the locals and Poppy blushed and grabbed hold of Sasha's arm.

'This is one day where you have to accept being centre of attention,' laughed Sasha, waving to the dishy barman, Ben, who had started working there the previous week. He was tall, blond and lethal, and the pub was now bursting at the seams to prove it. The ratio of women to men had doubled overnight. The landlord Franco was loving it, even though he still had his eye firmly on Billy, and looked surprised to see Ed by his side.

Luckily Ben was charm personified and great at his job, but Sasha suspected he was so good looking he would have been allowed to stay even if he'd been awful. She smirked at Demi who was admiring him as well. Poppy blushed as they stopped to chat to a few locals, but Sasha took one arm and Demi the other and they guided her to the back room and watched her face light up with joy. They'd worked really hard to pull this off, and with the addition of Ben the hot barman now coming through to serve drinks to their group, and the shimmering decorations, her night was almost complete.

Poppy was walking along and taking in all the photos with tears in her eyes. Ben smiled and winked at Sasha, making her grin. Who needed Oliver Taylor when you had a hot barman? They walked past a photo of Ollie and she felt dizzy for a moment and gritted her teeth, grabbing a fresh drink from the bar. Ben grinned at her and then turned to take an order from Maxine, who was suddenly preening and almost lying across the bar to catch his attention. Ben seemed more than happy to attend to her.

Before long Ben and Maxine were chatting like lifelong friends. He threw back his head and laughed at something she said. She was wearing a tiny white dress, which Sasha had tried not to disapprove of as there was only one bride, but she did have some sparkle as she'd liberally rubbed some sort of glitter powder all over her arms and chest, which made her shine as she moved. She was a beautiful woman and other than not quite meeting the dress code, Sasha was glad she was there to celebrate with them. Neither had mentioned Oliver and it seemed as if Maxine might finally have moved on, which was a relief.

A group of old school friends arrived, to a few squeals of delight from Poppy. Behind them were her mum and some of the café regulars who had become Poppy's family when her mum wasn't around so much as a child. Sasha and Demi went over to greet them

The DJ, who had been setting up when they arrived, suddenly turned on the tunes and Poppy's favourite mixture of 80's pop and soul music began to play. A few people from the other bar stuck their head around the door and Poppy went over to hug them. Soon the room was bursting at the seams as the whole pub seemed to have joined them. The folding doors to the function room were opened up and everyone intermingled.

'This is brilliant,' gasped Demi, as she finally came to a halt next to Sasha after a spin on the tiny dance floor with a guy who had earlier been sitting having a quiet drink after work. Most of the customers were local and they all wanted to celebrate with Poppy, it seemed. No one was following the protocol that hen night guests had to be part of the wedding party, and Sasha was loving it! If Dylan and his friends did turn up, which she doubted, then at least she wouldn't have to worry about them as she had a whole pub full of people as a buffer. Poppy was looking stunning in her shimmering white party dress with tiny Swarovski crystal spaghetti straps and a gorgeous fitted bodice and skirt. Her hair shone and her tiara and veil made her appear like the bride, at long last.

'It looks like the whole pub has joined us,' joked Sasha, taking Demi's drink and stealing a quick sip as she was parched. Barman Ben was being attentive, but their party had gone from a small function to an entire pubful, so it was all hands on deck.

Worry flitted across Demi's eyes. 'Do you mind? You worked so hard on tonight to make it perfect for Poppy.'

Sasha tucked her arm around Demi. 'We both did. Billy helped too. But look how happy Poppy is,' They both stared at their friend, whose face was a picture of joy. 'She hates being the centre of attention…'

'Unlike some of us,' joked Demi, poking Sasha in the ribs and making her laugh.

'But she's loving this,' said Sasha, with a smile. 'Good job Billy vetoed the idea of half-naked waiters, or we might have scared off most of the custom,' she laughed.

Demi grinned. 'Or encouraged them!'

'Who was the guy you were dancing with?' asked Sasha, watching the man in question chat to another customer by the bar.

'I'm not too sure,' Demi laughed. 'He said he'd come in for a quiet pint when we came in and all hell broke loose, so he decided to join in.'

'How's things with Allan and your dad? We haven't had a chance to talk recently.'

Demi turned to look at a few revellers who were linking arms and dancing. 'I honestly don't know. Mum and Dad almost fell out over it, but for now I'm just keeping my head down and trying not to upset anyone.'

Sasha was aghast. 'Demi! You can't do that. You have to stand up for what you believe in,' she said, taking Demi's hand and bringing her in for a cuddle, trying not to spill the wine from the glass she was holding.

'I can't risk doing more damage to my parents' marriage

and I'm honestly fine. If I get married and have kids, then I might decide to stay at home anyway.'

'Demi!' scolded Sasha. 'You can do all of that and still have choices. You could work from home later or continue to study online. Or you could start your own business like I have. If you want to be at home with your kids, then that's amazing too, but it has to be your choice and not Allan's. Do you think Allan's going to propose, then?' she winced as this was such a sore subject still.

Demi and Allan had been together for years and it seemed like he had no intention of ever changing anything. It was obvious his life was perfect as it was. A beautiful girlfriend on his arm and a job in her father's business. Sasha almost growled. She grabbed a fresh drink from Ben as he passed and took a huge gulp of the wine. Yet more people arrived, and amongst them she spotted a tall man with broad shoulders and a shock of black hair.

'Allan's just arrived,' said Sasha, trying to sound happy about that fact and not scowl. He was with Dylan, Ollie and Miles and a few of the other men. All the women in the pub turned to look, but she turned away and sighed. 'Bang goes the fun this evening.'

'Sasha!' said Demi in surprise. 'Don't you like Allan?' Sasha could hear the hurt in her friend's voice, so she paused to compose herself.

'Of course I do. I meant all the guys from the stag do arriving during the hen night. I love Allan. I just want to see you follow your own dreams – and not his.'

'I am,' protested Demi.

'Are you sure?' asked Sasha, then wished she hadn't as Demi sniffed and her eyes became glazed. 'Sorry, Demi. I'm just being a grouch because the boys have crashed our night.'

Demi turned and, for the first time ever, she didn't seem so happy to see Allan.

Sasha frowned and then turned away before her eyes started feasting on Ollie, who was wearing a denim shirt that made her mouth water. Barman Ben's hand slid around her waist and almost made her jump out of her skin as he asked her a question about the supplies of food and drink she'd provided for the party, which the whole pub now seemed to be enjoying.

Glad of the excuse to move away before Allan and the boys reached Demi, she touched Demi's arm to see if she was okay, but a smile was firmly back in place on her friend's face and she held up her glass for Ben to fill it from the open bottle of Prosecco in his hand.

'I'm fine… honestly,' she nudged Sasha with her hip. 'Allan and I love each other, I'm sure it's just a blip.' Sasha raised an eyebrow as this blip seemed to have been going on for a while – but perhaps tonight was not the right time for deep and meaningful conversations.

'We can talk about this another time,' Sasha said, allowing Ben to lead her away. She was just nearing the bar, with Ben ushering her through for a quick chat in the back room, when a pair of grey eyes caught hers. Someone didn't look too happy to see her going into the back room with Ben. She smiled a greeting and shrugged, then followed Ben into the stockroom and turned to him with a dazzling smile. 'What can I do for you, Ben?' she asked, her heart suddenly beating at what felt like a hundred miles an hour, which had nothing to do with the handsome man in front of her giving her an admiring glance.

'I'm so sorry that your party has been hijacked. Do you want me to speak to the manager about it? You put money behind the bar and bought the food, but it's being eaten and it's hard to tell who is one of your guests and who's from another part of the bar.' He held his hands up in surrender at the situation, and she laughed to try and ease the worry lines on his beautiful face.

'It's ok. The bride doesn't mind, and her fiancé and his friends have all just arrived, so there are even more people now. So much for a subdued but classy hen party, it's like a rave out there,' she joked, enjoying seeing a smile return to Ben's face. 'If the tab has been used up and the food's been eaten, then it means everyone's having a good time. They can pay for their own drinks now and as long as the bride's happy, which she is, then so am I.'

'And if you're happy, I'm happy,' he winked, making her laugh. 'The customer is always right. I was hoping I'd see you in here tonight. I was wondering if I could take you for a drink somewhere… somewhere other than the place where I work,' he grinned and cocked his head to one side as he waited for her answer.

'Umm… usually I'd have jumped at the chance, but it's complicated,' she apologised, blushing suddenly.

'The big angry guy at the bar?' he asked. 'He didn't look too happy at my hand on your waist.'

Sasha felt her skin heating up further and the back room suddenly seemed tiny. 'It's nothing really. We're old friends, but as I said, it's complicated.' She shrugged and started twiddling with her hair.

'Look,' said Ben. 'I need to get back to my customers, but if things ever uncomplicate themselves, then the offer stands.' He gave her a wicked smile and she couldn't help but laugh and follow him back to the bar.

Ollie was standing talking to a group of men and women, including Maxine, but his eyes followed Sasha as she joined Poppy and handed her a fresh glass of sparkling wine. Ben winked and then leaned in and gave Sasha a quick kiss on the cheek, which made Poppy raise an eyebrow and then giggle as she'd probably had a tad too much wine. Sasha shrugged and grinned back.

Suddenly the mood changed as a slow song came on and Dylan came over and pulled his wife-to-be onto the dance floor. A warm hand slid around Sasha's waist and Ollie asked her if she wanted to dance, not really giving her time to reply before they were swept along in the throng of people vying for space on the tiny dance floor. Sasha was pushed up against Ollie's chest in the bustle. He pulled her close and linked his hands behind her waist to protect her.

'Have you been avoiding me?' he asked. His deep voice was almost lost in the sound of the music. Sasha saw Maxine watching them and winced. But Maxine was then swept onto the dance floor by the guy Demi had been dancing with earlier and she left Sasha's eyeline, which was a relief.

When she didn't answer him and just rested her face on his chest for a moment, enjoying the feel of his heartbeat, he lifted her chin with one hand and their eyes met.

'Who's that guy you were talking to earlier?' Ollie's expression was pinched and he glanced around as if searching Ben out, but she could see he was back behind the bar.

'He was asking me about the bar tab,' she said honestly. 'And then he asked me out,' she added, trying to quell the triumphant swell of her chest and the frown on his face.

'What was your response?' he asked with a steely calm, capturing her eyes again and making her heart rate speed up.

'I said it was complicated.'

'Why?'

'You know why,' she sighed. 'It *is* complicated.'

'It doesn't have to be,' he said, pulling her closer for a second so that their hips connected.

'You're always busy. I'm always busy. You keep kissing me

and confusing me,' she mumbled into his chest, enjoying the feel of his hips linked to hers.

Ollie pulled back a little to look at her. 'Why is that confusing? I'm showing you that I like you, Sasha. I know we don't get much time together. We're both trying to build new businesses, but I want to make time for you.'

Sasha reeled back slightly in shock, but couldn't move far as his arms were still around her. She frowned and she realised Ollie was probably drunk. He'd been out for hours already. He'd never said anything like this before. They just snogged like teenagers behind the filing cabinets, for goodness sake. That wasn't exactly making time for her, was it? Fire started to seep into her veins, and not for a good reason.

'Why don't you, then? You seem to pick me up and put me down like I'm a toy. And you only tell me you actually like me when another man shows interest in me.'

Ollie started to grin as if that was absurd, but then seemed to notice the change in her, and grinned anyway. The man was that stupid? She tried to break out of his embrace, but the song hadn't quite ended and he wasn't letting go. She was tempted to stamp on his feet. Her heels were sky high and would certainly hurt.

Ollie could see she meant business and released her, but only to take her hand instead and lead her outside into the cool night air. She shivered suddenly, as her dress was made of silk – and she was still far too close to Ollie. He went over to a secluded table behind the pub and sat down. She put her hands on her hips and waited.

'Sasha,' Ollie said, pulling her onto his lap and wrapping his arms around her so that she wasn't cold any more. She sat rigidly on his lap, which was difficult when her hands ached to touch him. 'I don't like seeing other men with their hands on you because it makes me jealous,' he said simply, making her even more confused. 'I know we're not dating officially, but that's because you won't ever agree to be seen anywhere with me. I have to make an appointment at work to see you!'

She could hear the exasperation in his voice and frowned. Had she been avoiding him? 'I have to come over to your office with an excuse about wedding planning, to catch a glimpse of your gorgeous smile. Then when I do, I can't keep my hands off you,' he said as he dipped his head and captured her lips with his own, making her groan and pull his face even closer.

All thoughts flew from her mind until they heard laughter as someone came out of the pub and they sprang apart.

'I didn't realise I'd been avoiding you,' she said honestly as she got her breath back and leant her forehead against his, her arms still around his neck. He kissed her neck and she sighed in bliss and then caught his hands in her own. 'What is this?'

His eyes were glazed but he smiled at her and her heart melted. 'I don't know yet, but I'm fed up with hiding behind dustbins,' he laughed, nodding at the huge pub bins to the side of them.

'It's kind of sexy,' she laughed and quickly kissed his lips again before getting up.

'You're sexy,' he growled as he spun her back into his arms for another deep kiss, making the bottom fall out of her world, before he let her go again. 'I want people to know we're dating, and I want to take you out to dinner, and to bed,' he almost growled, as her skin fizzed with heat at his clear intention.

'Ollie!' she gasped.

'Sasha,' he grinned wolfishly. 'I've wanted you in my bed since we were teenagers and I'm finding it hard to be near you without wanting to throw you over my shoulder and take you back to my lair. I'll do this at your pace and I won't rush you, but when I'm near you I can't seem to stop kissing you,' he admitted, trying to look contrite and failing.

'You want to date me?' she clarified, ignoring the lust-filled visions of him naked in her bed with difficulty.

'Every inch of you,' he said, running his eyes over her and making her flush.

'Everyone will think I'm mad,' she blushed, looking at her feet.

He tilted her chin up again and when she looked at him, he was frowning. Her heart ached at the thought of hurting him, but she needed to put herself first. She didn't know if she could withstand falling for him again and him moving on. Maybe it was better never to start, but she had a feeling it was already too late for that.

'Why would they think that?' he asked.

'Look, let's keep this to ourselves for now and we can talk about what we want to do later.' She got up and straightened her dress and ran her fingers through her hair, hoping that the pub was so full that no one had missed them.

'Can I stay at yours tonight?' he asked, making her go pink again. He pulled her to him quickly and his lips touched hers to remind her of what they had. She caught her breath and her hand went to her heart as he pulled away. 'I know what I said earlier, but we can take things as fast or slow as you want. I just want to sleep with you in my arms.' This man would be the undoing of her.

The pub door opened again and they moved apart.

'Demi's staying at the flat tonight, and so's Devon,' she said with genuine regret. She usually adored having guests to stay, but now she'd pictured Ollie in her bed, the image wouldn't leave her mind.

Ollie sighed and took her hand but dropped it when they approached the door. He held it open for her and they wove their way through the throng of people, smiling and laughing and stopping occasionally to chat as they made their way over to Poppy and Dylan.

Maxine was standing at the bar with Ben and she noted Ollie's hand on Sasha's waist and looked pointedly at her. Sasha flushed. Ben just winked at her, which further infuriated Maxine. She quickly carried on tapping her number into Ben's phone, which was on the bar, and handed it back to him before flouncing away. Ben pocketed the phone and then asked Sasha what she'd like to drink. She looked at Ollie, but he was watching Maxine leave and didn't look too happy. Sasha's stomach clenched. Was this all a game to him?

She ordered two glasses of fizz and then handed one to Ollie and left him standing as she spotted Poppy and Billy and headed their way. She had no idea of what to feel. Ollie might actually like her, but was he really ready to leave his bachelor ways behind him? She didn't know. Sasha had berated Poppy last year for hiding her relationship with one of the notorious Taylor brothers, but she could finally understand why she had. Would he break her heart? Would everyone think she was stupid for falling for him once again, when she'd spent the past couple of years announcing to anyone who'd listen that she was finally over him? Now they'd all think that she'd been lying to them. She had been over him... hadn't she? Now she wasn't so sure.

Demi grabbed her arm and made her jump, as she was in a world of her own, which wasn't easy in a room full of very merry people and great music. The air smelt of a mix of aftershave, perfume and beer. The scent seemed to be driving them all crazy, loads of the revellers had their arms around each other and were dancing like mad to the current number one tune. It was one of those songs that made it impossible to sit still, the lyrics and beat speaking to people's souls and making them get up and move.

Everyone was smiling and suddenly Sasha grinned too.

She'd just been kissed by one of the oh-so-sexy Taylor brothers, who had told her he wanted to hold her in his arms. Poppy and Billy were also grinning and had glazed expressions on their faces when Sasha reached them.

Billy started singing at the top of his voice and then Poppy joined in. Sasha's heart swelled with love for these people. Today was all about Poppy, and Sasha was determined to make sure she had the best night of her life.

CHAPTER THIRTY

Sasha opened her eyes and then quickly closed them again. Her head was pounding and the back of her eyes felt like they had sawdust sprinkled in them. She could hear Poppy and Billy talking in her flat's little kitchen. Then she saw a pair of male feet sticking out of the end of her bed.

Her mind went blank for a second. There was someone snuggled up next to her. What the hell?

She gingerly lifted up the covers and then slammed them back down again when she saw Devon's sleepy face. How did anyone get to look that good, the morning after the night they'd just had? Then he woke up, smiled at her and pulled her in for a hug.

She snuggled into his arms as Billy, Poppy and Demi all piled onto the bed to join them. Sasha oofed and Devon moved over to make room for them all.

'I thought only Demi and Devon were staying over last night?' Sasha asked her friends. 'You two look far too bright-eyed and bushy-tailed after that final round of cocktails last night,' she croaked, pulling the covers up to her chin and looking pointedly at Poppy and Billy.

'Poppy kept trying to go home with her gorgeous fiancé and Ollie last night, but Miles had got all the boys hotel rooms in town as a stag night treat, so I gave her a piggyback here. It was hilarious at the time, but then we were too exhausted to leave,' said Devon. 'I thought this was a sleepy little town, but everyone seems to know how to party!' He blew Poppy a kiss.

'Billy decided that he'd rather be with us than that rabble at the hotel,' laughed Demi, snuggling into Devon's arms and then wriggling up to make room for Billy so that Sasha was almost pushed out of the bed.

'I'll get up and make us all some coffee, shall I?' she said sarcastically, glancing down and feeling glad that she'd been sober enough to throw on her silk pyjama shorts set the night before.

'Yeees pleeease,' they all chorused and she rolled her eyes as Poppy got under the covers too. 'Luckily it's a massive bed or you'd all be sitting on your arses,' she grumbled under her breath as she walked into the kitchen, switched on the coffee machine and grabbed some pods from the cupboard as the milk whisked away in the frother.

Sasha secretly loved that they were all there. She had actually collected a food shop that week, so she had supplies aplenty. For a moment there, she'd wondered if she'd succumbed to Ollie's charms, but that wasn't something she'd forget in a hurry. She was glad it was purely platonic bed-sharing with Devon. She frowned suddenly. Where was Ed? She'd seen Billy and Ed chatting in a corner for a while last night and then they'd hugged, but she'd also noticed how Devon always seemed to be around these days. He'd caused quite a stir in the bar last night with people asking for his autograph, but after a while people had left him alone.

As she got mugs out of the cupboard for the hordes of people in her bedroom, she thought back to the conversation she'd finally managed to have with Maxine. Max had been angry at first when she'd seen Sasha with Ollie, but after Sasha explained a bit about their past, she'd sighed and said she now understood, but admitted that she'd hated her for a while. Apparently Poppy had mentioned they had history, but had been very vague about it. Sasha paused halfway through pouring the first cup of coffee, as there was nothing really to tell, other than her own obsessive behaviour. Now that delicious barman Ben was on the scene, it seemed that Maxine had decided that Ollie wasn't worth fighting with a girlfriend over. Sasha felt like a weight had been lifted from her shoulders, as she'd have stepped away if Ollie had returned Maxine's affection... she hoped.

Maxine had gushed that she'd asked Ben to be her date for the wedding, which Sasha thought was a terrible idea as she'd only just met him, but she was glad that Maxine was happy. Sasha knew that half of Maxine's aerobic classes would happily follow her to the end of the earth, but for some reason, she wouldn't look twice at any of the really great men there. Sasha had occasionally met a few of them after a gruelling workout class for a cup of hot chocolate, in the hope of bumping into Ollie, which hadn't happened. One or two of the guys kept the conversation about Maxine, and Sasha thought they would make amazing dates for her.

Sasha had a horrible thought that maybe Ollie had made sure that Maxine saw his hand on Sasha's waist as a way to either get rid of Maxine, or make her jealous, but Sasha shook that thought away. She couldn't keep thinking the worst of him when he'd done nothing to deserve it. It was her own insecurities speaking – and they could keep their opinions to themselves and put a lid on it.

The crowd in her bedroom had started heckling for their coffee, so she grabbed a tray and filled it with mugs and some toast she'd quickly shoved into the toaster. To hell with the crumbs in her bed!

~

*S*asha put her feet up on the sofa later and tried to ignore the detritus of a good night out that was littered around her flat. Everyone had left, including Devon, who'd tried to prolong his stay, but Billy had offered to drive him home. Sasha grinned. She hoped it was because he finally realised how much Devon liked him and wanted to see his 'etchings', but it was more likely that he wanted to check out Devon's huge barn conversion – ever the business-man. She did have a hunch that Billy had a secret crush on their new friend. He'd barely spoken to Ed the night before and although Ed was staying with Poppy and Dylan, Billy hadn't invited him to join him at his place in the annexe above their garage. When she'd finally had a moment to sit in a corner of the pub and chat to Ed at the party, his eyes had longingly sought out Billy in the room and he'd told her how lonely he was without him. Billy wasn't making time to see if they could rescue the relationship, even though it had been pretty much his sole topic of conversation outside work for months, leading up to Ed coming home for the wedding.

Sasha's friendship group would hate to lose Billy, and Poppy would probably feel like she'd had a limb chopped off, but they all loved him too much to hold him back. They'd all thought Ed was his soulmate, however misguided he'd been for moving away without Billy and breaking his heart... or at least they had until recently. Billy was a lot stronger, but it seemed Ed was still never far from his mind. He hadn't dated anyone seriously since Ed left, and to Sasha that told a story of its own. She and Billy were like two peas in a pod, she sighed, thinking of Ollie.

She pushed herself up and put one foot on the floor, waiting for the dizziness to subside. The last two cocktails at the pub had been the worst idea, but by then she'd been high on adrenaline from kissing Ollie Taylor. After that she'd hugged and kissed everyone briefly on the lips, including the women. She gingerly got up and winced as she straightened her back. She frowned as she kind of recalled waving her arms around and asking everyone to get off the tiny dance floor, so that she could break-dance, and them all cheering. She gritted her teeth and grimaced. She might have even thrown her shoes into the crowd and seen one land on a light fitting. She gazed around the flat and saw her shoes innocently lined up near the kitchen counter, as if saying, 'nothing to see here'.

She sighed and started tidying, before deciding not to bother, and dumping the coffee cups and empty plates from the toast she'd graciously made everyone into the sink to wash later. Walking into her bedroom and pressing a button to open the blinds, she flinched as bright sunshine flooded the room. She wobbled slightly and then held onto the bedside cabinet for support.

Someone had made the bed after they had all eaten their breakfast in it, and she looked at it longingly, but knew she would end up spending the rest of her Sunday there if she got in now. She could see Ollie's gym across the road. There were already lines of cars in the car park and people standing around chatting next to the huge potted plants. The flat felt empty suddenly and she wished she'd told Devon he could stay. She'd wanted to have a moment to savour some memories from the night before, but in the cold light of day and with a hangover, the hours suddenly stretched in front of her, long and solitary. She wondered what Ollie would be doing. Having Sunday lunch with his parents, probably.

She straightened her back and decided to shower and

change, and then go across to do a very gentle swim, or see if there was a cancellation for one of the relaxation pods. She could even use the steam room or sauna, as she hadn't tried them yet and Maxine had said they were sublime. Then she'd be fresh and awake and wouldn't have time for the constant reruns of that mind-blowing kiss in the pub garden with Ollie. Would they be weird around each other now that they had gone way past friends who flirt and snog occasionally? Ollie had made his intentions clear and it was exciting, but scary. Supposing he broke her heart again and she didn't recover?

Stepping into the shower and turning her face towards the water jets, vigorously rubbing lemon and jasmine scented bodywash all over to wake herself up, she drew in a deep breath of the citrus scent and then yelped as some of the suds slid into her eye. She splashed her face with water and hurriedly dried her body and sopping wet hair, which hung like a glossy waterfall down her back. She was lucky that she had a natural wave in her hair, so she could literally dry and leave it. She had tried curling it a few times and had ended up looking like she'd stepped out of a wind tunnel. She'd mentally blocked out the time she'd offered to be a hair model for a friend, who had back-combed it into a tornado of strands. She winced at the memory of having Poppy, Anne and Demi take it in turns to carefully brush it out. It had taken hours, painkillers and many tears, to get them all through it.

She pictured Ollie running his hands through his thick black hair and gulped, before grabbing some work-out clothes from her wardrobe. Then she dashed some of her favourite Gucci perfume behind her ears. She'd treated herself to it with her first payment for her social media firm, STELLA. The company was still in its infancy, but already bringing in a little bit of money.

She'd spent a weekend visiting all the local shops and businesses and, because she already had Poppy and Ollie's gym on her books, she'd been able to show a portfolio of work and had secured three more clients. They only required a few hours of work a week each, so at the moment she was managing it all nicely. It was exciting to see an idea that she'd dreamed about for years becoming a reality. Ok, she wasn't a social media star, but she was building brands for other people and her own followings were steadily growing, too. She actually enjoyed both sides of the business, she didn't need to always be the one in front of the camera.

She took a moment to enjoy the exotic scent that she'd bought for herself with her own hard work and then grabbed her gym bag and phone. Her lounge smelt of burnt toast and took the edge off her euphoria slightly, but she grinned and thought about the sexy new swimming costume she'd bought the week before and couldn't wait to try at the pool. It had cut-out sections at the sides and was quite daring, but she loved it! It made her feel great and accentuated her curves.

She shut the door behind her and walked purposefully towards the gym, determined to enjoy the rest of her weekend and to walk into work the next day with a clear head, refreshed body and less confused mind.

CHAPTER THIRTY-ONE

*S*asha was looking dreamily at the huge swimming pool and spa area through the big glass windows in reception next to the café. The seats were strategically placed so you could sit and watch friends or be enticed to join them.

She almost did a double-take when she heard Maxine's shrill voice calling her from outside the first exercise suite. Sasha looked around for a hiding place, but there wasn't one. Maxine was hopping up and down, immaculately turned out for her gym class in pale pink leggings and matching crop top, showing off her impressively toned stomach. How come she wasn't hung over? Sasha fumed. She'd drunk more than any of them!

'Join my class,' said Maxine, waving her in. Sasha looked down at her gym gear and wished she'd thought to put on a pair of jeans and a T-shirt. She self-consciously straightened her hair with her hand and stared at the people splashing happily in the pool.

'I was going for a swim,' she said apologetically, as Maxine approached with a determined stride, her ponytail bobbing as she walked. Maxine just raised her eyebrows at

Sasha's gym wear, whilst ushering her into the class. 'Um, but I haven't bought a ticket…' Sasha mumbled.

Maxine laughed, having none of her excuses. 'You're Ollie's 'special' friend, she said with an undertone of bitchiness. 'I don't think he'll mind you having a class on him. Plus you work here some of the time, so effectively, you're staff.'

Sasha didn't quite like the evil glint in Maxine's eye, but sighed and followed her in. 'I'm hungover,' she tried as a last resort.

Maxine laughed loudly and ignored her protest. 'Then a little workout will help you enjoy the rest of your day.'

Sasha could imagine Maxine clasping her hands together and saying, 'Mwahaha!' at her friend's suffering. Payback was a bitch.

'You were throwing some shapes on the dance floor last night when you were trying to breakdance, so you definitely need to learn some balance. Half the time you were just face-planting on the floor.'

Sasha's head snapped up to see if Maxine was making fun of her, but she looked deadly serious. She gave a start of surprise when she spotted the barman from the night before standing at the side of the class. She gave in and began to limber up, and watched Maxine flirt openly with Ben, who seemed to be enjoying every minute, much to the clear annoyance of a couple of her regulars, but it made Sasha smile.

Ben seemed like he was good fun and he was certainly gorgeous to look at, so perhaps a good view would ease her hangover, she smiled, as he waved at her. Ben touched Maxine's arm, which made her simper, and then he came and settled himself into a space right behind Sasha, which made her wince, as he'd have a prime view of her Lycra-clad arse for the next hour.

She turned round to him and raised an eyebrow at his

choice as there were a few other spaces available, but he just grinned and shrugged, so she rolled her eyes and turned back to wait for the class to begin. She was surprised to see Dylan and Ollie's younger brother, Miles, walk in to join the class. She hadn't seen much of him for ages, then here he was twice in two days. But the women in the room who had been ogling Ben suddenly perked up even more. Miles was the most unassuming of the brothers, but he was just as handsome as the rest, with his thick black hair and strong lithe build.

Sasha knew Miles enjoyed running, but she'd thought he hated aerobics. She wondered what had brought him here? He stopped to chat to Maxine and Sasha wondered if perhaps they would be a match, then dismissed that idea. Miles was an entrepreneur who spent all his time on his tech business, and Maxine needed someone who would lavish her with constant attention. Miles was also the quietest Taylor brother. He didn't talk about his love life, even to Sasha, who could chat for England. He pretty much kept to himself and, although he was great fun to be around, he was a solitary and gentle soul.

She caught his eye and his face broke into a warm smile. He came over and gave her a quick hug before looking round for a space and taking one next to Ben.

'What are you doing here?' she asked, grinning, as no one could help but smile when faced with Miles.

He was an astute businessman and the town's most eligible bachelor after Ollie, now that Dylan had been taken off the market by Poppy. Sasha had no idea how he fought off the crowds of women who admired him daily. He'd been featured in countless flashy business magazines, but he was even shy about that. Sasha and Poppy kept copies, though, and Poppy had framed a couple and hung them proudly in her office on Cherry Blossom Lane. They were all proud of him. Sasha had sent one of the images to be made into a jigsaw and given it to him as a gift with a hint that he should get out more. He'd roared with laughter and then sent her a text with an image of the completed puzzle and a message for her to try harder next time. Most of the image was shades of black or grey so it must have taken him ages, although knowing Miles he might have had an assistant make it.

Sasha frowned for a second. She'd sent Demi a few copies of the articles, but her friend hadn't mentioned them. Perhaps Allan mightn't have liked them, as he was a bit proprietorial of Demi at times. Plus they both worked with cars, so maybe Allan felt competitive that he and Demi's dad just ran the biggest local garage, while Miles fixed supercars.

Sasha had never given it a second thought before, but she looked at Miles as he stretched in preparation for the class, and wondered. Sasha loved every bone in his body, so she'd only heard about the swoony women second hand, through town gossip. She did have eyes, though, and most of the women in the room were surreptitiously staring at him when they thought he wasn't looking. One or two offered him a bashful or brazen smile, and he simply smiled back and then went to find a workout mat. He was the epitome of zen. This was a trick Sasha had tried to learn from Poppy over the years, but never perfected. Her temper seemed to go from one to ten thousand in a matter of seconds, however hard she tried.

'Why are you here?' she whispered to Miles as he returned to his space.

'I'll tell you later,' was all Miles said, as he turned to nod at Ben, who she guessed he'd met at the hen/stag do. Then he looked back at her, raising his eyebrows as if asking why Ben was there. She frowned, but didn't have time to think as Maxine called out for the class to start.

It was as gruelling and incredible as always, even though

Sasha could only keep up with half of it and Miles had to prop her up at one point. Her hair was sticking to her face by the end and she was hot and flushed, but thankfully everyone else looked pretty much the same. They grinned at each other with shared pride at finishing another of Maxine The Destroyer's classes – that was what Sasha had overheard a few of the women call her after a particularly painful class.

Maxine grabbed her arm and hurried her to the side of the class before she could agree with the woman next to her that it had been a difficult session that week, as she tried to regulate her breathing and not pass out.

Maxine was speaking to her at a rate of knots and under her breath, which made Sasha's hangover come right back again as she tried to make the words unscramble in her brain. It was something about Ben being available and that Sasha had to get changed quickly and meet her in the café for a de-brief. Sasha glanced down at her sweaty gym gear in misery and imagined strolling into the café in her sexy new swimming costume, as that was all she had in her gym bag – that and a towel. She could go back to the flat and change, but Maxine was hissing at her to hurry up and practically shoving her out of the gym door with her hands on her back-side to get her moving. Sasha yelped and jumped forward to get to the changing rooms.

She'd only worn her gym clothes to try and blend in while she walked to the spa. Urgh! She gingerly side-hugged Miles as he strolled past and caught hold of her waist. She kissed his cheek and told him that a few of them were going to the café for a drink. She had enough to think about with Ollie, without Maxine chatting ten to the dozen about flirty Ben for an hour. That wasn't what she'd had planned when she'd decided to visit the gym for relaxation on her weekend. If Miles distracted Max, they might even find out they had a few things in common. Sasha liked Ben, but her 'bad boy' radar rang loudly when he was around and she already had her headache back. It was even worse now she was dehydrated from so much jumping around like an idiot.

When Ben had taken her hand and led her into the back room at the pub the night before, he'd had a sure smile and knowing eyes, as if he'd expected her to fall into his arms the moment the door was shut. It was a bit too practiced and over-confident for her. She thought of the way Ollie had told her he liked her and her heart melted. He hadn't assumed, he'd asked. He hadn't seduced, he'd held her heart in his hands.

She blinked as she looked at the cubicle she'd shut herself into for a quiet moment in the changing rooms. It was actually quite spacious and comfortable. She tutted, as there was no advertising on the back of the door, or mention of how to follow the gym or instructors on social media for exciting updates or upcoming events. It was an opportunity lost and she mentally added that to the list of things she needed to discuss with Ollie.

She felt her hands shake at the thought of it. Supposing he'd been drunk (she'd certainly had a few glasses of wine at that point), or changed his mind? They'd still have to work together – she'd invoiced him, at his insistence. Her face flamed and she came out of the cubicle and looked at herself in the mirror. She drew huge circles of concealer under her eyes and brushed her hair. Then she pushed open the door to leave – and stopped herself just in time. She'd forgotten to rub the concealer in, and looked like a deranged panda. She quickly smudged it and fluffed her hair out and was glad to see her clothes had dried. She spritzed herself with perfume and summoned enough energy to go and support Maxine's love life. To be honest, Sasha was grateful that her friend's laser-like stare had moved off Ollie and onto Ben, and that she herself had done her penance by taking the class with a hangover. She thought Max deserved love, but wasn't sure that Ben was the man to give it. A quick flirty fling maybe, but Sasha was pretty sure Maxine was looking for something more serious right now.

When she walked into the café, Maxine threw her head back and laughed at something Ben said and he placed his hand on her leg fleetingly. Both of them had changed and looked fresh and beautiful in casual jeans and tops. Maxine's fitted top was a designer brand that Sasha immediately recognised and Ben didn't look like he'd just finished an exhausting workout. Maxine's glossy hair was loose and hung around her shoulders and she'd applied lipstick. Maxine raised an eyebrow, as Sasha was still in her workout gear, but said nothing.

Sasha was surprised Ben was sitting so close to her friend, but Maxine just grinned as Ben jumped up and asked them both their coffee order. Sasha supposed she should have grown out of drinking hot chocolate and marshmallows, especially after a gruelling workout, but she hadn't, even though she could now drink a latte without pulling faces. She ordered a hot chocolate and ignored Maxine's disapproving stare. Maxine ordered a black coffee, which sounded disgusting and bitter.

Sasha slipped into the seat next to Maxine but her eyes darted to the door and she smiled widely and waved a bit manically as Miles strolled into the café, so he had no choice but to walk their way. Their eyes met in mutual understanding and he grinned mischievously. Miles was dressed in jeans and a crisp white T-shirt and she felt like most of the women in the room suddenly held their breath. The chattering background noise stopped as they all craned their necks.

Miles was oblivious as he was checking his phone, before smiling at them both and crouching down on his haunches so that he was at eye level with Sasha. He smelt divine! Like he'd just been doused in a zingy lime and mango shower gel, which he probably had. Her stomach rumbled and she quickly pressed her hand onto it to shut it up. Sasha had never fancied Miles, as she thought of him as a younger brother, but the same couldn't be said of Ollie. He'd always seemed exciting and dangerous. She scoffed at her own stupidity as Ollie wasn't dangerous, other than to her heart.

'Joining us?' she asked him.

Miles nodded to Ben who had just returned with their drinks and shook his hand. 'I'm meeting Ollie, but it's great to see you all, especially you, Sash,' said Miles, giving her a kiss, but looking directly at Ben, which was weird.

Sasha's heart rate shot up and she felt a bit weak suddenly. 'Ollie's here?'

'It is his gym, Sasha!' mocked Maxine, laughing coquettishly, rolling her eyes as if Sasha was a dunce.

Miles smiled at her, his eyes twinkling. 'You sound like you're avoiding him, Sash?' he asked.

'I'd hardly be here if I was avoiding him,' she said, her head held high. 'I just assumed he'd be out to lunch with your parents.'

'He had work to do. That's why I joined the class, which was great by the way,' he nodded to Maxine who flushed in happiness. 'I'm dragging my brother away from his desk for a drink, which neither of us need after yesterday, but we might find food too. Everyone thinks I'm a workaholic, but he's worse,' he joked. 'I'm just grabbing us both a coffee first.'

He kissed Sasha again and said goodbye to the others, which made several people bend their heads to go back to their gossip. Sasha watched him join the short queue at the till, along with most of the café's clientele who were acting as if a movie star was in their midst and chatting in hushed and reverent tones.

CHAPTER THIRTY-TWO

Ollie stretched his muscles out and rolled his neck, as Miles knocked on his office door and poked his head around it. It had been a hectic weekend but work couldn't wait. He had just employed a new manager for his other gym, so it meant he could be on site more to make sure this one grew steadily and any teething problems were sorted out swiftly. Ollie wasn't a man to sit on a problem – he usually acted very quickly to make it right. But his head was full of Sasha and the feel of her finally being in his arms, so although he had been working, he'd been mostly daydreaming, which was not ideal. Having Miles in front of him was a welcome distraction and he got up and embraced him, before Miles laughed and shrugged him off.

'I only saw you yesterday, you idiot,' joked Miles, ruffling his brother's hair so Ollie had to use his fingers to calm it back down.

'We don't see enough of each other,' said Ollie honestly. 'Except at the stag do, when you took off your shirt,' he laughed.

Miles blanched. 'That was Demi! She'd had a few cocktails and decided that anyone within reach should be at one with nature and donate their shirt. She had mine off before I blinked,' he laughed. 'Luckily Allan had left by then or he might have been upset, although he seems to think other men are immune to Demi's charms.' Miles shook his head at such idiocy.

Ollie looked at him with a knowing smile and Miles gave his brother a playful punch on the arm. Seeing Dylan happy with Poppy had shaken the other brothers up a bit. They worked hard to be successful, but there was more to life. There was a tangle of threads tying them all to their childhood friends. Ollie didn't want them drift away from that. What they found in each other had kept them together as a friendship group for a very long time. Perhaps there was a reason for that.

Miles patted him on the back to regain his attention. 'I've just been to Maxine's exercise class.'

'No way! That class is supposed to be excruciating!' said Ollie in awe. 'Aren't you hung over?'

'Yep,' said Miles. 'The things I do for you, brother,' he grinned. He eased himself into the chair opposite Ollie's with a groan, making Ollie laugh out loud. Miles was usually super fit, but he'd been slacking in that department lately as he had a new business idea and when he was like that, it consumed his time.

Miles sighed and rubbed his neck. 'I just saw that barman, Ben… we met last night at the party. He was with Max and Sasha in the café.'

'Ok,' said Ollie, knowing that his brother had more to tell him by his body language.

'I didn't tell you last night because we'd all had a skinful,' said Miles, clearly choosing his words carefully, 'but I overheard Ben betting with the other bar staff over which of them he could sleep with first, Maxine or Sasha.'

'What?' fumed Ollie, jumping up from his chair, which hit the ground with a thud, so he had to pick it up again. His fists bunched and his teeth bared in anger, he began pacing around the room.

'He said he was going to join the gym to 'bump into them', so I did too,' soothed Miles, catching his brother's arm to still him. 'Although I have honestly been meaning to for ages.'

'You didn't need to join. Come in for free!' said Ollie, his teeth still on edge and adrenaline pumping through his veins. Now he had a glimpse of what it could be like with Sasha in his arms, he only wanted more. He swore quietly and tried to regulate his breathing before his brother realised how badly this news had affected him. Miles knew Ollie had a soft spot for Sasha and was protective of the girls in their group, as were all the Taylor brothers, but Ollie had stepped way over that invisible friendship boundary last night and he had no intention of backing up.

'You're building your business, and I can afford to pay,' Miles joked, getting up and wandering over to the window to take in the view.

'Ok. Are you planning to be in the area more, or did you just join my gym to wind Ben up – which I'm all for, by the way,' Ollie ground out, while he stared out of the window too, his mind racing.

'I was looking out for Sasha,' said Miles, simply. 'She's like a sister – and Maxine counts as a friend of yours as she's working for you. Nothing happened there, did it?' he asked with a grin.

'No! I'd have told you if it had.' Ollie looked horrified. 'Sorry. Maxine's amazing, but...'

'But it's always been Sasha?' finished Miles.

Ollie didn't even try to hide it. 'Is it that obvious?'

'No, but Dylan and I have always known. Poppy does too.'

He added helpfully as Ollie winced. 'Thinking about it... Demi probably knows as well.'

Ollie puffed out his cheeks and leant against the window as Miles laughed at his brother's discomfort.

'How do you know what Demi thinks?' asked Ollie with interest.

'We're friends,' dodged Miles. 'We speak on the phone about cars and her dad's business, and we see how you are around Sasha when you don't think anyone's looking.'

Ollie regarded his brother at this but stayed silent.

'Why have you left it until now to do anything about it?' asked Miles.

He came and stood next to Ollie, shoulder to shoulder. 'I can see something has definitely changed between you. You're all tense and prickly, and so is she when you're around. What did you do?'

'I finally told her I like her. I'm not sure she's that happy about it,' grumbled Ollie with a sigh.

Miles shook his head in pity. 'Why didn't you tell her sooner?' he asked, sitting on the desk and leafing through a few business magazines, which made Ollie tut.

'I was scared she'd run away. A bit like she's doing now. An annoyed Sasha who talks to me, is better than one who ignores me.'

'Oh man, you've got it bad,' said Miles with pure glee.

'I know!' said Ollie in frustration, walking over and nudging Miles so he nearly fell off the desk onto the floor. Miles grabbed the sides of the table and laughed, before standing up.

'What are you doing here anyway? Other than stalking Ben?' Ollie said gruffly.

Miles looked out of the window across Cherry Blossom Lane and then turned to his brother. 'You all spend so much time here that I've started looking into property.'

Whatever he might have said, Ollie hadn't been expecting that.

'I've just bought a huge parking lot just down the road. It's nearer to town and is mostly waste ground, but I can see that as the town grows, they'll need more facilities.'

'Facilities for what?' asked Ollie, but he was grinning like Miles had just given him half of his chocolate coins on Christmas morning. 'Why didn't you tell us?'

'I wasn't sure it would go through, as there was a plan to possibly build a hotel there, but they bought a site further up the hill by the church. At the moment there are two derelict buildings on the site and some pretty dusty outbuildings.'

Ollie's eyes crinkled at the corners while he waited to hear more. He hadn't jumped up to go and thump Ben, and Miles was clearly impressed by his brother's restraint. As kids they had gotten into quite a few scraps and all knew how to handle themselves, especially Ollie who had always been into fitness, but they preferred to use logic rather than brute force to win an argument – unless absolutely necessary.

'So what are you planning to use it for?' Ollie asked. 'Surely you're not suddenly building a hotel? I know you're doing well, but that's a bit of a stretch.'

Miles got up and laughed. 'Poppy and Jared are the architects, I'd have no idea where to start. I've just invested in my first ever storage facility. I need somewhere big to put my clients' supercars while they're being serviced. And I have a few ideas about ways to grow my business.'

Ollie leaned back in his chair in shock. 'Wow! That all sounds great.' He got up and slapped his brother on the back in congratulations. 'I'm already proud of you, but that's amazing.' Then he thought for a moment. 'I'm surprised Jared hasn't snapped the space up, if it's building land.'

Miles grinned. 'Jared might be a hot shot, but I move

pretty quickly too. I've got other plans, but I want to firm them up a bit in my head first.'

'Are you moving into the area?' asked Ollie.

'I thought perhaps I could stay with you while I look for somewhere? But you do live in Dylan's house,' he said with a smile, his eyes sparkling. 'Maybe we both need to look for a permanent home?'

Ollie rubbed his shoulders with his palms and then sat back down at his desk.

'I can see how tired you are from the way you keep rubbing your neck,' said Miles. 'It's not surprising, considering you've almost finished setting up your second fitness centre. Well done, bro,' added Miles. 'Have you taken on too much, though? Mum and Dad have been worried too. You don't come home as much.' Ollie could hear the worry in his voice. 'Dylan did that last year to impress Poppy and nearly burnt out. Is this about Sasha?'

'Sorry. I'll make sure I pop home more. I'll call mum tonight,' reassured Ollie. 'Sasha isn't a problem, although she is the reason why I had my eye on this area already,' he grinned and Miles rolled his eyes. 'You know she's my social media manager now and she's streamlined all my advertising and did an amazing job with the launch of this site. I think it's why we're already so busy. She's brought in Devon, who you met properly last night, and she wants other influencers to post from here. She's convinced me to use one of the rooms for a hot desk site, so businesspeople can exercise and then get straight back to work, or post emails and check their social media if they need to. So many people work online nowadays. She's told me I'm missing a trick.'

'It sounds like a great idea,' said Miles in awe. 'Sasha was always interested in online trends, so it makes sense. Perhaps I need to talk to her about my new venture?'

'She'd love that, I'm sure!' said Ollie with a smile, hoping that might earn him some brownie points with Sasha and wondering if he could get her alone to tell her, even though it was Miles' news. He knew his brother wouldn't mind and he was itching to touch her skin and make her smile again.

'I'm buying the house and barn from Dylan,' Ollie said suddenly. 'He doesn't need it as Poppy's house is incredible. There's plenty of room for two, as it's huge! Dylan uses the workshop underneath the flat, but I'm out all day anyway. It'll be great to have all the Taylor brothers back together again.'

'Do you want to go and grab a coffee in the café downstairs to celebrate?' asked Miles, his eyes gleaming with mischief. Ollie grinned, but was already pushing himself out of his chair and grabbing his phone, picturing Sasha's face when she saw him, and picking up his pace to let Ben know very clearly the message that he obviously missed last night.

CHAPTER THIRTY-THREE

*S*asha ran her hands through her hair for what felt like the thousandth time and made a face as she took a sip of the now cold hot chocolate on her desk. The wedding was looming and tensions were running high. The office was a hive of activity, getting ready for Poppy to leave for her honeymoon, and as she'd never been away from her business before she was also getting a bit snappy. Sasha was trying to smooth over all the edges, but her own nerves were starting to fray.

Ollie and Miles had shown up in the gym café a few days before and joined them for a drink, but she'd felt an underlying tension. She hadn't known where to look or what to do when faced with Ollie, so she'd slapped on her brightest smile and chatted mostly to Ben, which seemed to upset Ollie for some reason. Ben hadn't been anything but witty and charming, so she didn't know what Ollie's problem was.

Since then she'd barely seen him, as there had been a glitch at the gym with the heating system going down, which was a huge problem with the spa and pool facilities. It had been rectified, but she'd glanced at him striding across the car park looking harassed. He had kept the rest of their conversations via email and about work. It was almost as if their kiss never happened. Now they were going to be sitting next to each other at the wedding, so they'd literally have to go back to being just friends, which would almost kill her, or decide what the hell they actually were to each other, if anything.

After the coffee, and as everyone else left, Ollie had tilted his head and asked her to follow him to a quiet corridor where he told her that Miles was moving into the area, which had surprised her completely, but he'd touched her face and looked at her longingly, before someone had walked by and they'd sprung apart... again. It was exhausting. Whoever said an illicit affair was exciting and sexy had a lot more energy than she did. She felt like she'd aged ten years in the past few months.

Ollie had said hello to his customer and then kissed Sasha's wrist briefly as they walked away. His lips had seared her skin and she'd gasped and she'd wanted more, but his hand had left hers and he'd sauntered off. How on earth anyone had time for a relationship, or even just sex, when they each ran their own business, she didn't know! Whenever she did fleetingly see Ollie he made sure to brush her hair from her shoulder or look into her eyes and set her soul on fire. She felt like she was a walking furnace that would explode if he didn't give her what she needed soon.

She'd bumped into Ben a few times and seen him at the pub after work and he was as flirty and outrageous as ever. You couldn't help but laugh at him, as he was so cheeky, but now Maxine had invited Ben to be her guest at the wedding. Sasha hoped she wouldn't get hurt.

Sasha shrugged and picked up the brand-new sparkly desk planner Poppy and Billy had bought her, after seeing her old dog-eared one in her drawer. Most of her schedule was online, but she still liked the feel of opening a book and seeing her plans laid out in her own neat handwriting. A younger version of herself would be proud of the woman she'd become, even if she wasn't actually famous or uber-wealthy. She had enough sparkle in her life right now with famous friends like Poppy and Devon and her own profile was steadily growing.

If Miles became her next big client, then she'd definitely owe Ollie a drink for suggesting him, and perhaps she might finally pluck up the courage to tell him that she liked him quite a lot too. He knew she lusted after him and seemed to quite enjoy that now, but after their chat at the hen night, she needed to open herself up to being vulnerable to him again too. She frowned, and then smiled as Poppy and Billy came into her office and perched on her desk.

'How's it going?' asked Poppy. She was in a pretty fitted shirt and jeans, looking fresh and relaxed, which was impressive considering their workload. Billy's hair had been cut and styled ready for the wedding and he smelt of coffee and biscuits. Her heart swelled just looking at her friends. She was so lucky to have them in her life, when she definitely wasn't as kind or considerate as they were.

'I'm doing ok. All the wedding plans have been finalised. Bonnie has been a godsend correlating it all since we hired her to run the reception. Your calendar is free for your honeymoon and when you get back, we've eased you in gently,' she smiled. 'But we know you well enough to realise that you'll just jump straight back in.'

Poppy grinned and nudged Billy with her shoulder. He glanced around and Sasha knew he was looking for food, he was such a scavenger. She opened her drawer and handed him a packet of chocolaty sweets. 'What happened to the healthy eating plan for the wedding?' she asked him.

'It's pre-wedding nerves,' said Billy, which made the girls burst out laughing.

'Aren't I the one who's supposed to have those?' asked Poppy, holding out her palm for some sweets.

Billy held them to his chest protectively. 'No! You're too calm,' he said whilst stuffing a handful of little chocolates into his mouth and chomping merrily. 'You're marrying the guy of your dreams and you can't wait! The pair of you don't stop smooching!' he complained mildly, with a half-smile.

Poppy dropped her hand and her eyes narrowed in on her target, as did Sasha's. They both moved closer and he ducked out of the way and ran to the door, hiding the bag of sweets behind his back.

Poppy stepped in front of him and blocked the exit with a grin, pinching a few sweets and chewing happily in victory. 'If you didn't spend half your life in my house instead of your flat, you wouldn't have to watch!' laughed Poppy, before she stopped and frowned. 'Is everything ok with you and Ed? I know you both eat with us, but that in itself is weird. Don't you want time alone now he's arrived for the wedding?'

Sasha thought back to how excited Billy had been for Ed to come back, and how he was behaving now. She was about to speak when Billy held his hand up for them to stop with the questions and stuffed all the remaining sweets into his mouth at once. Then the phone rang in his office. With a defiant backward glance, he dashed past them and almost dived over his desk to answer it and left the women staring at him as he tried to digest the food and speak at the same time. Sasha stomped over and placed a glass of water from the kitchen in front of him, which he took gratefully, and then she carefully closed the door to give him some privacy as a client had just stepped in through the front door.

Poppy and Sasha exchanged a glance that said they would talk about this later and Poppy went to her office as Sasha moved forward to greet the client and make sure they had a coffee before their morning meeting. There were only two days until the wedding now, and tomorrow would be taken up with running errands, so she needed to get her head back into the game and plough through her mountain of jobs, or she'd still be working while Poppy and Dylan walked up the aisle!

CHAPTER THIRTY-FOUR

*P*oppy sat in the bay window overlooking the side lawn of the Manor House Hotel that was hosting her wedding. She'd had to pinch herself that morning –she was about to become Dylan's wife. It was something her teenage heart had longed for, and look at her now. The room had beautifully high ceilings and the huge bridal suite had a sumptuous and decadent bedroom with a king size bed in the centre of one wall, artfully strewn with cosy blankets and the softest pillows. There were rose petals on the bed and a bucket of Champagne cooling on one of the bedside tables. The colour scheme was muted, in greys and soft greens, and it was oh-so-inviting. Poppy just about held herself back from jumping onto it for a snooze.

The past few weeks had been exhausting, but today would make it all worth it. Dylan supported her through thick and thin and she hoped he felt the same way about her. Next to the bedroom was a living room, with three velvet couches and little glass side tables that were full of dainty treats to tease her taste buds. Her stomach was a bit sore from stresses that had cropped up in the last few days, so she rubbed it and tightened the belt of her dressing gown.

Her hair had already been decorated with tiny wild-flowers and her make-up was soft and dewy. She'd wanted a couple of hours of quiet to gather her own thoughts and be ready for the day ahead and the questions that she knew would come with it. She sighed and picked up her flute of sparkling wine, sipping it and then pressing it against her forehead. She'd tried everything she could think of to quell her nerves, but they wouldn't budge.

The main room was full to bursting with vibrant flower arrangements with warm wishes from many of her clients and the heady scent filled the air and made her take a deep breath and re-centre herself. It was only a small wedding, but everyone had wanted to wish her and Dylan well, which brought tears to her eyes and filled her heart with love for her business and the people in it. All her friends seemed to be flourishing, too, and she wouldn't let any worries spoil her big day.

She jumped as someone knocked on the door, but she was actually glad of the interruption. She hoped it wasn't her mum, as she'd already been in and had her hair styled and had gone looking for Chris... her husband. That still made Poppy blink a few times in shock.

Some gorgeous curls appeared, then Demi's bright smiling face came into view as she stuck her head round to check it was ok to come in. Demi brightened everyone's day and Poppy got up to give her a hug and felt some of the tension leave her body. It would be ok. She could do this.

Demi grinned and Poppy handed her a glass of Champagne, which she took and sipped with a sigh of bliss. 'Yum. That's delicious!' she said, her vibrant energy filling the room. Her eyes ran up and down Poppy's body and she took her hand and made her twirl, which sent the ends of the robe belt flying in the air. 'You look stunning!' said Demi.

'I haven't got my dress on yet!' laughed Poppy.

'You always look beautiful,' said Demi, pulling her in for another hug and kissing her cheek. 'I can't believe you're the first one to get married,' she said softly, and Poppy felt her heart break in two.

'It should have been you first, Demi,' she said. 'You and Allan have been together for so long. Perhaps seeing the wedding will give him a kick up the bum,' Poppy joked, trying to lighten the sudden shift in mood for her friend.

'Or it might scare him off,' said Demi sadly, before she shook herself out of it and smiled again. Poppy's heart filled with love for this girl. Her eternal optimism couldn't excuse Allan for taking her for granted for so long, though.

'Then that would be his loss and someone else's gain,' Poppy said pointedly. She took Demi's hand and led her to the window, where they watched Ollie, Sasha, Miles and Billy walk across the gravel pathway. Demi's eyes glazed over slightly and then she brushed a stray tear quickly away. They both saw Ollie rest a hand on Sasha's bare back where her dress was cut away and watched her lean her body into his for a split second before they moved apart.

Poppy and Demi's eyes met in glee and they both sat there in silence for a moment, sipping their chilled wine.

'We could…' said Poppy.

'I know…' said Demi.

'Should we?' asked Poppy.

'Definitely,' said Demi.

'Throw them together?'

'Absolutely,' grinned Demi. 'It's about time!' Poppy pulled Demi up and they both rushed over to the phone that was on a huge cabinet in the lounge.

'Keep a watch,' said Poppy hurriedly, pointing to the main

door to the suite. Demi grinned and opened it to check the corridors and gave Poppy the thumbs up.

Poppy spoke into the phone and explained that there had been an unexpected guest and Mr Ollie Taylor would now have to share with the maid of honour. She bit her lip and tried not to laugh as she quickly asked for his things to be moved during the service and slammed the phone back down. Then there was a knock on the door and Demi opened it, her cheeks still flushed and her eyes full of excitement. It was Billy and Sasha.

Sasha looked from one to the other, as they were both a bit red in the face and giggling. 'What have you been up to?' she asked suspiciously.

'Nothing!' they chorused, as Demi grabbed the bottle from the chiller as a distraction and asked Billy to collect some glasses.

Billy looked devastatingly handsome in a three-piece suit, complete with one of the waistcoats Sasha and Ollie had chosen and a cream flower in his buttonhole.

Poppy's bouquet was filled with cream roses, with wildflowers to represent the field. Her dress was cream silk with expertly made cherry blossoms scattered at the bottom and neckline. The dress was backless and flowed over Poppy's slim body like a dream as Sasha and Demi lifted it over her head and did up the tiny buttons at the back. The design was simple but effective.

Demi and Sasha walked over to their golden silk bridesmaid dresses, hanging in protective covers in the wardrobe in the main bedroom. They slid into them and the three of them stood side-by-side, arms linked, looking at their reflections in the huge gilt mirror by the main door. Tears filled their eyes. Billy called them back into the lounge and the mood was broken, but not before they'd given each other a quick squeeze of the waist and a kiss on the cheek.

Poppy smiled as Billy settled himself on a couch nearest to the silver food trays and began nibbling on a miniature pastry straight away, between sips of Champagne. 'I didn't have time for breakfast,' he laughed at Sasha's raised eyebrows. 'It takes time to look this good.'

Poppy grinned and went to stand opposite him. Her stomach ache was back and she knew she needed to speak to them all together.

Sasha and Demi tried to sit down with Billy, but their delicate dresses didn't really allow for lounging around, so they propped themselves up on the arms of the couch. Billy asked Poppy about her morning and told them about his adventures in the hotel grounds while he'd checked everything was set up correctly with Sasha. 'We caught two staff members snogging in the formal gardens,' he laughed.

'They almost jumped out of their skin when we bumped into them,' said Sasha reprovingly, as if she'd never snogged anyone she shouldn't. Poppy stared out at the beautiful formal gardens through the window and knew it was time.

'What's happening with Ed? You didn't arrive together this morning,' said Poppy.

'We've spoken about our relationship, or whatever it is that we have now, and we've decided to stay as friends. He's staying here tonight, so he got a room here last night as well.' Poppy's mouth dropped open in shock. 'Ed's going home tomorrow and we're ok about it, which has surprised both of us.'

'Why?' asks Demi, with a gentle smile. 'Is it anything to do with a certain superstar who seems to hang around with us all nowadays?'

'That's a long way to come to get dumped,' said Sasha.

'Sasha!' said Demi, spluttering her drink and mopping her chin down quickly so as not to get Champagne on the front of her dress.

'Well, it is,' repeated Sasha. 'We all know that Ed wanted you back, Billy. What an idiot for letting you go in the first place. There's only one Billy,' she said ferociously and they all grinned and clinked glasses to that. Sasha filched a petit four from the plate and turned it from side to side to try and work out how to eat it. 'Plus, now there's Devon,' she added guilelessly, watching her friend closely and then stuffing the tiny cake in her mouth, munching furiously as if she'd never been fed.

Billy sighed and handed the plate of pastries to Demi, who took one and admired the intricately iced design before tasting it. 'Ed knows I don't want to move abroad. He's settled now, but my career has grown thanks to you and Poppy,' he nodded at Sasha who flushed at the compliment. 'Ed and I still care about each other, but it wouldn't work.'

'He didn't try hard enough when it mattered,' said Poppy with insight and Billy shrugged.

'So, about Devon...' giggled Sasha, poking Billy in the ribs. 'Is it a bit uncomfortable, having two beaus at Poppy's wedding,' she joked. 'Although the bride does too, as Jared's here!' she almost doubled over and they all started to laugh, while Poppy pretended to be indignant.

'Jared and I are great friends now, as you well know, and he realises nothing will ever happen so he's moved on. It's not like he was in love with me or anything.'

'It was just lust,' joked Billy as Poppy flushed and they all laughed again. 'Anyway, I think he might have a thing for Verity. I've just seen them arrive together!' They all rushed over to the window and craned their necks to see, before realising that they might mess up their outfits. Then they demurely pretended they hadn't just been behaving like ten-year-olds.

Sasha turned to Poppy suddenly as she watched some more guests arrive and get out of parked cars. 'Devon's just got here. He drove with your dad. I didn't know they knew each other.' She frowned. 'I know we all love Devon, but how come he was such a late addition to your guest list?'

'Sasha!' scolded Demi again. 'That's none of our business.' She winked at Billy, who blushed.

'Is he your date, Billy?' Sasha turned to him, but he looked bemused.

'Ed's at the wedding, Sash. We all love Ed, even if his choices over the past couple of years have been questionable. I wouldn't do that to him,' said Billy, his face flushing. 'Plus, I'm not sure if I'm ready to date anyone new.'

'He's my brother,' blurted out Poppy suddenly, and the room went silent.

'What?' they all chorused, and everyone sat down in the nearest chair in shock.

'Devon is Glen's son,' explained Poppy, with a pained expression on her face. When no one else spoke, Poppy sipped the dregs of her drink and gazed out of the window. A member of staff tapped on the door and stuck their head round to tell them that the ceremony would be starting fairly soon and to check that they were all ready. Billy got up to say thanks and then rushed back to sit by Poppy's side, his face still a picture of shock.

'Why didn't you tell us?' he asked, clearly trying to mask the hurt in his voice. Sasha looked like her chest was constricting and she might pass out, so Poppy quickly poured her a glass of water from the crystal jug on one of the side tables. She sipped it gratefully.

'I haven't known for long. Glen introduced us recently, but of course we'd already met.'

'*That* was why he was so interested in you, and connected with me on social media?' asked Sasha. Poppy watched her eyes fill up with tears and she grabbed a tissue from a box on the desk to blot her eyes. 'Has our whole friendship been a lie?'

Poppy put her empty Champagne flute down and came over to take Sasha's hand. 'He's been watching my work for years, he knew who I was. I influenced his own choice of career, apparently. He struck up a conversation with you because he loved your timelines and sense of humour. My posts have always been pretty dry, which is why I employ you to post for me,' she soothed, pulling Sasha in for a hug, but then pulling away. 'I don't want to crease your dress,' she said gently, brushing the tears from her friend's cheeks and trying not to ruin her make-up.

'But I helped him get to you,' said Sasha sadly. 'Is that why he boosted my business too... so we'd be indebted to him?' Her bottom lip wobbled and her eyes filled with more tears. Her face crumpled and she cried for the loss of what she'd hoped was a true friendship. 'The whole thing was built on a tower of lies,' she said, mournfully. 'He's spent hours and hours at my flat asking questions about us all.'

Poppy could see her friend's heart was breaking and her own heart ached for her. The past few days had been a strain for Poppy. She knew Sasha cherished her friendship with Devon, they'd become close very quickly.

Poppy pulled Sasha into another hug and dried her tears with a tissue that Billy handed her. His own eyes were misted over and Demi looked upset too. 'It wasn't like that, Sash. He adores all of you. He didn't know how to approach me and decided ordering a light panel would be the best way, which was actually quite smart.' Poppy frowned at the protective streak she felt for her younger brother.

'Devon didn't know that he'd fall in love with my best friends or that his dad had finally plucked up the courage to reach out to me as well,' she soothed carefully, her stomach still tight with knots. 'Then it was a bit too late for him to tell me. Both he and Glen worried about how I'd react to the fact that Devon grew up with a mum and a dad, whereas I didn't.'

They all sat back in silence for a moment while they digested this news. Poppy smiled tightly as the manager of the hotel knocked and came into the room to check on the bride. Poppy indicated that everything was fine and she'd be down in a moment and then got up and went to the window. They all followed suit and watched the arrival of more guests outside in the glorious summer sunshine. Billy was white as a sheet.

'I really didn't want to have to tell you all today, but I only found out a few days ago myself and I'm still processing it all,' apologised Poppy, taking his hand.

'You seem remarkably calm, considering what you've just been through,' noted Demi, knocking back the last of her drink and pulling some make-up out of her handbag to repair Sasha's face.

'I don't have much choice... it's my wedding day,' Poppy tried to bring the mood back up with some light humour, but it failed miserably. Not even Demi was smiling.

'Does Dylan know?' asked Billy.

'He was there when I found out,' said Poppy with a sigh. 'I've got to get used to my husband being there for me.' This made them all smile finally and Poppy could see Sasha's fury start to thaw and the ends of her lips try to turn upwards.

'Does Ollie know?' she asked.

Poppy gave her a knowing smile and she blushed. 'No. Neither does Miles,' she looked at Demi.

'Why are you looking at me? I wasn't thinking of Miles,' frowned Demi, while the others pretended to be busy suddenly and began picking up things to take downstairs, as they could hear restless chatter from the hotel staff.

'I am sorry,' Poppy told them, beckoning them all into a group hug. 'I didn't know how to tell you without hurting you, so I can kind of understand how Devon felt.' She stood back and then kissed them all in turn. 'I learned a lot from my own behaviour last year. I don't ever want to lie to any of you. I know my wedding day isn't an ideal time to share something like this, but it's the first time we've all been together.' She handed them each a small gift-wrapped package and watched them discover a little silver heart with all their names inscribed together.

'I love you all and I already love my brother, which is a bonus because I always dreamed of a sibling to hold my hand. Especially as he's besotted with my best friend,' she winked at Billy and then laughed at Demi and Sasha's cross faces, before they all burst out laughing.

It felt good to dispel some tension and Poppy decided that her friends, especially fiery Sasha, would have to unpack their feelings later.

Today was about the amazing wedding they were about to attend and the gorgeous Taylor brother that she was going to become a lifelong partner to, she hoped. If Dylan didn't turn up at the altar, she'd go to the ends of the earth to find him.

She had a feeling that Sasha might now know that feeling a little too well and as for Demi, Poppy didn't think she was quite as immune to the Taylor charm as she imagined, either.

CHAPTER THIRTY-FIVE

*T*he wedding was a huge success. Sasha drank a few delicious cocktails and enjoyed dancing to the band she'd booked for the event. Her head was swimming a bit, but she was still alert enough to know she'd spent most of the time after the speeches checking that Poppy was enjoying every second of her day and then being swept onto the dance floor by Ollie, whose tie had been loosened and who looked devilishly handsome in his almost midnight blue best man's suit. His shirt was undone at the collar and she'd barely managed to restrain herself from licking his neck, he smelt so divine.

Now her shoes were hanging from her fingers and she'd begun to sober up. Poppy and Dylan had retired to their suite and Sasha was feeling the pain of working such long days whilst planning her best friend's wedding from the ground up. Her bones ached and although there were still quite a few revellers drinking in the bar area, she needed to change her shoes and rest for a minute or two on her bed.

Her head was a bit fuzzy but she couldn't work out what the receptionist was saying. Something about Mr Taylor's things being moved to her room and an unexpected guest. 'What unexpected guest?' she asked, wondering what Ollie was playing at. She jumped as a hand snaked around her shoulder and she turned to see Ben standing next to her, looking dashing but dishevelled after throwing some shapes on the dance floor.

Ben pulled her into his side and kissed the top of her head, making her sway towards him to keep her balance. 'I'll happily share a room with you if there's been a mix up,' he said smoothly, as Ollie appeared from the bar entrance and his eyes met hers. He looked at Ben who let his hand drop and moved away slightly. Ollie came up next to her and she could feel the heat from his gaze.

'Is there a problem?' he asked the receptionist, never taking his eyes off Sasha.

'I was just explaining that your things have been moved to Miss De Luca's room,' she nodded her heard towards Sasha. 'Due to an extra wedding guest. Mrs Taylor specifically requested it earlier today,' the young woman behind the desk said, her face flaming under Ollie's gaze, which was now directed at her. She handed him the key card that Sasha had been just about to collect.

'That's fine,' he said, suddenly jovial, so Sasha rolled her eyes. His arm wound around her waist to pull her close. 'Do you need anything, Ben?' he asked, suddenly solicitous.

Ben's eyes narrowed and he shrugged. 'I was just checking out my own sleeping arrangements, but it seems that your sister-in-law has organised me a room.'

'Aren't we both lucky that Poppy is so thoughtful?' said Ollie, pointedly, as Sasha noticed Maxine wander into the foyer and look around for Ben. Finding him, she grinned widely and then grabbed his hand to pull him back onto the dance floor. He winked at Sasha and let himself be led away, slinging an arm around Maxine's shoulders as they reached the door.

'We can't share a room,' said Sasha when Ben was out of earshot. Her head was still spinning at the idea. 'Don't look so smug,' she chided when Ollie didn't stop smiling. He'd been drinking all night too, but didn't seem too much the worse for wear. He'd clearly paced himself better than she had.

'Why can't we?' he asked innocently.

Demi walked past and headed for the stairs and Sasha caught her arm. 'What happened with my room?' she hissed under her breath. 'Ollie's in it!'

Demi giggled and wobbled a bit so Ollie helped her to reach the stairs. 'Poppy said you're the only people who could share and get her out of a tight spot with the rooms.'

'Why can't you give up your room?' asked Sasha petulantly.

'Allan's already in it!' laughed Demi. 'He was snoring for England last time I checked.'

Sasha frowned. 'He left you at the party on your own?'

'I do know everyone, and he doesn't,' said Demi, with a slight slur. 'Plus Allan hates things like this.'

'Weddings?' asked Ollie, with a frown, as he practically picked Demi up and carried her upstairs as Sasha trailed after them. He set Demi back on her feet and reached out for Sasha's hand, which she took reluctantly.

'He just isn't good with crowds of people, so he went to bed early,' explained Demi as they reached her room. She kissed them both goodnight and Sasha and Ollie walked on to her room, which was further up the hall. They stopped outside the door and stood staring at each other for a moment. Ollie pressed the card to the lock and the door opened, so he gently led her inside. His things had been hung up in the wardrobe and his toiletries were set out alongside hers in the bathroom.

Suddenly Sasha felt herself sober up and her skin felt hot and clammy. She'd fantasised about having Ollie in her bedroom for years and yet now he was actually there, she felt tongue-tied and could only look at him from under her lashes. His hair was a bit mussed up, his collar was undone and his tie was loose, making him look hot and sexy. She didn't often see him in a suit, even when he was running the gym, but the sight of him made her throat feel suddenly parched and she cleared it and moved to the window to shut the curtains. Ollie came up behind her and wound his arms around her, making her sigh and sink back into his embrace. He bent his head and trailed kisses along the back of her neck and she groaned and turned round to face him, her pupils dilated. His lips captured hers and his fingers reached into her hair to hold her to him. Her own hands slid around his back and into the top of his waistband, making contact with warm skin. He drew in a sharp breath and pulled away slightly, his arms linking behind her back to keep her close. His eyes were alight with passion and his lips plump from her kiss.

It had been a long day and although she had been feeling almost dead on her feet minutes earlier, she now felt truly alive in his arms. He brushed a stray curl out of her eyes and then turned her around. He kissed her gently on her shoulder and undid the back of her dress so that it slid to the ground in a pool of silk. She tried to repress the urge to hide herself as he turned her once again and his gaze feasted on her almost naked body. Fire lit in his eyes, but instead of making the mad passionate love to her that she'd dreamed about for years, he gave her one searing kiss and then picked her up and placed her gently into the bed and pulled the covers over her. Her head was still fuzzy but by the time she tried to think what had just happened her head hit the pillow and she fell into an exhausted, dreamless sleep.

~

Sasha was sure that the inside of her throat had been rubbed with sandpaper and her head ached like hell, but she also felt like she'd had the best night's sleep that she'd had for weeks. The wedding planning and being Ollie's date for last night had taken its toll on her nerves. He'd insisted on holding her hand from time to time and a few people had raised eyebrows and a couple had asked if they were together.

Obviously they had just been partnered to help Ollie get away from Maxine, but at the time it had almost felt real. That was why she'd drunk one too many glasses of Champagne and had clearly needed some sleep. Now she blinked a few times to try and wake up, but then felt someone move in the bed beside her and froze. The room was still dark, but it must be early morning, as she could just see a line of light forming around the edges of the window blinds and open curtains.

Suddenly a warm arm snaked around her and then settled on her waist under the covers, just below her naked breasts. She didn't dare move until his breathing regulated and she knew he was still asleep. She looked down and realised that there wasn't a wisp of clothing between them! Memories of Ollie having to share her room, and then kissing her, flooded her mind. She'd tried to pull him into bed, but he'd stopped her saying they'd both been drinking. Then he'd given her that searing kiss and had undressed her. Clearly he'd undressed too – but she'd fallen straight to sleep! She winced and tried not to wriggle. His hand was now cupped around her hip and her blood was starting to warm up for different reasons.

She turned her head slightly and couldn't help but take a slightly longer than was necessary peek at the very hot man in her bed! He'd clearly wanted to her to know what was to come and for his body to be imprinted on her mind so that she couldn't see anything else. It worked. Now she was wide awake. She groaned out loud and tried to move from under his arm, but he pulled her into his side and cuddled her into his chest in his sleep, so that her bottom snuggled into his groin, which wasn't as asleep as the rest of him.

Humiliation burned that he'd turned her down the night before, even though she knew he was attracted to her, but at least when she finally got out of bed she could run for her life and never see him again. She'd have to move town, or country, to be far enough away to be able to look at another man and not see Ollie Taylor naked and in her bed. Oh hell, it was embarrassing.

Before she could think further, Ollie's breath was in her ear and his hand was sliding up her side, to touch the skin right under her breasts. She gasped in shock and tried to move away, but he was already kissing his way down her neck and she could still feel his hard body pressed into her back.

Then his hands cupped her breasts and reached for her nipples and she closed her eyes in bliss before snapping them open again and wriggling round to face him, which seemed to make him happy as he immediately captured her lips with his.

Those same hands reached for her derriere and his mouth moved to her breasts, which was doing incredible things to her insides. Before she knew what she was doing, her own hands wound into his hair and she moaned and called his name so that his mouth kissed a trail to her own and he pulled her body into contact with his own so that she was in no doubt of his intentions.

He looked at her for a moment for a nod of consent, before grabbing a condom from beside the bed. He'd clearly left it there last night in the hope of today's events. Then he threw the covers aside with a flourish, making her shiver in anticipation. He dipped his head to explore every inch of her body, setting fire to her senses and pushing any other coherent thought out of her mind, other than the sensation of hot mouth on warm skin.

CHAPTER THIRTY-SIX

*S*asha woke again to sunlight streaming through the curtains. She stretched luxuriously and then grinned to herself at the gorgeous man in her bed, who had done incredible things to her body and left her in a state of sated bliss a few hours before. He was now fast asleep by her side but his leg was thrown over his edge of the covers. She took a moment to admire the firm lines of his backside before frowning and realising what this meant. They both knew, now, what the other looked like naked. She slipped out of bed and threw on a few clothes, pausing to make sure Ollie was still asleep, before picking up the key card and closing the hotel room door behind her.

She crept along the corridor and tapped on Demi's door, knowing she was an early bird whereas Allan slept like the dead. Within a few moments the door was opened and a ridiculously perky-looking Demi opened the door and eyed her dishevelled state up and down before grinning like she'd won the lottery. 'It worked, then,' she giggled as Sasha pulled a mean face and then threw her hands up in exasperation at her friend's obvious glee.

'It did not work!' seethed Sasha. 'Now I'll never be able to get over him,' she said through gritted teeth. 'I lusted after that man for years and the reality was even better than the fantasy. I'm ruined for another man for life! What the hell am I supposed to do now?' she hissed under her breath, not wanting to wake anyone else up to witness her misfortune. 'This is your fault.' Sasha pointed a finger straight at Demi's nose but her friend was still giggling behind her hand.

'Stop being so dramatic and go back to bed! You never surface at this hour normally, so why waste time when there's a sex god in your hotel room?'

Sasha stuck her nose in the air and sniffed, but actually she did quite like the sound of that idea. She flicked her hair over her shoulder and gave Demi one last glare, before turning back to her room.

'Invent a new way to get over a hangover,' laughed Demi at her retreating back.

Sasha didn't know why Demi wasn't taking this seriously, but hearts had been broken for less. She was right about not wasting a moment of being naked with Ollie, though, and Sasha's body was already tingling with anticipation. Perhaps her heart could withstand one more encounter with him. That man had some moves!

Sasha crept back to the room but Ollie was already up and showered, and was drying his wet body. Her mouth dropped open and her heart felt like it had stopped beating, he looked so delicious. But for some reason he wasn't smiling. 'You ran out, and then changed your mind?' he asked scathingly.

She frowned in confusion and felt adrenaline fill her body, ready for an argument. It was fighting against the powerful scent of freshly showered naked man.

'I wasn't running out,' she huffed, kind of liking sexy angry Ollie too. 'I just had to drop something to Demi's room for a second. But… now you've mentioned it, I'm not looking for something casual any more.' She hated the words as soon as they came out of her mouth, knowing he might leave.

'And I am?' he asked, his eyes boring into hers.

It was hard to concentrate when his towel kept slipping down on one hip and giving her tantalising glimpses of what was below. 'Um… I er… aren't you?'

'Sasha,' he said, and the tension seemed to dissipate from the air. He walked over and took her hand, leading her back to the bed, where he pulled her onto his lap. She squeaked in surprise as the towel mostly fell away, which was kind of hot!

He kissed her on the lips and then her neck and then her lips again, making her mind go to mush.

'I've been wanting this for as long as I can remember,' he said, picking up her hand and kissing his way up her arm to her chest where her top was askew as she'd rushed to dress. She sighed in pleasure and wriggled a bit on his lap to get comfortable, which made him draw in a sharp breath and hold her still.

'The only things that stopped me were waiting for us to both be single at the same time, or you working for me.' He said, as his eyes went dark and filled with lust as one of his fingers trailed a lazy line across her collar bone and then reached up to cradle the back of her neck and move her closer.

Her gaze moved down to his naked chest, which still had a trail of water running down from his wet hair. 'I'd have resigned if I'd have known about your policy about dating staff,' she said, suddenly unable to meet his gaze, but wanting to be honest. She flushed but let her own fingers follow the trail of water.

'I wish I'd told you sooner too,' he grinned, dipping down and capturing her lips with his as he undid the front of her top and slipped it over her shoulders, following a path to her breasts.

'I've got to go finish my bridesmaid duties,' she said lamely, while he laid her down on the bed with him and his hand trailed along her thigh and her own hands reached for him.

'I want you for breakfast,' he growled suddenly and she giggled and her hands slid around to cup his taut backside.

CHAPTER THIRTY-SEVEN

'Shall we tell everyone?' asked Ollie, kissing his way up her neck while she tried to put a top on while his hands were wandering under her freshly laundered shirt. She laughed and slapped his hands away.

'I have to go! I'll end up with creases,' she laughed. 'I'm useless at ironing and I had to bribe Demi to press this for me to wear today. I usually buy stretch to fit,' she joked with a wink, making him grin, but drop his hands finally.

'Do you want to tell everyone?' he asked again, serious now. Her heart ramped up and she fleetingly wondered if they could keep it to themselves for now, as everyone would have an opinion. Then she sighed at his earnest stare. She could see her response would mean something to him and she wanted to get it right. She was fed up with mixed signals. They were grown up enough to work out for themselves if this was a fling, or perhaps something more.

'Yes. I don't want to hide and I've learned the hard way from Poppy not to keep a Taylor brother romance a secret. Let's tell them when we're sure.'

He looked at her enquiringly. 'You're not sure?'

She gulped as she watched his eyes turn dark and stormy. She put her hand on his chest and could feel his heartbeat. 'Of course I am, but it's new and I didn't expect this to happen.'

It was his turn to raise an eyebrow in question and she flushed and smiled. 'Ok, I hoped it would. Especially after our conversation at the hen night, but we'd both been drinking and I wondered if you had beer goggles on.'

Ollie pulled her to him so that their hearts were beating next to each other and his arms were wound around her, making her almost swoon on the spot. Damn, this man knew how to melt a woman's resolve!

'I knew exactly what I was doing,' he growled and kissed her deeply so that she was certain of his meaning. She tried to draw in some extra air and put her hands on his chest to get some space between them before they ended up in bed again. If she hadn't promised Poppy that she'd be there to greet her guests for breakfast, then she'd have gladly dragged him there herself.

She grinned and cupped his face with her palm, like she'd dreamed of doing for years. 'Let's just enjoy this for today, then we can tell everyone and they can comment as much as they like.'

She went up on her tiptoes and kissed his lips briefly, then grabbed her key card and left the room before she changed her mind and led him into the shower again, like she had earlier that morning.

She closed the door behind her, with one more daring quick kiss in the doorway when Ollie had crossed the room to pull her back briefly before letting her go. She sighed and looked up as another door in the hotel corridor opened. Ben grinned wickedly as he saw her and she flushed, hoping that he hadn't seen her and Ollie. He was leaving Maxine's room, which was a few doors down from her own. Sasha had been in there the previous day to drop off a list of last minute jobs before the service.

Ben slung his arm around Sasha's shoulders as she walked past and he joked that they clearly both had a good ride, which made Sasha's blood boil and she threw his arm off her in irritation. She heard a gasp behind them and looked behind her. Maxine's flushed face was staring back at her from the door to her room.

Sasha felt sick as her eyes met Maxine's in a moment of understanding. Maxine held a finger up to her lips and shook her head to tell Sasha to stay quiet and not mention that Maxine had overheard Ben's crude comment.

Sasha turned back to his smug face in disgust. She wanted to slap his silly cheeks for being so insensitive, but that was for Maxine to sort out. Sasha stopped at the front desk in the guise of checking all their guests were ok, as a way to avoid going into the breakfast room with Ben. She sent a quick text to Demi to get her arse to Maxine's room to check she was ok.

After thirty hectic minutes of saying hello to all the guests and checking that Poppy and Dylan had all they needed, she tried not to react when Ollie arrived and sat down with his brothers and the bride. She felt his warm hand touch her leg briefly under the table and they locked eyes and grinned for a split second before she had to get up again to answer a question from a member of staff about the bill.

Then Demi and a very pale-looking Maxine arrived. Sasha winced as she looked at her friends, but Maxine's head was held high. Both she and Demi went to sit with Ben, who was chatting to Ed and Billy. Sasha hurried to join them in case war broke out over the croissants and jam spilled all over the table. Her stomach rumbled and she wondered if she could save one of the pastries before Maxine started hurling them at Ben's face.

They ordered hot drinks and Billy turned to Maxine with a smile, which faded when he clearly noticed how agitated she looked.

'Are you ok, Max?' he asked, reaching for her hand and frowning at Sasha quickly, who winced.

'I'm fine,' Maxine said carefully, her eyes not leaving Ben's, who suddenly didn't look so sure of himself. 'I overheard Ben bragging about us sleeping together last night and it's left me a bit bewildered,' she said loudly enough for the people on the next table to hear. They tried not to look too eager for any gossip from the aftermath of such a great party, but did lean their way slightly. Billy's eyes met Sasha's and she pulled a face and shook her head about him stepping in. All colour drained from Ben's face and his smile dropped away.

'I'm not ashamed. I'm a grown woman and can sleep with who I like,' she continued. 'But the bewildering part is what there was to brag about?' she finished triumphantly as Ben's face flamed and the group next to them sniggered into their napkins to try and hide their mirth.

Ben got up and came round to stand next to her. He put his hand on her shoulder, but she shook him off. Everyone on the next table had stopped talking now and Ollie got up and came and stood behind Sasha, who had also pushed her chair back and was trying to block Poppy's view of any impending arguments.

'I didn't mean to insult you,' Ben hissed under his breath to Maxine. 'I just meant that I'd had a really great evening.'

'And you decided to announce that to anyone in the corridor?' she asked, not giving an inch.

'I didn't know you were there,' he said woefully, his embarrassment showing on his face.

'Clearly,' said Maxine, her voice as cold as ice.

'I think it might be a good idea to let Maxine cool off and

give her some space,' said Sasha, glancing over her shoulder at Poppy, who was laughing at something her mum had said and hadn't noticed the altercation.

'I'll give you a call later in the week,' said Ben, his confident smile firmly back on his face.

'You might find that her number's changed, though,' said Demi helpfully and Ed snorted into his coffee cup. Ben's smile dropped and he closed his eyes for a second before he said sorry to Maxine again and quietly left the room.

'Right, everyone,' said Maxine brightly. 'I'm exhausted from wasting my energy on that idiot. Who is going to get me a full English breakfast?'

Ollie grinned and his hand brushed Sasha's back briefly. 'Breakfast is on me,' he joked as he turned and wandered over to the free buffet that had been laid out.

Sasha finally felt the anxious knot of tension dissipate and breathed in the delicious scents of fresh toast and crispy bacon. Her stomach rumbled again and she leant in to hug Maxine with pride in her voice. 'You rocked it!' she laughed. 'Are you really going to ignore his calls?'

'I haven't decided yet,' Maxine laughed back. 'But I'm definitely feeling a lot better about it than I did an hour ago. It depends on how much grovelling he does and if he means it when he says he's sorry. We did actually have a great night, but he needs to learn how to treat a lady. Bragging isn't attractive.'

'Too right,' echoed Ed and Billy. Sasha enjoyed seeing them together, but wondered if Billy had changed his mind about Devon after Poppy's revelation that they were siblings. Sasha's own siblings drove her bonkers with their squabbling, but she loved them dearly. Devon and Poppy would have to work out a whole new dynamic to their relationship, but if anyone could do that, it was her incredible best friend.

She heard Ollie laugh at something Miles said and looked

his way. Her heart began to beat faster every time she saw him and now she could picture him naked, she would be constantly walking around grinning like she'd won the lottery. She wanted the world to know how much he meant to her. They were both feeling a bit vulnerable about their new 'relationship' or whatever it was, but now that she had him firmly ensconced in her life, she intended to keep him there for as long as she could.

CHAPTER THIRTY-EIGHT

*S*asha noticed the time on her phone as she picked it up to scroll her social feeds. She'd been daydreaming about Ollie again and not concentrating on her work. She looked at a couple of photos of them both together and grinned to herself. She got up from her desk and opened a window. It was a warm summer's day and she adored the scent of flowers mixed with sunshine that filtered in from outside at this time of year. The sky was a beautiful shade of bright blue and only a few dainty clouds sauntered by, when they could be bothered.

Her online timelines were doing well and she now had a very healthy following. Her posts were shared everywhere. She'd opened an account for a hot new online application that everyone was talking about and really enjoyed being in front of the camera making fresh and exciting videos each day. She found coming up with original content surprisingly easy, but she guessed that her job and surroundings helped. They had a whole host of glamorous parties and events to attend, and it literally took a few seconds to record a new post.

The office was running smoothly without Poppy and Dylan while they were on their honeymoon. Sasha sent Poppy one daily message with a rundown of everything they were covering, but only included a list of completed tasks, so that the happy couple could relax and enjoy their time together on the tropical island they'd flown to.

It sounded like they were having an incredible time. Dylan had pulled out all the stops to make his wife happy. They weren't just sitting on a beach, although it was a stunning resort that looked like paradise with its palm trees and infinity pool. Dylan knew his new bride loved anything creative and had booked them into trips to see local artists, craftspeople and galleries.

Sasha had posted a few of their images on social media and was already thinking of ways to write blogs for their website about how doing what you love can bring such joy to your life. She adored her new role and was excited to think about her own network of influencers which was slowly growing. She could offer her new customers complete packages of marketing ideas, but also posts on how those products would benefit their own client base through her influencer strategy. The changes her ideas had brought to her own life over the past year were testament to small differences leading to great rewards.

Ollie was a lot happier since their night at the wedding and he popped to her flat most evenings after work. She smiled at the memory of him running a deep bath filled with rose petals for them both after a long day at work and then insisting on drying every inch of her body personally. The man was insatiable! Not that she was complaining. She barely went to the gym now she had Ollie in her bedroom. His workouts left her muscles worn out but zinging and full of wanton lust for more.

Miles was about to move in with him, so he'd be busy for

the next few days. They still hadn't officially told anyone they were dating, but she felt that it was pretty obvious by the way she wasn't growling about him and by how many times he dropped by to 'borrow milk', she sniggered. Billy just shook his head at their antics, but he seemed to be in his own little love bubble since Ed had returned home and they had said their final goodbyes. Ed had dramatically pleaded with Billy again for a second chance before he travelled home, after seeing him with Devon at the wedding, but it was too late, sadly. Billy and Devon were both smitten.

Devon stuck his head around her office door and she beckoned him inside. 'You free for lunch?' he asked brightly.

They hadn't seen each other to talk seriously at the wedding, but he had taken her aside and apologised for not telling her about his connection to Poppy sooner. She wasn't quite sure how she felt about him now, but it wasn't like he was going away anytime soon, so she needed to clarify if there was a friendship to be salvaged at all from this mess. She checked her online calendar and then saw Billy leaning back in his chair in his office and egging her on to go, suggesting she should leave with a nod of his head. She harrumphed and wanted to sulk, but if she said no she'd seem churlish. She grabbed her bag and chucked her phone inside, before pushing back her chair dramatically and sticking her tongue out at Billy, who grinned and blew them both a kiss.

'Where do you want to go?' she asked, as she followed Devon out into the bright sunshine and felt a wave of heat brush over her skin and make her draw in a breath of calm. She'd been dreading this meeting and had been hoping it would just sort itself out at some point. For someone who was usually very upfront with her opinions, she was now wary about what she said or how she behaved around Devon, when before it had been the most natural thing in the world.

'The pub?' he suggested as he took her hand and led her up the hill along the line of cherry trees. She looked at their interlinked hands and her stomach crunched, then she sighed and followed him to The Cherry Tree, whose garden was overflowing with vibrant flowers tumbling from window boxes and brightening up the hedges.

Sasha tried not to be stroppy, but she really felt like sulking for a long while yet. Devon led her to a wooden table in the back garden of the pub with a deep blue branded parasol, and then went to grab their usual food order, which gave her a moment to catch her breath. When he returned with two huge glasses of rich red wine, she sipped hers gratefully and waited silently, so he knew something was drastically wrong.

Devon hung his head. 'I'm sorry.'

Sasha waited to see what else he'd say, but was itching to butt in and remonstrate over his recent actions.

'I'd been trying to think of a way to contact Poppy for years,' he said finally, 'but I still didn't think it would happen after you connected with me. I'd seen your timelines and laughed at your posts – they're so entertaining, Sash. It was only once I felt that I knew you a bit through social media and I thought we'd get on, regardless of my sister, that I agreed to meet. When we did become friends, in a way it made things even more complicated because I cared about you as well.' His fingers played with the stem of the wine glass and a small dog came over and sniffed his shoe, which made him smile and reach out to stroke her soft fur, before she was recalled with a sharp whistle by her owner.

'You should have told me at the start,' she grumbled, looking at him angrily over the rim of her wine glass, wishing the dog was still there as a distraction.

'I didn't know how,' said Devon honestly. 'I was desperate to meet Poppy, but didn't know I'd find a best friend too.'

Sasha looked up sharply to see if he was lying to her face, but his forehead had frown lines and he appeared quite distressed. A few people were looking their way, which always happened when Devon was around and even the dog's owner was grinning and talking animatedly to her friend, possibly about her dog meeting someone famous, which finally made Sasha grin and forget her woes for a split second.

Sasha let her hair fall over part of her face so that he couldn't see her turbulent expression, but he gently brushed it aside and lifted her chin. 'Can you forgive me?'

Sasha chewed on the inside of her lip for a moment, then sniffed and took another sip of her wine. 'I suppose so,' she said finally as relief filled Devon's face and he scooted round to bring her in for a big squashy hug. He kissed her cheek and hugged her again, just as Jared came into the garden and looked around. When he spotted them he beamed and headed their way. Sasha scowled.

'Has he upset you as well?' asked Devon, getting up to shake Jared's hand as he approached.

'No,' she sighed dramatically, 'but whenever he's around my workflow gets messed up and I have to spend days re-organising everyone's calendars.' She got up and let Jared hug her in welcome, but he laughed at her not-so-welcoming grimace.

'I come in peace,' he said, placing his glass of wine next to hers and then holding his hands up in surrender. Sasha grinned finally and they all turned as their panini order arrived. Sasha noted that Jared had managed to add an extra sandwich for himself quick-smart and vowed to ask him about that skill.

'Have you two made up?' he asked glancing between them. Devon looked at her hopefully.

'I guess so,' was all she said before picking up her lunch

and biting a huge chunk off, savouring the flavour. She was suddenly ravenous. The boys clinked glasses in celebration and then tucked in as well. They took a moment to enjoy the delicious fillings of slow roasted tomatoes and thick mature cheese with homemade pickles, produced in the pub kitchen.

Jared put the remainder of his lunch back on his plate and stared at Sasha, sipping his wine. 'Spill,' was all she said, trying to remember he was their biggest client as well as a friend. He put his glass down slowly, clearly considering his words carefully, meaning he was serious about whatever he was on the verge of saying.

'I've been hearing about the success of your social media campaigns, and as you know I'm a fan of your work.' Sasha's eyebrows shot up as she hadn't known this. 'I'd like you to come on board with my next building project.'

Sasha squeaked in shock and took a huge gulp of wine, gasping as it burnt the back of her throat.

'How would that work?' she asked. 'I've got my own company now and I already work part-time for Poppy.' Her mind was whizzing with possibilities, and she couldn't help the light of excitement that was shining from her.

'I thought I could become a client, like Ollie is, or maybe your brand could come under the umbrella of my parent company? It's something we'd need to discuss at length, and not over an admittedly delicious panini, or while the girl from that table over there is weirdly throwing titbits of food this way for her dog,' he joked, as they all turned to see the woman blush at being caught trying to snag Devon's attention again. 'I just wanted you to think about it before you get too busy with other clients,' said Jared, his voice animated.

They both looked up as Ollie approached with a beer in his hand. Sasha had texted asking him to join her and Devon, as she'd been worried about a confrontation and thought he might ease the way. Now she flinched and wished she'd done her usual thing of dealing with things on her own. She'd been trying to consider Ollie more, but putting him and Jared together for too long was never a good idea.

Jared got up to leave as Ollie drew closer. Jared shook his hand as he reached their table and then gave Sasha another warm hug, which she knew would put Ollie's teeth on edge, even though he was still smiling.

'If you come to my office,' said Jared, 'we can go over the small print and decide how us working together more often can fit into our diaries.' He went round to shake Devon's hand and then left them all at the table, mouths agog, the dog now sitting on Devon's lap.

'You're working together?' asked Ollie before he'd even sat down or said hello, which immediately made her hackles rise.

'He's just mentioned it and Sasha's thinking about it,' said Devon helpfully, setting the dog back on the ground and waving to her owner who giggled and blew him a kiss.

Ollie nodded and sat down next to Sasha, putting his hand on her leg and leaning in to kiss her on the lips. This made her jump as they still hadn't told anyone publicly about them, and even she wasn't sure if they were a couple or just casually dating. Ollie frowned and then shrugged and drank a mouthful of his beer as he watched Jared's retreating back.

'You've been photographed out with Jared a lot lately,' commented Ollie, making Devon excuse himself to go and pay the bill before they headed back. He put a hand on Sasha's shoulder as he passed and winked at her as she gazed forlornly after him.

She bit her lip and stared at Ollie, her skin fizzing just through her knee touching his. 'I'm trying to build my own brand. You know what that's like, after the success of your place.'

Ollie put his arm around her and snuggled her in close. 'I

know. Working with Jared's a great idea.' When she looked sceptical, he hugged her close. 'Really. I'm proud of you, even though we're usually too busy tearing each other's clothes off to talk seriously.'

She flushed and he kissed her nose and then her mouth again, for a little longer than he probably should in public and when they were so hot for each other.

'I want everyone to know we're together. Why haven't we told anyone?' He said, leaning back and taking a photo of them both with the beautiful tree-lined hedge behind them.

She smiled and looked at the image. 'We look like a couple.'

'We are a couple,' he said firmly.

'Are we?' she asked, butterflies suddenly taking wings in her stomach.

'I think so. It's what I want, if you do?'

'So we're going official? Dating? Boyfriend and girlfriend?'

'Yes.' He dipped his head for one more kiss as Devon returned and coughed loudly, grinning down at them before slapping Ollie on the back and helping Sasha to get up.

'Finally!' laughed Devon. 'I'm new round here and even I can see that you two are made for each other.'

Sasha laughed and kissed his cheek as they walked out of the pub together.

'All we need to do now is to find out what exactly is going on with you and our beautiful Billy!' she chortled, enjoying Devon's flushed cheeks as he suddenly seemed quite keen to drop her back at the office.

CHAPTER THIRTY-NINE

*P*oppy was looking glowing and relaxed, with a deep suntan and a permanent secret smile on her lips after her honeymoon. Sasha had one too, and Billy knocked his hip with hers to wake her out of her daze. 'Whatever it is those Taylor brothers have, I want some!' he joked, handing Sasha a mug of hot chocolate and Poppy a coffee.

'You don't need anything. You've got Devon,' quipped Sasha, inhaling the heavenly scent of the rich dark chocolate and taking a sip in bliss.

'I saw that Jared came in earlier, when I looked in the diary,' said Poppy. 'Please tell me that he hasn't made more changes to our latest build project?'

Billy and Sasha exchanged glances and he excused himself as he suddenly had a call he absolutely had to make in the next ten minutes. Poppy frowned and stared after his retreating back before looking at Sasha with a question in her eyes. 'Want to tell me what all that was about?'

Sasha led Poppy to the little terrace outside and sat down, waiting for her friend to follow suit.

'This seems serious,' said Poppy, her voice showing her concern. Did something happen while I was on my honeymoon?'

Sasha fiddled with the handle of her hot chocolate mug and stalled for a moment. 'Jared wants me to work with him.'

Poppy's mouth fell open before she snapped it back shut and narrowed her eyes.

'Of course he does! The git,' she laughed, breaking the tension and making Sasha feel like her chest was less constricted. She hadn't been sure how to broach the subject with Poppy, and Billy had been no help whatsoever. He'd just said they'd hate to lose her and given her a hug of congratulations.

'Jared always has his eye on the ball with up and coming talent,' said Poppy. 'It's how he found me. I shouldn't be surprised because I was half-expecting it.'

'Jared already has an internet team, but he loves what I'm doing for this brand with you, and he wants me to look at some of his newer projects. This could be an incredible opportunity for me, but I don't have your business experience in how to handle him. He's a bit overwhelming,' Sasha sighed.

Poppy grinned. 'He does have a magnetic personality,' she teased. 'Plus those big sexy eyes?' she batted her own eyelashes at Sasha in jest.

'I'm dating Ollie,' said Sasha quietly.

Immediately, Poppy jumped up and rushed to hug her.

'Sasha! That's the best news ever! Officially?'

'Yes,' she grinned. 'Officially.'

'Since when?'

'Since a few days ago. It was your fault.'

'My fault?' asked Poppy innocently, suddenly finding a speck of dust on her top and focussing on that.

'The hotel room mix up at your wedding?'

'Um… Oh that… Such a tricky dilemma, organising guests,' she giggled suddenly.

'Jared loves winding Ollie up,' said Sasha, shaking her head. 'If Ollie is anywhere near, he cuddles me a fraction too long. I used to love it, as it definitely made Ollie jealous, but how can I work with him?'

Poppy sat down opposite her friend again. 'Show Jared your boundaries. He probably does it because it's clear to everyone how much you like Ollie and Jared is very protective of us all, however much he jokes and flirts. He's showing Ollie that other men are interested if he's not.'

'He's trying to help me?' asked Sasha in surprise, her mind rethinking most of her meetings with Jared.

'Well, he does love cuddles and winding the Taylor brothers up, but more than that, he looks out for his friends. Once he knows you're serious with Ollie, he'll step back. He's great fun to work with and a whole new world can open up with his contacts.'

'I quite like it when Ollie's the teeniest bit jealous,' admitted Sasha, before they both started giggling like schoolgirls.

'Let's talk through what Jared has offered you and see how it can work with the rest of us, if that's what you decide,' said Poppy. 'I'd hate to lose you, but you've got to follow your own path.'

Sasha got up and gave Poppy a big hug, before going back to her office and opening a drawer and pulling out two A4 writing pads she'd stored there just in case this happened. Poppy laughed, and her sunkissed hair swung round her face, making her look even more beautiful and happy.

'Ever the organiser,' she joked, drawing a line down the middle of the sheet and writing pros and cons on either side, to get them started on deciding what would work best.

CHAPTER FORTY

*S*asha woke up in her gorgeous flat and took stock. Today was her birthday and her stomach was full of excited butterflies. It was her first birthday in ages with an official boyfriend, and now she was a fully-fledged business owner in charge of her own destiny too. It felt good to be exactly where she was in her life. She still felt a tad unsure of how secure her relationship with Ollie was, but her feelings for him were growing daily, which scared the living daylights out of her at times. She was trying to overcome her fears and live in the moment, and that was what she intended to do today.

She looked at her phone and scrolled through a few messages. She'd hoped for a few more, considering her new career, but it was still only 9am. She needed to get up and get ready to go and have coffee and cake with all her noisy family back home. Then there was going to be a relaxing dinner later with her friends from Cherry Blossom Lane. Poppy had told her that she'd booked a table at the Italian restaurant and that there would be ten of them, including Jared and Ollie!

The previous day, she'd sat with Poppy for hours, planning away. In the end Billy had come and joined them and they'd ordered pizza. They'd run through how she could manage her new clients, plus work for Poppy, and have a big client like Jared. Sasha didn't want to rely on him entirely. She needed diversity, and in the end she'd decided to offer to run two of his new campaigns to test the water and make sure he was happy with her ideas. She could still work for Ollie, which was crucial as with their hectic schedules this was precious time they got to spend alone. It often involved her sitting on his lap and having long smooches during their lunch hour. They'd actually spoken about him staying over at the flat a few nights a week, instead of him travelling home after they'd eaten together or slid between her sheets. Her body craved him constantly and she wondered if she was falling deeply in love with the man she'd fantasised about for years.

She responded to the few messages on her phone and ran herself a fragrant bath, scattering in some heavenly scented rose petals and inhaling the heady aroma as the tub filled. She picked out two outfits from her wardrobe, one for the family gathering that was comfortable to travel in, and then a knockout red dress and gold dangly earrings that caught the light for later. She imagined Ollie unzipping the dress and licked her lips before sighing, wondering if she pretty much filled his every waking thought, too.

Flicking on the kettle for a quick cup of hot chocolate, then testing the bath water to make sure the temperature was perfect, she placed her drink on the side and wondered how she'd feel sitting at a meal with her friends and her boyfriend. She wasn't quite ready for him to accompany her home to meet her mum and dad, but as they'd all grown up together, she was pretty silly to be holding off. She knew they liked him and he adored all her sisters, even when they had given him grief for not paying her enough attention. At least she now knew why – he was just so busy! His business ethos meant they had taken a long time to get together, but Ollie was certainly worth the wait! She knew that she was the one that he wanted, and he was certainly all she'd ever dreamed he could be.

$\sim$

*S*asha took one last look at her phone as she slid into her new red dress. She styled her hair with two clips at the sides so it hung in curls down her back. Then she spritzed herself with her favourite sultry perfume, and enjoyed the scent of sandalwood and rose that filled her senses. She'd received a huge bouquet of flowers from Ollie, and a delicate gold bracelet with two entwined hearts on it. The bouquet was adding to the lovely aroma in the room. He'd also sent her a text saying her was looking forward to seeing her that evening, which made her shiver in anticipation.

She felt an undercurrent of nerves about Ollie and Jared being in the same room, though Poppy had assured her that Jared would behave now that he knew she was dating Ollie. She glanced at her quiet social media feeds one more time before shrugging and grabbing her handbag and keys. It was only a short stroll into town, where everyone was meeting her at the restaurant. She was tired from a day with her family, but it had been heart-warming to hug them all and see how well they were doing without her watching over them. She did miss them. It was far quieter in the flat without her sisters, but she needed her own space. They had all come round to her decision now, and were happy for her. They hadn't even told her off when she'd announced who her new boyfriend was. It had been the opposite, in fact.

They'd all chatted at once about how much they loved Ollie now he'd 'come to his senses… at last' and 'seen what they'd all seen for years', apparently. Perhaps she wouldn't be quite as scared to bring him home with her next time?

She jumped as someone came out of the shadows. He'd been leaning on the wall waiting for her, a lightweight jacket slung over his shoulder. She tried to regulate her breathing, but the sight of Ollie never ceased to make her heart beat faster. He grinned at her and walked her way.

'Did I scare you? Sorry.' He leaned in and pulled her into his arms, his lips meeting hers and making her groan as he moulded her body to his.

When they eventually parted, she tried to still her beating heart and the rampant hormones flooding her veins. She looked up at him and smiled, before snuggling under his arm as they strolled into town. 'I thought I was meeting you there?'

'I couldn't wait that long,' he said, cheekily, stealing another swift kiss. 'I haven't seen you alone for days and Jared's going to be there tonight, so I wanted to get you on my own before he starts trying to wind me up,' he grinned.

She glanced at him, but his smile was genuine and she could see he was joking. She loved the feel of his arm around her shoulder as they walked. She paused for a moment.

'He knows about us now. I've told him that if we're going to be working together, he's got to cut out the extra-long hugs.'

Ollie started in surprise, but his grin widened. 'You told him that you're my girlfriend?'

'I told everyone,' she said with a grin, butterflies taking flight again in case she'd read the situation wrongly. But he swooped down for another kiss and picked her up so that her feet left the floor as he swung her around. When they separated this time she felt breathless and giddy.

'You approve?'

'Of course! I'd already told all my friends so you couldn't change your mind.' He laughed and she swatted his backside as he tried to jump out of the way. He pulled her into his arms for a reassuring cuddle as they reached the restaurant and then they both took a steadying breath and they headed inside, hand in hand.

~

*S*asha's dinner was in the side room reserved for private functions, and she stopped in awe on the threshold when she saw how beautifully it had been decorated.

There was one long table in the centre of the room, draped with a pristine white tablecloth. In the middle were small intricately designed grey ceramic urns, overflowing with flowers and greenery, interspersed with candles. Their gentle light flickered off the sparkling wine glasses and reflected around the room.

Once she'd greeted her waiting friends, Ollie pulled out a chair at the head of the table for her. She was warmed to see all her favourite people. In front of her was a pile of beautifully wrapped gifts. She took her time opening them and sighing over everyone's thoughtfulness as the first course, bruschetta with marinated tomato, was brought in and handed round, making her stomach rumble as it smelt delicious. Sasha's heart filled with love for these people. Chatter soon filled the air as the main courses arrived, and they all tucked in to heaving plates of carbonara and huge plump pizzas.

As the plates were cleared away, Sasha sipped her wine thoughtfully. She'd noticed a projector screen on the back wall earlier and she wondered if they held some kind of classes or seminars there during the day. Ideas began ticking through her mind about how any of her clients could use the space for functions. Then Ollie gently touched her arm as the screen sprang to life. Sasha jumped out of her daydream and then frowned. 'What's this?'

'It was Ollie's idea,' said Poppy with a grin, reaching out to hold her hand. 'Jared and Devon helped too,' she added with a wink.

Sasha's jaw dropped. Ollie had worked with Jared? He grinned and leaned in to kiss her briefly on the lips, making everyone smile.

'Happy birthday, Sasha,' he said with love in his eyes, and they all turned to the screen.

Images of Sasha with other people started filling the screen and she was stunned to silence. Her phone started dinging with notifications and she didn't know where to look first. She glanced at her phone and saw that the same posts were currently going live on social media.

Many of the faces on the projector screen were famous people who she'd met through networking or at parties, or through her friends. She couldn't believe what she was seeing. Her account was literally blowing up with posts, and the hashtag #SashasBirthday was trending. People she didn't know were seeing the posts on other people's timelines and were jumping on to say happy birthday too. It was a chain reaction, and the screen filled with images over and over again, until the last image said #SashasBirthday, happy birthday Sasha, from everyone who loves you.

Tears filled Sasha's eyes. She felt choked up with emotion and didn't know what to say, other than thank you, but she couldn't get the words out. She got up and hugged and kissed everyone more than once until Poppy touched her arm and handed her a glass of Champagne, and they all toasted to her birthday and her success.

Then Ollie took her hand and led her outside to catch her breath. 'We've got to stop meeting like this,' he joked, pulling her in close and slipping his jacket over her shoulders.

She kissed him with all the love and longing she felt, and it took a while for them to come up for air as he matched her passion for passion.

'Thank you,' she said, when they finally parted. 'No one's ever done anything like that for me before.'

Ollie kissed her nose and hugged her close. 'You deserve it. Everyone loves you and it's about time you realised how much.'

Sasha felt like she stopped breathing as she looked up at the man she loved. 'Even you?'

'Especially me,' he growled as he kissed her again.

'This must all have taken you ages,' she sighed happily. Her phone dinged and she frowned and looked at the screen. There were some photos there that Poppy had promised to send her from the hen night. She must have just remembered. Sasha noticed Demi and Miles in the background of one. They had their heads bent closely together. Sasha and Ollie looked at each other and smiled conspiratorially. 'Do you think they know? she asked him.

'He does... she doesn't,' he said simply. 'I'm not sure we should interfere?'

'They did, with us and the wedding rooms,' she protested.

'You're right. Maybe with a bit of meddling from us, Demi will see that he's the one that she wants?'

Sasha grinned and she leaned in and kissed her man one more time, troublesome friends forgotten... for now.

ABOUT THE AUTHOR

International bestselling author and award-winning inventor, Lizzie Chantree, discovered her love of writing fiction when her children were little. She now writes books full of friendship and laughter, that are about women who are far stronger than they realise. She lives with her family on the coast in Essex. Visit her website at www.lizziechantree.com or follow her on Twitter @Lizzie_Chantree

For more writing news, subscribe to my newsletter: www.lizziechantree.com

I really hope you enjoyed reading The One That He Wants, Book 2 of The Cherry Blossom Lane Series. Book 3 will be available soon!

If you liked reading my novel, please consider leaving a review. Many readers look to the reviews first when deciding which book to choose, and seeing your review might help them discover this one. I appreciate your help and support. Make an author smile today. Leave a review! Thank you so much. From Lizzie :)

facebook.com/LizzieChantree

twitter.com/Lizzie_Chantree

instagram.com/lizzie_chantree

PRAISE FOR LIZZIE CHANTREE

'Books like this are the reason I love reading.'

'I'm happy to read that this is the first of a series of three books and I will be first in line for the next one when it's published.'

'After reading this wonderful book, I am now very much looking forward to the next instalments.'

'A bunch of lovely, well-told characters with just the right amount of humour thrown in too. This book will keep you turning pages until you reach the last one and then leave you looking for another novel by this author.'

'Chantree has a way of creating an intriguing and seemingly innocent plot that slowly draws you in and all of your emotions are set afire.'

'Take a few scoops of family drama, drizzle it with some hot men, scatter some sprinkles of misunderstandings along with a wafer of romance, and you get Lizzie Chantree's new novel, The Little Ice Cream Shop By The Sea. I really enjoyed reading this and devoured it in a day!'

'Well, what can I say about this book? It's gorgeous, clever, surprising and enthralling.'

'If you haven't had the pleasure of reading one of Lizzie's books yet - treat yourself!'

'If this was a TV play I would have been shouting at the telly and weeping 'discreetly' – I loved it – a tormented family where each family member has a story – SUBLIME – 5 stars.'

THE LITTLE ICE CREAM SHOP BY THE SEA

Escape with an uplifting, feel-good romance, set by a sun-drenched beach.

CHAPTER 1

Not again! Genie Grayson wanted to scream and throw her hands in the air. Instead, she stuffed her fist in her mouth and turned away. She'd thought she had her terrible phobia under control – she was a perfectly sane twenty-two-year-old – but the last few weeks had been stressful, and this was her Achilles heel. She looked around furtively to see if anyone had noticed, but there was hardly anyone enjoying breakfast in her family's seafront restaurant.

The evil seagull had dropped a lump of cheese onto her pristine outdoor tablecloth. After flying right into the restaurant awning. It had obviously been at the beer that always ended up in the gutters after a busy night at one of the clubs further down the beach.

Genie rarely admitted to having this issue, as who in the world, other than herself of course, had a problem with cheese? No one who managed a restaurant and ice cream parlour, that was for sure. Not a responsible professional who served food all day and had to be surrounded by the awful stretchy stuff that smelt like her grandad's old socks after a day on his feet.

She knew if she recited the alphabet backwards she'd be ok. She'd had years of practice. She usually got to about W, and then her pulse slowed down and she was able to take a deep breath and move on. She looked up and saw the gull sitting on the wall above the restaurant, its piercing red eyes like lasers. She shushed it away, but it just turned its back on her.

She often wondered if she had an allergy to wild animals. She'd tried to pet one at a zoo on a school trip and got bitten, then her hand had swollen up and she'd been rushed to hospital, even though she'd been fine after a few hours. She'd avoided zoos ever since. She gave the jungle a wide berth too. It wasn't too difficult from her current location on the coast of Essex, but she wasn't taking any chances. Cheese, on the other hand, was impossible to dodge. Not only did she work in kitchens, she cooked when her dad had a day off. Luckily, their bestsellers were their huge breakfasts, and plates of fish and chips.

Genie knew that if she gave into the urge to shove the offending messy table into the road, she'd get herself into all kinds of trouble with her parents, and probably the local council. She was already on their radar for changing all the restaurant's lightbulbs to a deep shade of red one weekend, to create an ambience. She'd had a formal letter the following week suggesting she might be moonlighting as a sex worker. That was slander! She might be a bit busty, and she was down on her luck, but she was too tired to blink some days. She just plastered on a smile and worked through it. Takings really had to pick up, at the restaurant though. They needed more customers.

She had to find a way to calm down and reasonably work out a plan of action, either by talking to her mum, Milly, about their current dilemma, or by finding a boyfriend and having some hot steamy sex to take her mind off things.

While she pondered that thought, she grabbed the tablecloth by the edges with a couple of forks and shoved it behind the counter into the washing basket, quickly re-covering the table with a fresh cloth.

Genie smiled brightly at two school mums who were perusing the menu but her grin dropped as she turned towards the kitchen at the back of the little restaurant. She wondered if anyone would notice if she stood in the middle of the room and screamed. Probably not.

The mums were the only two customers, and they'd already caught her cursing in Spanish under her breath as she wiped down the tables when they'd arrived. They had looked at her in confusion. She'd picked up a 'learn to speak Spanish' course at the charity shop the week previously, in the hope that she might one day travel abroad with friends. She'd also thought it might help if they ever got a foreign customer, however unlikely that seemed. But when she'd got the disc back to the house, it was a home-made knock-off copy and the only vocabulary was swear-words. She hated being conned, so she'd resolutely learned the whole tape, which consisted of about fifty phrases that all sounded mightily dodgy. They were great for easing frustration, though, as no one else knew what she was saying. She hoped. She'd looked up a few of the words, but then been worried her parents would question why she was Google-translating so many profanities. She didn't want them to start to wonder if that council letter had been spot on.

Usually, the breathtaking panorama of sandy beaches and the endless skyline across the road were enough to lift her spirits. But today she felt she might as well go and bang her head against a wall, instead of trying yet again to reason with her parents. The family business *had* to be brought into the twenty-first century. She knew she had a temper and didn't always explain things clearly without combusting into flames, but they still treated her as if she was nine years old.

All she was asking of her parents was that they let her try out a few new business ideas and a handful of new ice-cream flavours. She didn't want to reinvent the wheel. Their business hadn't changed for decades. They still had the same chairs and tables, and even the menus, that her grandad Gus had installed. Her parents' restaurant, Graysons', offered bought-in, basic puddings, but Genie had seen massive growth in big gooey ice cream desserts presented in glass mugs or tall glasses. She didn't see why they couldn't try this. They had a prime site on the seafront, for goodness sake! She could feel her temper begin to rise again. Then she remembered – their customers. She didn't want to scare them away. She twirled round to face them again with another smile.

Her parents were worried about upsetting her grandad, who ran the ice cream bar. He only offered about six flavours these days. She had spent much of her time with him and her grandma when she was growing up. Her parents had stepped in to take over the business when her grandma had died a few years previously. Her grandad had begun wandering around the small garden at the back of the restaurant and shouting at the plants, raging at the loss of his wife. In the end, they'd explained to customers that he was an inventor seeing if upsetting plants stunted their growth. It was the only explanation they could come up with for his behaviour, which was becoming more and more erratic.

Their regulars knew about Genie's grandma and understood Gus's sorrow and anger, but occasionally a new customer would start to glance around to see if there were spaces to eat elsewhere, which meant even less income for them all. Genie missed her grandma Vera terribly, as she had always let her sit with them after school. Genie would perch on a high stool behind the ice cream counter and Vera would tempt her with her latest ice cream concoction and cuddle her, while Gus served a steady stream of customers anxious to get Vera's new flavours before they sold out.

With Genie's parents selling breakfasts and lunches, and Gus and Vera on ice cream, the restaurant had worked like a dream. Then her grandma died and Genie's parents had taken the reins, working harder than ever to cover their grief. They looked more frazzled as each year passed. Genie was used to coming home from school to the empty house they lived in, up the hill, as her parents were always working. Soon, she was roped into doing her homework at the restaurant, and then it seemed a natural progression for her to help out. She'd been doing that since she could walk anyway. She loved the restaurant and was proud of her family's heritage. She needed to spread her creative wings, though, and felt that since Vera had passed away, Gus was wilting. She wanted to keep her grandma's spirit alive, and Gus needed Genie more than her parents did right now.

She spent her weekend evenings making batches of ice cream for him to sell, though he kept telling her she should be out partying with people her own age, not keeping an old man company and trying to keep his business alive. He was bored one night and bought two whippy-type machines for simple, smooth ice cream and declared that she wouldn't need to help him anymore. It broke her heart. She could see that he was trying really hard to manage alone, but he was struggling with his memories of his beautiful wife and the happiness she'd given everyone with her smile and her amazing ice cream flavours. He just couldn't replicate them.

Genie had asked him about trying different recipes, but he'd harrumphed and told her that if she thought she knew better, then she could get on with it. And besides, he'd added that there wasn't enough business to try new ideas. He liked his whippy ice cream machines and they did sell a fair amount of cones, but there was no love in the ingredients. Vera used to sprinkle chocolate chips, lemon rind, tiny bites of apple and many other incredible ingredients into her mixes to make you feel like you were eating a mouthful of magic. Your tongue would tingle and most people came back to order more. People visited from miles around to try her latest flavours. Recently Genie had decided to try to keep the tradition going. After five generations of her family running this business, she was determined to make it shine again, in honour of her grandma.

As far as she was concerned, Gus had given her the green light. She'd always worked hard for her parents and was determined to turn their fortunes round. All the shops along the seafront were looking a bit tired these days. She felt they'd get stuck in a time warp if something didn't change.

She tried to calm herself down. She chanted a mantra in her head that she'd heard on the radio that morning. It was supposed to make you feel zen, but it soon irritated her now she couldn't get the stupid phrases out of her mind.

Her parents had often told Genie she was too bossy for her own good, but then, she'd had to be. Her schoolwork had suffered and she'd failed most of her exams, because she was always helping out at the restaurant or washing and cleaning at home while her parents were at work. Her parents had despaired, but what else could they have expected?

It was why she hadn't yet found a home of her own, even at her age. Her parents had moved into her grandparents' Georgian seafront property when Genie had been just two. The house and the business were their lives. She secretly couldn't imagine living anywhere else, but she'd never tell her mum and dad that. Her grandad had moved into the annex, which was separate from the main house. He'd recently paid a man to put a fence up between the two buildings, saying he needed more privacy. Genie suspected that he wanted to be able to hide away with his grief. She felt that she couldn't express her own sorrow, as she had to keep everyone else's spirits up. Her dad walked around looking permanently grumpy and her mum often wrung her hands, which in turn made Genie anxious. Genie did the restaurant books, so she knew that they could just about scrape by for now, but how long that would last for, she had no idea. They needed something to change – and fast.

Maintaining the house, her family and the restaurant was a full time job. Although none of the whole parade of restaurants were up to date, they were still quite busy as very few bars and eateries were allowed on each stretch of beach. They rarely came up for sale, tending to stay within a family. Everybody was friends with everyone else, but the décor in each venue was old fashioned, as far as Genie was concerned, and their clientele was getting older too.

That was fine, Genie respected older people, but a few tended to sit for hours, hogging the tables, and they didn't spend much money. She'd almost poked an elderly man's eye out once when she'd thought he might be dead and was checking he was still breathing. Thank goodness, he'd woken up with a start. As an only child, she loved it when there was a mix of ages mingling around. Her dad was an only child too, so there were no siblings to help him run the restaurant. It had fallen to Genie and her mum. But since Vera had died, it felt like the life and soul of the place had gone with her.

The school mums, who were regulars and probably their youngest customers, checked their designer watches to see how much time they could spend relaxing before rushing off to pick up various offspring. It was still only 9.30am, so she wandered over to take their order and chatted amiably, as she did with all their customers, biting back her frustration.

It was hard keeping up a cheerful face with the customers, when she knew that the restaurant's takings were down again that quarter. The quiet worry that seemed to be with her most days was starting to make itself more apparent. Even if it meant more of her mum's death stares, or her dad's rolling eyes, she was determined to turn the family's fortunes around.

CHAPTER 2

Ada stared out at the beautiful sea view in front of her, but couldn't really take anything in. Tears threatened to spill from her eyes, but she was tougher than that. She refused to feel sorry for herself.

Since her darling Ned passed away last year, she'd been determined to stay in the apartment they had bought together when they knew he was unwell. He'd wanted to come back home to the seaside town he'd been born in. Although it had meant leaving their friends and family behind, he yearned to wander along the sandy beaches and sit and watch the seagulls. He wanted to wriggle his bare toes in the sand and eat melting ice creams as the sun went down.

The months before he went were bittersweet. He had been at peace in his hometown, so she couldn't be cross with him for leaving her alone. She'd never lived here before, though, and the endless beaches and little shops and eateries dotted around were a far cry from her past life, full of interesting people and endless social engagements. Here she had a beautiful home, but her family lived abroad and she could not – would not – let them know how much she was still grieving, and move home. Here she felt close to Ned. She could run her fingers through the sand and picture him next to her doing the same. The joy on his face, when he'd recounted stories of his childhood in the old fishing town and told her of his summers building sandcastles on the beach and riding the waves with his friends. She remembered it so well.

They had only visited his birthplace once before. But as soon as he was diagnosed with his illness and given such a short time to live, he suddenly craved home.

To her, home was their huge house in America. Ned had been a celebrity photographer and they had moved often, but they had settled down in the States. She had adored the huge rooms with high ceilings and the warmth of the sun that eased her old bones, but here she was, in a new place, a place that wasn't really home for her.

Her sons called her almost daily, but so far, she'd refused to go back. Ned was here with her, she could feel him, even though she couldn't see his kind face anymore.

He would be telling her to get onto that plane and stay with their children, but they were busy. They had careers and families of their own. What would they want with a heartbroken old woman, wandering around their houses looking lost and frequently bursting into angry tears? They didn't need her dragging them down, when they were coping with their own grief. Ned had filled the room with his presence and people clamoured for his attention. He was one of those souls that others gravitated towards, to bask in the glow of his golden personality. She had been well used to it, though, and his gaze always found her in a crowded room.

She knew she could get through this, but she would have to do it in her own time. They would all probably demand that she visit them, or they would descend on her at Christmas, so until then, she had almost a year to compose herself and to let the outside world think she was recovering. She was an actress. She could do this. She would make damn sure that by the time her boys got here, they'd think she was coping beautifully, rebuilding her life and staying strong. She gripped the handrail of the panoramic balcony on her penthouse flat and gazed through a sheen of tears at the waves kissing the shore. She tried to feel some of the peace that Ned had found here.

Movement caught her eye on the promenade below and she recognised the young woman from one of the breakfast places along the beach. She was looking mutinous, even from this distance, stalking back and forward and muttering to herself. Her hands were bunched into fists and she was brandishing one of them at a very innocent-looking bush, before she swung a kick at a plant pot and then hopped about holding her toes. Ada couldn't help but smile. She had met the girl and her parents a few times and exchanged pleasantries, but Ned hadn't really wanted to eat out. She'd only been there alone, when the isolation had got too much for her. Perhaps she'd go there today and try and chase away her demons. If Genie – she remembered the girl's name at last – was in a bad mood, then they could be grumpy together. She might even have a little chat to the hedge as she walked past, too. It wouldn't answer back. She was pretty sure everyone in her building thought she was an eccentric recluse, so no-one would bat an eyelid to see her talking to a plant.

The little cafés and bars along the seafront were quaint and beautiful and looked as if they hadn't been touched by time, which was charming. Ada did think that they could do with a few modern touches, like softer cushions on their seats for frail bottoms like hers and maybe the odd tweak to the menus as a change from cooked breakfasts and chips. The beach was popular, though, and the street below was often bustling with people. It was just the restaurants that seemed eerily quiet. She couldn't understand why, as the prices were very low for the huge plates of food that were served. Seaside fry-ups were usually a crowd pleaser. They were too heavy for a little woman like her, though. She wished they offered something a bit healthier. Perhaps she ought to ask for a children's portion, but she always felt embarrassed to do that and ended up leaving at least half her meal.

Maybe if she went for brisk walks along the shoreline, then her appetite would return. She knew she was wasting away here. Her children would be horrified if they could see how much weight she'd lost. She always hid most of her body behind a table when they video-chatted with her. She wore a bulky jumper and stuck a smile on her face and told them she was *fine*.

She straightened her back, which ached slightly from all her tossing and turning at night. She often thought she must be searching for Ned in her sleep, as she woke up feeling like she'd done a workout. She felt the worse for it, not better. Her building had a gym downstairs and a spa, but she'd never ventured in. She used to swim every day at her old home, but now she worried that she'd pass out through exhaustion while in the pool, and hadn't plucked up the courage to risk it yet.

She occasionally wondered if she should just let herself drift off and be with Ned, but she was stronger than that. She would survive this. Brushing a tear from her eye, she turned and decided that she needed some fresh air. In fact, today was going to be the day when that huge breakfast at Genie's restaurant didn't defeat her.

CHAPTER 3

Genie smiled politely at the little woman in front of her, who was becoming a regular. She had beautiful skin, and her soft grey hair was always pulled back into a perfect chignon, but her eyes were so sad. Genie didn't know her well enough to ask her if she was ok, but she could feel the unhappiness emanating from her, even though she always looked up at her with a bright smile.

Today she was working her way through a huge plate of food and had been bravely tackling it for the last hour. She had only got about a third of the way through, and looked exhausted. Genie had once asked her parents to offer smaller portions for different sized appetites, but they had told her not to be silly, their prices were so cheap and no one would want a smaller plate for the same money. Genie secretly thought they overloaded the plates too much. If they would just take two or three ingredients off the breakfasts and add them as extras, they would make much more money. People could still have a hearty breakfast, but the pound or two on each plate for beans, mushrooms, and extra toast would make such a difference to their bottom line. It would give them a chance to improve everything else.

Genie took Ada the fresh pot of tea she'd asked for and gave her a warm smile. There was something about her that drew Genie to her. She wanted to reach out and give her a supportive hug. Instead, she whipped the plate away as soon as the lady put her cutlery down and was rewarded with a grateful glance. A woman that size probably ate muesli for breakfast, lunch and dinner.

Genie looked down at her own ample hips and bulging bosom and decided that she was going to try and take her nextdoor neighbour's dog out for a morning walk along the shore more often. She'd also try not feel so stressed that she couldn't be bothered to cook a proper meal at night. Her parents loved food that was quick and easy to whip up, but Genie enjoyed fresh ingredients and spent ages scanning new recipe ideas and trying out different flavours at home. It didn't have to take an age to make a meal from scratch – as long as it didn't contain cheese. If it did, she had to put on gloves to handle it. This often caused her to spill most of the ingredients. She'd then have to put on wellington boots to sweep up the disgusting, cheesy tendrils before they touched her toes. Genie's parents had lost a bit of weight recently, but this might have been because they were stressed out about the businesses along the seafront, rather than her delicious evening meals.

She eyed her dad's not-quite-so portly stomach. She was pleased to see he was in slightly better shape these days. He wasn't as grumpy either. Her mum, on the other hand, always made an effort with her appearance and scolded Genie about being such a slob. But Genie didn't have time to spend ages shopping with friends for the latest fashions. Besides, her clothes usually stank of grease from the fryer in the back kitchen by the time she got home, so she had given up on that years ago. She was clean and presentable at work, with her long dark hair pulled back in a ponytail to keep it away from the food (and cheese) and a fresh blouse and skirt every day. Even that seemed an effort.

She had piercing blue eyes that customers often stopped her to ask about, and long silky black lashes, which meant she didn't need much make-up. Her skin was slightly tanned from working outdoors, even at this time of year. Half the chairs and tables were inside, but the other half were under an awning. This could be swept back at the touch of a button, allowing diners to sit in the sunshine. The British weather was actually good this year, so the awning was open for a lot of the time, even though Christmas wasn't all that long ago.

Genie glanced up from a table she was clearing. Trudie, from one of the other restaurants further along, had popped her head in to say hello. She glanced around to see if they were busy and grinned a hello at Genie.

'Hey Trudie, how's business today?'

Trudie paused to say hello to Ada, which surprised Genie, as she'd thought the older lady pretty much kept herself to herself. Ada greeted her politely and then turned back to her tea.

'We're really busy,' said Trudie. 'And I've run out of milk already. I forgot to send the order today. We've got a coach party in and they're causing havoc, moving all the tables round.' Trudie smiled happily.

Genie knew she wouldn't mind a huge crowd. These businesses were used to being packed to the rafters at weekends, but being busy on a weekday and not having to pace up and down the road looking for customers was a complete bonus.

Genie grinned at the other woman's infectious smile. Everyone along the parade called her Tantalising Trudie, because her hips swayed mesmerizingly as she weaved between tables. Trudie kept Genie sane and was always dropping in for a chat with her or her parents. Genie had tried to copy Trudie's sashay once and had tripped over and almost landed face-first in the lap of one of their male customers. She'd looked up to apologise, and seen Bob from the local council office staring disapprovingly down at her, his face bright red. She wouldn't be trying that move again in a hurry.

Everyone along this parade of restaurants got on so well. It was what had kept Genie going when her own friends stopped coming to the restaurant and she had fewer people of her own age to chat to. Trudie was more her mother's friend than hers, but they still got on really well.

'Of course!' she responded to Trudie's appeal for milk. 'I'm sure Dad ordered enough and we're quiet today, so I'll grab you a couple of cartons.'

Trudie smiled her thanks and pulled out a chair and sat chatting quietly to Ada, who seemed pleased at the interruption. When Genie returned, Trudie jumped up, waved her thanks and jogged back to her own establishment, waving to Genie's dad who had just come out of the kitchen with huge breakfasts for a table of two.

Click here **to continue reading book 1 in The Little Shop By The Sea, series!**

ALSO BY LIZZIE CHANTREE

Romantic Fiction

The Cherry Blossom Lane Series

Book 1

My Perfect Ex

Book 2

The One That He Wants

Book 3

Coming soon!

The Little Shop By The Sea Series

Book 1

The Little Ice Cream Shop By The Sea

Book 2

The Little Cupcake Shop By The Sea

If You Love Me, I'm Yours

The Woman Who Felt Invisible

Ninja School Mum

Babe Driven

Love's Child

Finding Gina

Shh… It's Our Secret

Non-Fiction